G000128105

LETHAL DOSE

Dangerously close to catching a killer

ROBERT McCRACKEN

THE BOOK FOLKS

Published by The Book Folks

London, 2021

© Robert McCracken

This book is a work of fiction. Names, characters, businesses, organizations, places and events are either the product of the author's imagination or are used fictitiously. Any resemblance to actual persons, living or dead, events or locales is entirely coincidental. The spelling is British English.

All rights reserved. No part of this publication may be reproduced, stored in retrieval system, copied in any form or by any means, electronic, mechanical, photocopying, recording or otherwise transmitted without written permission from the publisher.

ISBN 978-1-913516-11-6

www.thebookfolks.com

Lethal Dose is the fourth novel in the DI Tara Grogan mystery series. Details about the other books can be found at the back.

CHAPTER 1

Guy

I called her Holly, it being close to Christmas. You don't have to know her real name. None of your business. I give all my girls a name that suits them. This one looked like a Holly, so Holly was her name.

Ten to nine. I knew it wouldn't be long. I'd checked every night for a week, and I didn't usually get things wrong. Not like this. You see, we're all creatures of habit. She wouldn't dare be late.

It was one of those nights when there's hardly a sinner about. Dark, the wind whipping the rain into your face. A night for being home in front of a warm fire, cup of cocoa, a nice horror movie on the Blu-ray. But not for me. I love being out in bad weather; it makes my work so much easier.

Three minutes to the hour and she rounded the corner into the avenue. From forty yards off I couldn't make out what she was wearing, but at this stage it didn't matter. She was already chosen. I squeezed hard on the rubber ball in my right hand. Saved me touching myself.

I sat tight in my van. No need to rush; no need to panic. Big old houses on this street hidden behind overgrown hedgerows. Most of them no longer occupied by families, taken over by charities or dentists, and one I noticed was the office of a bloody shrink.

I knew she hadn't seen me; her head was down, uncovered, long dark hair soaked, but still blowing in the gale. Her flimsy denim jacket gave little protection, her skinny jeans darkened from the rain and her suede ankle boots stained with the dirty water off the pavement. Only ten yards to go.

As she passed between my van and the hedge, I opened the door, jumped out and was around the back of the vehicle just in time to meet her.

Never give them a chance to scream.

Before she could even squeak, my hand was on her neck. Under her throat and pushing upwards. Try screaming now. I stepped closer, forcing her back. Not a thing could she do about it. Her eyes bulged, doing all the yelling for her. Pitifully weak hands came up to fight me off. No chance. When you control a body by the head, you control all of it.

I slid open the side door of the van and forced her inside. She kicked out. It made a noise, not very helpful, but it was a dark and windy night. No one here. No one to care. I had a strip of gaffer tape ready, dangling from the bulkhead. Heavy duty stuff. Still gripping her neck with my right hand, I stuck the tape across her tiny mouth with my left. Releasing her throat, I grabbed her by the wrists. Again, nothing she could do. I had a cable tie ready and waiting and, in a second, her hands were secured behind her back. Another cable tie around her ankles and then I shoved her down on the mattress. Finally, I took a syringe from my bag, made a quick jab to her arm, and at last I could draw breath and relax a little.

I left her in the back, trying to scream, trying to kick her way to freedom. In a few minutes she wouldn't be able to do either. A last look around the empty street, then I climbed behind the wheel and we were off.

This country is littered with lonely places. Easy to find. Twenty minutes later, I bounced over a stony track that in a few yards became grass and sand, and I rolled to a halt on a little rise overlooking the Irish Sea, the tide on the ebb, white foam peaking on the waves. So romantic it was. I heard her body thud against the side of the van when I came to a halt, but I knew by now she was completely powerless. Out of it.

Climbing in beside her, I switched on the overhead lamp, its dull yellow glow showing up the pale face against dark clothes and hair. She was still conscious. Only just. Her eyes were lazy and rolling in her head. I pulled off the tape and cut the binds on her hands and feet. Couldn't do much with her while she was all tethered. I saw her trying to focus, trying to visualise what was about to befall her. Yet she no longer possessed the fear to call out. She would never remember. Wouldn't have to. I pulled off her wet jacket, her boots and her tight jeans. She couldn't lie there all night in soaking wet clothes; she'd catch her end. I paused for a moment to look at her neat little body. Not much of her, but that's the way I like them. If they're too big then most likely they're too strong and will put up a much bigger fight. A size eight fits the bill for me. And before you start getting the wrong idea, I don't do bloody kids.

I kicked off my shoes and pulled off my trousers, then I edged closer to wee Holly and lay beside her, pulling her close to me, passing my warmth to her beautiful body. Stroking her long damp hair, I slid it away from her cute face and watched her drift in and out of sleep. She had blue eyes, a slender nose, small mouth and thin lips. She had the sort of face that made her look clever, confident, a girl who found it easy to have friends and to attract lovers. But I didn't give a shit about that. Now she was with me. I'd watched her for weeks, catching the morning bus to work, walking to her office in the city, hurrying with girlfriends to lunch at Starbucks. Home to mum for tea twice a week, Saturdays at the pub, usually with a crowd of girls and blokes. I knew as much as I needed to know about Holly, and I'd used all my knowledge to arrive at this moment.

When I felt us both warmer, I rose to my knees and removed her jumper and T-shirt. Reaching underneath her,

I released her white bra and pulled it away. There wasn't much there, but it's a small price to pay when you go for petites. Finally, I slipped her panties down, sighed at the beauty before me then did what I had to do. I'm not telling you all the details. I'm no pervert, you know.

Sometimes, if you get the dose just right, they come around slightly when you're doing the business. I swear they're so spaced out some of them, not knowing what is happening to them, they actually get into it and enjoy it. With some, though, you don't get any feedback; they just lie there and take what's coming to them.

I'm no super-stud, but I know how to enjoy myself. After the first time, I take a break, catch my breath, lie beside her again, caress her sleeping body, and if I feel like it, I'll have another go. It's just that when it's finished, I always feel deflated, like the thrill was all in the anticipation and not in the doing.

I held Holly for a few minutes more and then removed another syringe from my bag. Most girls won't remember anything when it's over, but I can't take the risk. They have to go. With the second jab there would be no coming round for Holly.

I'm really just an average guy. You won't have heard of me. That's the way I want to keep it.

CHAPTER 2

Tara

Tara pulled in behind the car she knew to be that of Superintendent Tweedy. Another early start, a flat grey sky and a tumbling sea three hundred yards over the sands of Crosby Beach. She lingered in her car noting the figures, upright, gazing to the horizon – *Another Place*, the statues of Antony Gormley keeping watch on a stretch of Lancashire coastline. A hundred lonely figures in a lonely place. And to what had they recently been witness?

A white incident tent stood over whatever had transpired here. From a hundred yards she recognised her colleagues DS Alan Murray and Superintendent Harold Tweedy as they emerged from the shelter and paced slowly around, looking out to sea, then along the beach.

She gave a deep sigh, her stomach already knotted as it usually was when faced with these chilling scenes. There had to be better ways of getting by in this life. Gathering her bag from the passenger seat, she yawned then opened the door into the stiff wind tearing along the strand. A couple of uniforms stood by the roadside, ready to keep the public and the press at bay, although why anyone would want to stand on a beach at this ungodly hour and watch a few crime scene professionals come and go from a tent was beyond her.

One of the uniforms smiled thinly and nodded as she walked by, no doubt bemused at the appearance of such a young-looking detective inspector. She often had to show her ID to confirm that she was indeed old enough to be classed an adult, never mind a police officer. She stepped carefully over a bank of uneven grass and onto the sand. The wind cut at her face, the chill stealing down her neck as she walked briskly toward the scene, hands thrust deep in her anorak pockets.

'Morning, ma'am,' said Murray, much too cheerful for Tara.

'What's the story?'

'Morning glory.'

'Pardon?'

'It's a song, ma'am. Oasis?'

Murray received a glare for his trouble. Tara was in no mood for quips. Even a smile was hard to come by at a crime scene. Murray should have known better.

'One male, dead. It's not pleasant, Tara.'

Again, the glare as Murray reverted to first names. He frequently overlooked her rank of detective inspector to his sergeant.

'I suppose I should take a look now that I'm here,' she said, walking towards the open flap of the tent. At that point Superintendent Tweedy approached, his thin, lined face and pale complexion all the bleaker in this exposed location. She thought him rather like one of those emaciated Dickensian characters loitering on the streets of London or running some godforsaken boarding school in the middle of nowhere.

'Good morning, Tara,' he said warmly, his manner filled with more compassion than his looks. 'Brace yourself. This is not for the faint-hearted.'

She replied with a dull 'sir,' then followed him to the shelter. At first, she saw nothing but the pathologist and two scene of crime officers all clad in white coveralls, but as they stepped aside, she felt her stomach rise and a pain shooting through her head. An arc lamp suspended from the overhead pole of the tent shone down on very pale skin on the legs of the victim, weather-beaten, bleached already by sand and salt air. This gave way to a mass of deep red pulp at the crotch then a trail of blood down the torso, where the body disappeared beneath the damp sand. No head or arms visible, most of the upper body was buried. The man, for that is what this carnage of human flesh had once been, had been planted naked, his legs hanging askew, prised apart and bent at the knees.

'The genitals have been removed,' said Tweedy in that matter-of-fact way that only her boss could manage.

Tara forced herself to look again at the profusion of blood and tissue between the victim's legs.

'We found his other bits further along the beach,' Murray put in. 'Not sure if they were dumped there or if they got moved after the event.'

'What do you mean?' Tara asked.

'Well, the seagulls are at them now.'

'See what you can do about that, Alan,' said Tweedy. 'If you've seen enough, Tara, we can step outside.'

She had a final inspection of the body, not a vision to slip easily from the mind, then she stepped into the breeze with her boss. Murray bounded off to scare away the seagulls feasting on what was left of the victim's genitals.

'Do we know who he is, sir?' Tara asked.

'A coat and pair of trousers were found near the promenade. There was a wallet and a mobile phone in the pockets. We think it's Terry Lawler; I'm sure you've heard of him, Tara?'

Instinctively, she gazed over the sand to the gathering posse of press and media. Terry Lawler used to be one of them.

'I haven't seen him for a while, sir.'

'He went freelance a couple of years back but seemed to retain the ability to rattle cages and get up people's noses.'

'Any ideas on motive or suspects?'

'I believe that's where you come in, Tara. Knowing Mr Lawler as I did, I'm quite sure he managed to acquire a few enemies in the course of his journalistic career.'

'Yes, sir. If I can get a look at the wallet and phone and start from there.'

'That's fine. We'll meet at ten in my office and see what we've got.'

Tweedy strode off towards Murray who was trying his best to keep a pair of large herring gulls away from the severed remains of the murder victim. Tara forced herself to re-enter the tent to have a word with Dr Brian Witney, the duty pathologist.

It was a timely entrance, for the body, having been photographed, was now being freed from its mooring in the ground. The two SOCOs shovelled sand away from the torso, while Witney held firm to the victim's legs. When he finally came free, the body slumped, face down.

Witney and the SOCOs quickly turned him over, and Tara got her first look at the battered face of the man they believed to be Terry Lawler. Copious amounts of sand remained on the head and clung to the thick strands of hair. Dark, congealed blood mixed with sand smothered the mouth and nose, and both eye sockets were filled with the gruesome blend. Again, that surge of painful shiver coursed through her, not helped in any way by the rising stench of rotting seaweed.

'What do you reckon, Brian?' she asked.

Witney stood upright, groaned a little, massaging his lower back. He was a man in his fifties, unshaven, tall and once athletic but now heading for a weight problem. He peered down at her over his thick glasses and smiled.

'I'd say he's been dead about five hours. Hard to be entirely accurate with half of him in the ground and the other pointing skywards.'

'Do you think he was dead before…'

'Before the castration? Don't know yet. My guess is he was beaten, buried and, while technically still alive, the killer did the cutting.'

'No sign of a weapon?'

'None so far, but I would say it was a fairly sharp knife. Looks a clean cut.'

His factual, non-emotional language provoked yet another shiver that she failed to disguise.

'You OK, Tara?'

'I will be. Thanks, Brian, keep me posted.'

'Will do, Tara.'

Witney stared longingly as the detective left the tent. She was happy to be out of there and walked quickly towards her car. Murray and Tweedy were still talking as a SOCO went about the beach gathering the remaining pieces of the murder victim, placing each portion in a separate evidence bag.

Tara was already pondering the implications of this murder as she reached the relative sanctity of her car. If it were Terry Lawler out there, well-known Liverpool journalist, he would not have been short of enemies. He was renowned for exposing corrupt public officials, the seedy side of celebrity and some of Merseyside's big criminal noises. But she got the feeling that this was not an act of revenge. If that were the case, he'd have been shot, or stabbed and dumped in an alley. This killer was making a bold statement, sending out a message. Why else would Lawler have been half buried on a beach and his privates cut off? Was it possible to make him any more dead by castrating him after he'd been buried?

She looked again at the Gormley figures and wondered if the upturned body of the victim was a sick and twisted artistic statement.

CHAPTER 3

Guy

Before I go any further let's get one thing straight. I'm no serial killer; I'm just tidy.

When I choose a girl, I choose carefully. I don't take shortcuts. I don't make mistakes. Success is all in the planning. Do something stupid and you'll spend the rest of your life in a prison. I'm not a sad ugly bastard, you know. I can get girls the normal way, like any other bloke, but I don't always get the one I want. If there's some beauty out there who won't look twice at me then I take her without permission. It's like stealing a car. What pillock ever sets out to steal a beat-up Clio? No one at all. They're going to take a 5-Series, a Merc or a Jag. Stands to reason. And choice is all-important. Look around. Take your time; pretend that you're going shopping. Girls are like apples on the trees or blackberries in the hedgerows, ripe for the picking. And the best fruit is always the most difficult to reach. Don't rush into anything. Choose the wrong bird and you're finished before you get the chance to make it a career.

'Act in haste, repent at leisure.' My granny used to say that. She wasn't talking about killing, though. I used to play Draughts with her when I was a kid, and she was nearly eighty. Ma used to leave me at her house during school holidays, while she went to work. I always made the first move that popped into my head, and Granny would punish me so bad. I'd lose half of my counters simply by not taking the time to plan my moves. I only started to win when her mind had gone a bit. Sometimes she didn't even know that she was playing the game. So, here's a piece of free advice. It's better that the girls don't realise they're in a game, your game. That way they'll never know they've lost until it's too bloody late.

It's so easy when you know how. OK, maybe for the first couple you feel a bit nervous, in case something goes wrong. Do your homework. Think it through. Run the whole plan over in your mind, and when you think you have everything sussed, go over it all again. First time I did it, I even had a couple of dry runs, just to be sure. What I'm trying to tell you is plan it well and you won't ever get caught.

I suppose it's like everything else in life that is wild, exciting and a bit of a blast. The first time is the best. After that you're always trying to re-create the first one. But you won't ever do it. That ruthless buzz and the anticipation of what lies ahead are gone. It's like your first kiss, your first goal for the school team, your first job and your first shag. Make the first one great; savour it, because it won't get any better. Besides, if you're not careful, your first may be your last.

So now you have two of my rules. Don't ever rush into it, and don't let her know that she's in the game. Simple.

There are lots of pretty things in this world. Remember when you were a kid and, perhaps on your birthday, your da takes you to a toyshop? There are so many wonderful things in there, it's impossible to choose, but you know that you're allowed only one toy. It has to be the right one. Has to be memorable. Holly was just like that. She was a beauty. I planned my time with her, she didn't know she was part of my game, and when I was done, I knew I would never forget her. Perfection.

Once Holly had departed this life, I wasted no time. I moved her, bent her double so that she was almost touching her toes. Have to do it before the rigors set in. Then I bound her hands to her feet. That way she would fit perfectly into the holdall. I use those big sports bags, the type that have wheels. Makes it easier to transport. Once I had her packed inside, I threw in her clothes, her boots and her handbag. The stuff I'd been wearing went in too. When I had changed into fresh jeans and shirt, I drove off, making for Mother Freedom and the early tide.

My grandfather built her. He used to work in the shipyard on the big tankers and built wee boats in his spare time. When I was a kid, he would sail us across the water to Scotland for long weekends. Before he died, he gave her to me instead of my da. My da had no interest in boats. Not much interest in anything, except pubs and bookies.

I don't keep her in the same port for long periods. Too many bloody snoopers asking if she's for hire for a lads' fishing trip. Bloody hooligans, if you ask me, out for a piss-up, and not much fishing ever gets done. And I seldom put into the same port I've just left. Don't want people making connections.

That morning, with Holly in the bag, I drove to Bangor in North Wales, to Port Penrhyn. Mother Freedom sat close into the quayside, fuelled up and ready to go. She's a thirty-foot motor cruiser, fibreglass hull painted white and royal blue. Sometimes, just to get away from it all, I take her round the coast, Cornwall, Sussex and even up the east side to Scarborough and Whitby. Besides, moving the boat provides me with more options to search for women. I've been all over the country.

I parked the van on the quayside as close as I could to the boat and began loading my gear aboard. I wheeled Holly along the quay and then lowered her by rope the six feet onto the open deck. There was no one about, although several cars were parked close to the harbour master's office. Ten minutes later, I was out of the harbour in a dull grey morning and into the Menai Strait. Thankfully, a calm sea because, although I love to sail, I can get seasick from time to time especially when I come to a stop and I'm just bobbing about in the swell. An hour later, I was about two miles off Amlwch on Anglesey.

When I prepare the boat for a trip like this, I load a dozen or so rocks, each one not so heavy that I can't lift them but heavy enough to do the job.

I slowed the engine right down and began packing the holdall with the stones. The whole package was now too heavy for me to lift, but all I had to do was lever it over the side. Young Holly was at the bottom of the sea before anyone had even reported her missing. Job done.

CHAPTER 4

Tara

When they arrived at St Anne Street station, DS Murray gave her the wallet and mobile phone of the victim. The mobile didn't seem so promising; it had been smashed and the SIM card removed. Someone had taken steps to prevent information being discovered. Tara wondered why they hadn't simply taken the phone with them after the killing.

She sat at her desk with the wallet sitting in front of her. Her feet were chilled to the bone.

Murray obliged with a mug of coffee and took a seat on the other side of her desk.

'Definitely Lawler then?'

'I think so,' she replied, picking up the wallet. It was black, imitation leather and folded in three parts so that it would fit neatly into a trouser pocket. There were several credit cards inside, each with the name Terrence Lawler on them. She set them to the side and then removed some cash which amounted to forty-five pounds in two tens, a twenty and a five-pound note. Next, she examined three receipts, but they were merely for petrol from Sainsbury's. Tara would have expected to find a driver's licence, but it seemed to be missing. Lastly, she found a couple of business cards tucked away behind the photograph of a woman. One advertised EB Property Management in bold blue lettering with an address in Warrington and a name of Evan Blackley, company director. The other had the name Paul Macklin, solicitor, with an address in Castle Street, Liverpool.

She paused for a moment to study the small picture of the woman. Late twenties, early thirties, Tara guessed. Cropped black hair, grey eyes and red lips with the merest smile on the pale face. Seemed like a passport shot, and probably not the most flattering of the woman.

But it was a start, and that was more than she usually got with murder cases. There were another forty minutes until Tweedy required their presence in his office, so she lifted her phone and dialled the number of the solicitor. It cut immediately to voicemail inviting her to leave a message or to contact another number for urgent matters. She took a note of the number, but when she tried that it also reverted immediately to voicemail without further contact details. She re-dialled Macklin's number and this time left a message for him to contact her at St Anne Street station.

Tweedy called his team of detectives earlier than planned, so Tara didn't have time to call EB Property Management.

All the case meetings held in Harold Tweedy's office took place in an atmosphere of relaxed formality. Tweedy had the manner of a Sunday school teacher combined with that of a high court judge. He didn't stand for any nonsense but wasn't in the business of stressing out his officers either. He stood behind his desk, while his staff sat around it, all of them aware of the leather-bound King James Bible sitting upon it, a text that Tweedy was often found reading. First name terms were always his way but, despite the informality, everyone knew that he expected their full attention and dedication.

'Alan, perhaps you could start us off.'

Murray cleared his throat, sat upright from his slouched position and set about explaining the circumstances of finding the body on Crosby Beach. Tara got the feeling he relished telling the story of gulls tearing at the flesh of the victim's private parts. At times he was the station jester, liked to think he was the lad. She, however, knew him well beyond that. Shaven head, thick neck, bulbous eyes, grey suits, and shirts straining at the stomach, he was divorced, cynical of fresh starts, and even more so on his chances of promotion to Inspector. Tara's early rise to that rank had long since been an irritation to Alan Murray. But she had learned to tolerate his attitude and respect his ability as a detective.

DC John Wilson recounted the details of finding the wallet, mobile phone and clothing of the victim on the sand, closer to the road than where the body had been discovered. More than ten years younger than Murray, Wilson seemed to be headed in the same direction as his peer. A more athletic build, he also was divorced and getting re-acquainted with the free and single life. Tara would have regarded him as quite attractive if it wasn't for him being a work colleague and that he was moving in a direction similar to Murray's, playing the field with no interest in commitment. For all that, Wilson was never less than courteous and carried out her instructions to the letter.

'Do you have anything for us, Tara?' Tweedy asked.

'Not much so far, sir. I've had a look through the wallet, a couple of contacts to follow up. The mobile phone was smashed, and the SIM has been removed.'

Tweedy had begun recording details on the large whiteboard fixed to the wall behind his desk. All known facts would be replicated on a similar board in the operations room.

'Approximate time of death was five hours before he was discovered, so that makes it around two in the morning. It was dark obviously, but it's worth checking for anyone who was walking on Crosby Beach around that time. John, I'll leave you to check out residents in the area.'

'Yes, sir,' Wilson replied.

'For now, pending a positive identification, we will work on the assumption that the victim is Mr Terry Lawler. Tara and Alan, I'll leave you to follow up on the leads and to contact family members.'

With all instructions meted out, they were dismissed. Tara had the image of the woman in the photograph uppermost in her mind. Perhaps it was Lawler's wife or partner. She hated delivering bad news to a relative. When she got back to her desk, she checked her voicemail and found that Paul Macklin had returned her call. He seemed as good a place to start as any.

'Let's go, Alan,' she said breezing by his desk on her way to the door.

'Where to, ma'am?' Murray was already on his feet wrestling to don the jacket of his suit.

'To see a solicitor.'

CHAPTER 5

Guy

I put in at Bank Quay in Caernarfon in the early afternoon. I scrubbed down the small deck with harbour water and made sure I hadn't left anything of Holly's lying around. I don't take souvenirs, knickers, shoes, a lock of hair or anything like that. I don't save pictures from the newspapers; I don't keep any information I gather on my girls. Everything is destroyed. Call it data protection. I don't even keep count of the women I've had but, in my head, I can still visualise each one. And I can recall the names I gave them; after all, they're my girls. My bag is strictly in the lovemaking. Beyond that I remove all traces of my contact with a girl. And finally, I don't get a buzz in leaving cryptic clues for the peelers. What eejit scrawls words on walls, or leaves ancient symbols, riddles or voice messages? Psychos with a death wish of their own, that's who.

I caught a bus from the station in Caernarfon back to Bangor and then collected my van from Penrhyn harbour. From there I drove to the civic amenity site on the Llandygai Industrial Estate, where I dumped the mattress, and then to the self-service car wash at Tesco. I power-hosed the back of the van inside and out and, after stopping for a burger, I was home in Liverpool by eight o'clock. By the end of the week, I'd sold on the van at an auction, and any evidence that Holly and I did the business in it had completely gone. That's how tidy I am. I wonder what *CSI Miami* would make of that? No crime scene and no body. Figure that one out, you smart arses.

It's a pity about Holly, though. Nice girl. If I'd brought her round instead of putting her to sleep permanently the chances are, she wouldn't have remembered a thing. But you can't be too careful. My DNA would be all over her and inside her. Can't be doing with that. Some clever dick would realise what went down, and in no time, I'd be staring at the four walls of a cell in Liverpool Prison. No, sad though it is, they have to go.

Just so you know, I don't get any buzz from killing. I do it as humanely as possible. It's a necessity, not a part of my thrill. Apart from grabbing them by the throat, there's no violence. A wee jab of China White: fentanyl, and they doze off. I do my thing, and finally I apply the lethal dose. Most of the time it's China White. That's stuff more potent than heroin. An intravenous shot of 2 milligrams is the lethal dose. I used a little more to make sure. Holly just slept on. She didn't suffer, never knew what happened, never had to live with the trauma. Sometimes I feel for the family, but hey, thousands of people go missing every year in Britain, and some are never found. At least Holly's family will believe they have hope.

Time to start looking for the next one.

CHAPTER 6

Tara

Murray pulled into a lay-by outside the offices of PDP Solicitors in Castle Street in the city centre. A sign of blue lettering on a white background above the door stated that the firm specialised in property law, and criminal and family legal aid. The ground floor of the four-storey building was occupied by a coffee and sandwich bar, the PDP offices were on the first and second floors.

Tara told the girl working in the cramped reception area that she had an appointment with Paul Macklin. They were shown through immediately to an even smaller office with two desks and a tiny, frosted window. The walls were crammed full of files and papers in lockable cabinets, and several imposing law manuals adorned a single shelf by the windowsill.

Paul Macklin, a weedy man in his thirties, with narrow eyes, pointed nose and dishevelled mousey hair, glanced up from behind a computer screen. His maroon tie sat askew, his blue shirt open at the collar. He looked neither pleased nor particularly interested in greeting his visitors, his mind seemed to be somewhere else and he looked stressed.

'Mr Macklin? I'm Detective Inspector Grogan and this is Detective Sergeant Murray. Sorry to disturb you, sir, but we'd like to ask you a few questions.'

'Sure. What case?'

'I beg your pardon?'

'Which of my cases are you interested in?'

He was back gazing at his screen. The arrival of two detectives had not raised any alarm with him. It appeared they were merely interrupting his train of thought.

'Nothing like that, sir,' Tara replied. 'Can you please tell me if you know a Mr Terry Lawler?'

'Terry? Course I do, we're mates. What's he done now? Which politician has he shat upon today?'

When Tara didn't respond immediately, Macklin finally looked up from his screen.

'When did you see him last?' she asked.

Tara noted the concern slowly descending upon the bony face of the solicitor. His mouth remained open, revealing crooked teeth.

'Last week. Why?'

'Have you spoken to him since then?'

'No. A couple of texts maybe. What's he done? Is he all right?'

'Are you aware of any activities he's been involved in recently?'

'What's going on? Is Terry all right? If something's happened to him, I'd like to know. We've been mates since school. Played footie in the same team.'

'We can't confirm at the moment, but we believe that we found the body of Mr Lawler this morning on Crosby Beach.'

Macklin paled. He stared pleadingly at Tara who duly noted his reaction to the news. She repeated her previous question.

'Do you know anything of Mr Lawler's recent activities?'

Lost in thought, the solicitor stared at the floor.

'Em, no, not really. What I mean is, Terry dabbled in a lot of things. Especially since he went freelance, he had a lot of potential stories on the go.'

'Can you think of anything in particular?'

'Why? He hasn't been murdered, has he?'

'If it is Mr Lawler we found this morning, then yes, we believe he has been murdered.'

Macklin rubbed frantically at his face with both hands and breathed deeply.

'I don't know. We had lunch and a pint last week, but he never mentioned anything.'

'Nothing troubling him in particular?' Murray put in.

Macklin shook his head, no.

'What did you talk about?' Tara asked.

'Usual stuff, football, music, women.'

'Was Terry married?'

'Used to be,' Macklin scoffed. 'Gwen. She got tired waiting for him to become reliable. They divorced about three years ago. They had a daughter, Maisie. She'd be about fourteen now. Gwen remarried.'

'And Terry?'

'Na. No way. Said he wasn't going down that bloody cul-de-sac again. God, I can't believe Terry's dead.'

'Do you know of anyone who'd want to do Mr Lawler harm?'

It was a nervous laugh but ironic just the same.

'How long have you got, Inspector? Terry named and shamed a lot of people over the years. Some of them got put away; others are still running the bloody country. Don't you know anything about Liverpool? Stop any punter on the street and they'll have a Terry Lawler story for you. Take your pick of enemies, from druggies to city councillors, celebs to ex-girlfriends. I loved him to bits, but he could be a right bastard when he put pen to paper. He exposed the dubious secrets of a lot of people.'

'One last question for now, Mr Macklin. Is there anyone close to Mr Lawler that we should contact? Do you have an address, perhaps?'

'No one that I know of except for Gwen. Parents are both dead. His sister, Ruth, went missing five months ago. No one's heard from her since. He has another sister, but she has learning difficulties. His ex-girlfriend, maybe. Her name is Lynsey Yeats. They split a few weeks ago. I can get an address for you. Apart from them, there's me. I suppose I was his closest mate.'

'Then perhaps we may have to call on you to identify the body,' said Murray.

Tara glared at her colleague. He had a tendency toward insensitivity when handling delicate situations.

'Do you have an address for Terry?' she asked.

'He lived at Lynsey's place until they split, but he still kept his own flat. Not that it's up to much. Wasn't so good at looking after himself.'

Macklin checked an address book he had lying on his desk, then scribbled quickly on a torn scrap of PDP-headed paper.

'Terry's address, Gwen's address and Lynsey's,' he said, handing the note to Tara.

'Thank you, Mr Macklin. We'll be in touch if we need to speak again.'

Macklin nodded weakly as Tara and Murray left the office. He returned immediately to his computer screen.

'Do you think it's strange that Macklin had the addresses of both women?' Tara asked Murray when they returned to the car.

'Hard to say, ma'am. He gave the impression of being very close to Lawler.'

'Mm. I wonder if he was also close to the women.'

CHAPTER 7

Guy

Gemma was eighteen. I found that out the first time I laid eyes on her. It was her first day at Queen's, and I watched as she walked through those big gates on University Road. Not a care in the world, dear love her. Three girls together, students, they had that student look about them. Sort of dressed down, understated in jeans and flat shoes, and nice wee tops showing bear arms, because it was unseasonably warm for late September in Belfast. They had big hair, all three of them. Freshly washed, tumbling down their backs, one blonde, the other two, dirty fair. But the hair was enough to start me off, spoke volumes to me, especially with Gemma. Everything about her was dripping in sex appeal. Her hand tossing those blonde locks over her shoulder, the wispy smile, aloof, arrogant. Somebody who knows rightly that they're a dick-teaser. Someone who takes satisfaction from boys gawking at her as she walks by. The stupid wee nerds in her new class wouldn't stand a chance. The likes of Gemma already had a boyfriend who, if he wasn't from a rich family, was likely to be loaded before he hit thirty. She was in a different league; money attracts money. I was going to have to look into all that.

It was the first time it ever occurred to me how much I wanted a girl. And I tried things the normal way, honest I did. I walked up to Gemma in a bar crowded with freshers on the Malone Road and offered to buy her a drink. She politely declined. I tried again later on when I had a few pints in me, and she'd had a few vodkas.

'I would really love to buy you a drink,' I said. 'With a view to getting to know you better. What do you think?'

'No thanks,' she replied. 'I can buy my own drinks.'

'I'm only trying to be friendly, like. We're both new here. It's good to make friends.'

She flicked that rapturous hair back and glared at me with a sarcastic smile. Big eyes, blue and confident stared me out. I realised then her smile was a fuck-off smile. It was a smile that told me that I was not at her level. I was a pauper not a prince.

'Sorry, I didn't realise I was talking to a stuck-up bitch,' I said and backed away. Her mouth dropped open as if she'd never heard such language before, but I couldn't believe she'd got to that age without anyone ever telling her she was a stuck-up bitch. And I was quite sure with that big gaping mouth of hers that some bloke must have inserted his manhood in it long before then.

That little encounter was no reason to give up on Gemma. But it was the first time I realised that if I couldn't get my way with a girl, I would just have to take matters into my own hands. That night I had no idea how to go about it or what it would eventually lead to. But I knew that Gemma would soon be mine in a way that probably wouldn't suit her. Fuck her, I gave her a chance and she didn't take it.

Having made it my intention that one day I would take Gemma, she wasn't to be my first. That dubious honour went to a wee girl I called Millie. Millie by name and millie by nature, if you know what I mean? If you don't understand the colloquial Belfast term, then go and look it up. I can't be arsed explaining every detail. Suffice to say, Millie hailed from a more working-class background than the stuck-up Gemma.

I was on the bus when I spotted her. Luckily, it was stopped at a red light. I had been watching a fairly nice Asian bird pushing a buggy with a gurney wee brat in it. She had a nice arse and long black hair, which had first caught my eye. Apart from that, she wasn't up to much. A little too big as well.

There was a bloke on the news recently. He had been captured on CCTV trying to abduct a young girl who was walking home late at night. He tried to carry her into some bushes, but she kicked and struggled until he couldn't hold her any longer. Finally, she pulled herself free and ran off. You see what happens with no planning, no forethought? The daft eejit should have picked on someone a bit smaller. At least then he might have stood a chance.

Just before the lights changed to green, Millie stepped out of the chemist shop that the Asian woman with the sprog had been about to enter. She was delightful. That was the first time I realised that I would be going all the way without even asking.

So, you should see already, that they will come to you. It doesn't require a lot of searching. Remember though, that having considered all the practical aspects of choosing your girl, she has to be right for you. After all, you are going to make love to her. No point in wasting your energy on some cheap slapper who isn't worth the time of day. I'm not one of those guys who tries to rid the world of hookers. Where's the fun in that?

Millie took a lot of hard work. She was a complete stranger to me but only for as long as that first sighting lasted. In seconds, I was off the bus and, staying about forty yards behind, I followed her along Strandtown as she meandered through the afternoon shoppers, popping into the odd store herself, first a jeans shop and then a bookstore. By the end of that day, I knew her real name was Linda Meredith. She had tanned skin and long, shining black hair with a fringe threatening to cover her eyes. Her face seemed a little too serious, her jaw square and her mouth quite small and taut. She wore tight, pale-blue jeans and pink and white trainers. Most important of all, to me that is, her arse was neat and very rounded, stretching the denim of her jeans into such fabulous shapes. It was a hot day, and she wore a cropped yellow vest which did not come anywhere close to meeting the waistband of her jeans. I stared at her exposed flesh and could see the tiny bar of gold, which seemed to stand guard at her navel. It was all I could do to stop myself from groping her, right there in the bookshop. But if I wanted her, I would have to be patient.

Incidentally, I saw her name on the debit card that she handed to the assistant after buying two books and a magazine. She bought two of those modern frolicky type novels, you know the ones where modern girl meets sexy modern guy who cheats on her, and she rebuilds her life to become strong and independent? Just as soon as she's accomplished that, she meets her all-time Mr Right and lives happily ever after. Bless. She also bought a copy of *Hello*. See how observant you can be, once you pick your girl?

The most important thing to find out about her is where she lives or, failing that, where she works. That done, there's no stopping you. Don't forget that once you have that information, you must make sure she doesn't get the creeps, thinking that some pervert is watching her every move. You're not some amateur stalker. No point getting caught for peeking through her window or breathing heavy down the phone. May as well get hung for a sheep than a lamb. That's another thing my granny used to say, although at the time I never quite understood what she meant by it.

So, after that first sighting it took me nearly three months to set the whole thing up. By then I knew that Millie was single, nineteen and working as a hairdresser in a city centre salon. She lived at home with her parents and younger brother who was still at secondary school. But more important than all of that, I knew that on weekdays she left home around twenty past eight, walked up to the bus stop on the Holywood Road, around the corner from her home, and boarded a bus headed for town. What I'm saying is, you have to slip into her routine. You have to be prepared for long periods of hanging around. Sometimes it is only to make one sighting of her or to check one simple fact. But don't ever raise her suspicions. Each time you're on the lookout you must alter the routine. Standing opposite the bird's house day in, day out for a week, I mean, how daft is that? Somebody will notice. And when it comes to disappearing time you can be sure that some old hag from two doors down will tell the peelers about the strange git who had been lurking about in the street.

When you get a lucky break, take full advantage of it. One morning I got on the bus with my Millie and sat two seats behind her. She got off at a stop in the city centre. I stayed on board, watching until she disappeared down Upper Arthur Street. Next morning, I was already waiting when she stepped off the bus. From a distance I could follow her until she reached her workplace, which turned out to be a salon in Church Lane. After that I checked lunch breaks, knocking off time and then her evening and weekend routines. Whenever she did something different, something unexpected, like going to the cinema or the pub, then I had to re-check everything. That's how you build up the information. I should have been a spy.

With experience you can be working on two or three girls at a time. Find yourself the odd private place and you can get off just in the watching of your precious beauties. But no photographs and no touching the merchandise for a quick taster. And remember, another wee rule of mine, you must space out the snatches. It would be totally stupid to do more than one in a month and in the same town. You're not a serial killer. Each one is unique; no patterns, no traces and you don't get caught.

Six weeks after my first sighting of Millie I had enough information to fill a book, and she had spoken to me on three occasions. You might think I'm mad, getting so close, but it's all right as long as you don't raise their suspicions. She must never make any connections. The first time, all I did was to let her get on the bus before me.

'Thanks,' she said a bit under her breath with the hint of a grateful smile.

I was dead chuffed. 'No problem,' I replied.

Next time, nearly three weeks later, was a repeat of the first, but you see how much time had passed? She would never connect those two occasions.

'Thanks,' was all she said. No sign of her remembering that first time.

A few days further on, I went into a Subway and she was there, ordering an Italian meatball sandwich for lunch. I managed to glean a whole load of information from the brief conversation that she had with the young girl behind the counter. The pair of them seemed well acquainted, and within a few seconds I learned about her forthcoming plans for going to a music festival in Edinburgh. Her mention of a date for leaving home also left me with a deadline to meet. She remained in the shop as I was being served. The shop assistant was babbling on about the previous night's episode of *Coronation Street,* and Millie was mostly nodding in agreement.

'I suppose you fellas don't bother with the soaps?' the girl said to me.

'I watch them sometimes,' I replied. Millie didn't seem interested as she lifted her lunch from the counter. 'Is that Phil Mitchell still in it?' I asked.

Millie smiled. It was almost a laugh.

'He's in *EastEnders*,' she said, heading for the door.

She had scarcely looked at me, but I certainly took note of her. She wore black trousers, flat-heeled calf-length boots and a black blouse through which her bra advertised her cute breasts. I watched her lovely arse sidle out the door. I felt overwhelmingly turned on. Everything I saw confirmed that I had made the right choice, and I could hardly wait for the moment.

The next thing that I have to tell you might seem obvious. Only a moron with brain fade would try to nab a girl in broad daylight or in a place where there are lots of people or cameras. All I can say is, once you know her well, then you know automatically when and how to get her.

I did a couple of dry runs before I lifted Millie. I knew that she walked home from the gym on Tuesdays and Thursdays. Sometimes on Tuesdays another girl would accompany her. She was quite nice, too. I called her Penny, for future reference. But on Thursdays Millie was always on her own. That was her routine. I'd checked it for weeks, and not once did it change. For my practice run I walked the route that she took, but I did so on a Monday night. Then on a Thursday I covered the mile or so an hour before she was due. Do you see what I'm getting at? I could examine the route for the best spot on a night when I was unlikely to come across Millie. Then I could check out how many people were about that area on the evening that she actually walked home alone. Simple. She didn't stand a cat in hell's chance.

Here is my final rule, and this is the one that will save your bacon. When you take her, do the business and dispose of her long before anyone even suspects that she's gone missing. Don't think you can hide these girls away somewhere, dipping in and out whenever you feel like it. Too many things to go wrong. Someone will eventually notice your antics. And there's always the chance that your girl will manage to escape. Then you'll be screwed and not in a nice sexual way.

In the end, wee Millie was so bloody easy. She walked quickly. Small steps. Wiggly bum. It was dark and quite cold. Her boots were silent on the pavement as her shapely wee legs hurried her along, past the shopping centre. I knew that on Thursday evenings, after working in the salon until seven-thirty, she went directly to the gym. She exercised for an hour and a half and then walked home. Her route never altered. She liked to cut corners. Out of the gym, down the Albertbridge Road, crossing over into the Ballymacarrett Walkway. The houses had gone from there years ago, and an open pathway ran parallel to the Newtownards Road. At this time of night there were never many people about. Always be wary, though, of bloody late-night dog walkers. They're a curse, although it's useful to pose as one the odd time, to get some of your reconnaissance done without attracting attention.

I was already waiting as she turned the corner into the walkway. I had to take her at this point. A hundred yards further and she would reach the Holywood Road. Once there, Millie would be safe. If somebody was lurking, I could abandon the lift. If not, then my lovely Millie was all set for the time of her life. I would put such a wonderful smile on that cute face, good enough to take to her grave, except that she wouldn't be having one of those.

My heart was thumping and reverberating through my head like a boiler ready to explode. I could see my Millie, traipsing along the flagstones. I gave her two more steps. Then I jumped out of my van.

I hit her once. Hard. Not enough to knock her out or for her to go sprawling on the ground. That's far too awkward. No, I hit her a thump on the back. It knocked the wind out of her. That way she couldn't scream. Quickly, I put a knife to her delicate throat, just enough to prick her into submission. This was the trickiest part, because already I had a hard-on and just wanted to take her, right there. But that's a mug's game. I told her that if she was quiet then she wouldn't get hurt. I gave her the pill. A bloody godsend they were, but I had to force it down. Opening the back door of the van, I pushed her inside. Parcel tape across her mouth and two cable ties, one for her wrists, the other for her feet. I shut the door, and off I went.

By the time I reached the spot, up in the hills above the city, forest all around, a proverbial lovers' lane, the tab I gave her was taking effect. She was conscious but woozy. She wouldn't put up a fight like that. It gave me that precious time to appreciate her beauty. Millie was especially hot that night. She had a beautiful freshly showered smell. Her hair was light and wispy, probably from having just been shampooed and blow-dried following her work-out at the gym. Her skin was cool and pale, and as I peered into her brown eyes I could tell, despite her drowsy state, that there was some recognition on her part. Or at least she was processing something in that lovely wee brain of hers.

When I pulled off her coat, I could hardly believe my luck. Her shoulders were bare. She wore only a delicate, black lace vest and below decks she sported tight, black leggings. You may not think so, but it was my idea of heaven. My hands were all over her. She lay on the cold floor of the van, her eyes now closed, her breathing shallow. For a second, I lay perfectly still trying to listen for her breathing, watching for a rise and fall in her chest. I thought I'd killed her before I'd even taken my chance. I placed my hand on her chest just beside her left breast. I breathed a heavy sigh of relief when I felt a gentle pulse. You see, at that point, Millie being my first, I wasn't sure if I could go through with the killing part. I was a lover not a killer. But my logical thinking had convinced me that any girl once taken had to die. I couldn't take the risk of her remembering something when she came round.

I laid her out nice and pretty, got her clothes off and her legs apart. I thought, do anything you wanna do.

'You're only young once, son,' another thing my granny used to say.

CHAPTER 8

Tara

They arrived in Lymm outside a pair of sturdy wooden gates and an intercom. When Murray announced who they were the gates swung open, and soon they pulled up outside a mock Georgian red-brick house with a double-garage to the left-hand side where a silver Ferrari sat gleaming in the afternoon sun.

'Not short of a penny or two then?' said Murray, his eyes fixed on the sports car, while Tara's interest rested firmly on the house and the woman standing with arms folded at the open front door.

Before climbing out of the car, Tara glanced at the photo of the woman from Lawler's wallet. As she approached the house, she realised the woman at the door was definitely not the woman in the photograph.

'Mrs Gwen Blackley?'

'Yes.'

'I'm Detective Inspector Grogan and that is Detective Sergeant Murray,' said Tara, indicating her colleague who couldn't resist the opportunity to inspect the type of car he could only ever dream of owning.

Hands in pockets, he wandered around the vehicle, bending to peer inside, kicking the tyres and stepping back to take in the vision before him. He looked more like a know-it-all punter perusing a used-car lot.

'How can I help you, Inspector?'

'If you don't mind, may we come inside?'

Without a word she led Tara indoors with Murray jogging across the drive to catch up. They were shown into a front sitting room, laden with three huge, cushioned sofas, a long dark wood coffee table in front of a white marble fireplace. The room was bright, neutral colours but for a fiery-looking landscape of sun on hills, in reds and oranges, hanging on the wall above one of the sofas. To either side of the fireplace were pictures of family, and several of a man Tara presumed to be Evan Blackley – professional footballer of twenty years ago, famous for leaving Liverpool at the height of his career to join one of the Milans. Tara couldn't remember which one. She had a passing knowledge of football, particularly where Liverpool was concerned, but it didn't extend to the European theatre. Besides, it was a bit before her time. Blackley's world fell apart somewhat, when he got mixed up in a betting scandal, and there were allegations of match-fixing. He was soon on his way from Milan, and made a stinted return to English football, finding himself on short-term contracts with a Premiership club before dropping to the lower leagues. Nowadays, he made his money from property, although, Tara reckoned, he must have hit some difficult times with the financial crash of recent years. And now she was seated in Blackley's house about to inform his wife that her ex-husband had been murdered.

'And what brings the police to my door all the way from Liverpool?' said Gwen Blackley.

She was very presentable, wearing an expensive-looking royal blue dress and, Tara guessed, designer shoes. She looked to be in her twenties but had to be older. At least thirty-five, Tara thought. Her face was not unfriendly but seemingly well used to dealing with difficult situations, experienced in public circles. Even at home she wore full make-up on her small, rounded face. She displayed perfect white teeth and a thin nose. She had the air of being an actress or a model, but Tara already knew her to be neither, working instead in PR, and nowadays in her husband's business.

'Am I right in saying that you were formerly married to Mr Terry Lawler?'

Despite nervous smiles, and an attempt at cheerfulness, it appeared the question was sufficient to strike alarm into Gwen Blackley.

'Terry? Yes. What's he done?'

'We believe that Mr Lawler's body was found on Crosby Beach early this morning.'

'No, that's not Terry,' said Gwen Blackley dropping into the middle of a sofa. Her face had already paled. 'Terry would never do that.'

'Do what, Mrs Blackley?'

The woman's expression became distant, vacant, as if peering into her past to the life she had once shared with Terry Lawler. Her eyes were fixed somewhere beyond a spot on the cream carpet.

'Mrs Blackley?'

'Kill himself. He'd never do that.'

'We believe that he's been murdered.'

Tears flowed then, and Murray was despatched to fetch a glass of water and some tissues.

'I understand this is a shock for you, Mrs Blackley, but, if you don't mind, I need to ask you some questions.'

Gwen Blackley nodded, and thankfully Murray returned quickly with the water and a piece of kitchen roll.

'When did you last see Terry?' Tara continued.

'About two weeks ago, end of August. We both took Maisie back to school after the summer holidays. She boards.'

'Have you spoken to him since then?'

'Briefly, last week. There's a concert coming up at the school. I was inviting him to go, although I doubt if he would remember when the time came. Not what you'd call reliable, is Terry.'

'Did he mention anything that was troubling him?'

Gwen shook her head slowly, dabbing at her eyes with the kitchen roll.

'Did he sound in good spirits?'

'He sounded like he always did, Inspector – preoccupied. Maisie is the only common ground between us nowadays. Apart from our daughter, Terry's head was always somewhere else.'

'And your present husband, Mr Blackley?'

'Evan? What's he got to do with it?'

'Did he have any contact with Mr Lawler?'

She looked indignant at the question, her tears drying. Maybe her defences were up, Tara thought.

'Evan and Terry don't, didn't, see eye to eye. As far as I'm aware they didn't have any contact.'

'I used to watch Evan Blackley play at Anfield,' said Murray. Gwen didn't seem impressed. 'Pity what happened in Italy.'

'A long time ago, Sergeant.'

'Before you met him?'

'Yes.'

'Seems like he's doing all right now,' Murray replied, gazing around the room.

Gwen Blackley was not about to grace the remark with any kind of reply. She merely winced.

'If you don't mind, Inspector, if you have no further questions I would like to go and see Maisie, to break the news.'

'Yes, of course. I'm very sorry for your trouble. I'll leave you my card. If you think of anything that might help us find the person responsible for Terry's death, please get in touch.'

'Cool customer that Gwen Blackley,' said Murray on the drive back to Liverpool. 'Did you notice that she didn't ask anything about how Lawler was killed?'

'Mm. Cool customer or very good actress.'

An hour later, they were standing in the home of Lynsey Yeats. If Gwen Blackley had given the appearance of a well-presented affluent lady, then Lynsey Yeats moved within a much different world. Tara's first impression was of a twenty-something who, though tall, looked more like a teenager, a schoolgirl but already with a lifetime of experience. Her face, pitted with acne scars, was pale and sick-looking. Her eyes sported poorly applied liner, thick and smudged, and it was difficult to work out any natural colour of hair with traces of pink, green, blonde and more recently, it seemed, a chestnut brown, cut with a deep fringe that threatened to obscure her vision. She looked pissed off, permanently, a scowl more easily summoned than a smile. Her style statement was visible in the tattoos of creeping ivy and butterflies around the base of her neck, up to her left ear and all the way down her right arm to the wrist. Tara would not have been surprised to learn there were several more under the red vest and black jeans.

'Haven't seen that bastard in weeks,' she replied to Murray's question. 'And he owes me money.'

She sprawled in a well-worn blue leather armchair, badly mismatched with the brown mock-velour sofa. Neither Tara nor Murray chose to sit. It was hard enough coping with the heavy stench of fried food, cigarettes and filthy cat litter. A television, hanging from a wall, blared out MTV, and Lynsey didn't seem inclined to lower the volume.

'Did you break up? I believe you used to live together?' asked Tara.

'Told him to sod off. Only brought me grief, no money and he was a crap fuck.'

'Did you row about something in particular?'

'What is this? What's the bastard told you? Did he tell you I was on the game? Is that it? Bastard.'

'No, Lynsey, this is a murder inquiry. Terry's body was found this morning.'

'Serves him right,' she snapped, although Tara could sense a slight change in her tone, shock at the news or a defence going up in the face of having to answer questions.

'When did you last speak to him?'

'Told you, it was weeks ago.'

'No, Lynsey, you said that you hadn't seen him for weeks.'

'Same thing.'

'Did Terry call you?'

'No.'

'Did you call him? Ask him to come back?'

'No way. Like I said, we were finished.'

With little further to discuss for the moment, they left the house on the Treadwater Estate in Netherton and headed for the last call of the day in Bootle.

It was a terraced house in a dull street but, at some point, an opportunist developer had managed to convert it into two flats, one on the ground floor the other on the first. Lawler's was the one above. They didn't have a key, but Murray was intending to put his shoulder against the door confident it would give under the strain. They needn't have worried; even Tara could have forced the lock. When Murray shoved, the door banged against the inside wall, and they stepped inside.

Opposite the door was a bedroom, to the right a small bathroom and beyond that a living area with a kitchen combined. Not a lot of furniture, an armchair and sofa, an old portable TV, electric cooker and small fridge. A desk by the window was piled high with paperwork. The place had more the feel of an office, where perhaps the odd sleepover occurred rather than it being a permanent habitat. Tara felt a chill as if the rooms had not experienced any heat in recent months. Vertical blinds at the single window were closed to the street outside, the floor covered in stained carpet tiles.

Murray had disappeared into the bedroom, while Tara set about an exploration of the desk, a home assembly affair too old for Ikea and possibly for MFI also. Buff folders were piled high on it. Some contained newspaper articles written by Lawler, but most consisted of notes and scraps of paper, typed and many handwritten. She didn't know where to begin or whether there would be anything worth finding. The walls were covered with posters, one of Blur, one of Beyoncé, and a few headlines from the national dailies, again presumably Lawler's work. She moved from the desk to the kitchen, opening the fridge to find it empty but for a tub of butter and the dregs of a plastic carton of milk. A cupboard above the sink held a few cans of tomato soup, tea bags and a near-full bottle of vodka. Murray called her from the bedroom.

'Thought you might want to see this,' he said, staring at the wall in front of him.

Tara stood beside him and examined the collage of pictures fixed with masking tape to the water-stained wallpaper.

'All girls,' she said.

'Some have names on them and towns. What do you reckon?'

'Your guess is as good as mine.' She took several photographs of the wall with her mobile. 'I suppose we should take them with us, and we can work on the significance tomorrow.'

They began peeling the photos from the wall. Tara counted twenty-nine; some were good quality glossy photos of young smiling girls, a few were scanned copies of prints and some had been torn directly from newspapers. Murray worked quickly and soon had most of them sitting in a pile on the single bed. Tara reached for the last picture and stopped to look at the grainy news cutting of a girl with cropped dark hair. She lifted her bag and pulled out the photograph she'd taken from Lawler's wallet earlier in the day. She was convinced it was the same girl in both photographs.

CHAPTER 9

Guy

Millie didn't die so well. The pills took ages to work and still she was breathing. I couldn't stay there all night waiting for her to snuff it, and I had no pills left. I had to make the tide or else I would be stuck with her for another day, and I was already feeling edgy, wondering if I'd done the right thing, that maybe I should've let her go. Chances were she wouldn't remember, not properly. Couldn't prove it was rape.

In the end I pushed her coat into her face, holding it tight against her nose and mouth. She didn't resist, and when I thought she'd stopped breathing I fetched the coal sacks from the front seat of the van. I managed to slip her legs into one and pull it up to the top of her thighs. With the other, I placed it over her head and down to her waist. I was disgusted with myself that they didn't meet in the middle. The only other material I had with me was a roll of heavy-duty polythene. It was far from ideal, but I cut a piece and rolled Millie in it, saving a second piece to wrap the bags of stones I'd already placed on the boat to weigh her down.

This was my first time, remember; I hadn't planned as well as I'd thought. I was worried about somebody seeing me carrying her to the boat. But if I didn't make a move soon it would be daylight and my opportunity would be gone.

In those days I kept Mother Freedom in the wee harbour at Groomsport. It's where my grandfather kept her, and it was handy to home. The village was quiet; it was after two in the morning. Cars lined the main street, but there was nothing stirring. I turned left off the street and rolled quietly down the hill toward the harbour, the car park deserted, the surrounding houses in darkness. The good thing about Groomsport harbour is that it's possible to drive a car right onto the quayside. Mother Freedom was moored close up to the wall. I eased the van past the slip on to the quay and killed the lights. I jumped out into a chill breeze and glanced around. All was quiet and safe unless some randomer nearby couldn't sleep and was peering out the window. But I had no choice other than to go ahead. I was past the point of no return. To be honest, I was past it when I put the coat over Millie's face.

I dragged the package from the van, holding it where Millie's head and shoulders were so that as I pulled her out her feet dropped from the van floor onto the ground. She was heavier than I'd imagined. It was one thing bungling her into the van when she was conscious, but now she was a dead weight. I could do little but trail her over to the edge of the quay. It had been my intention to somehow carry her aboard Mother Freedom, but I was knackered, and she was heavy. It took all my energy to bend down, gather the whole package in my arms and rise again to straightened legs. Felt like a weightlifting exercise. I reckoned, with a slight push outward, I could drop her onto the deck of the boat. If I missed then Millie was in the water, and I was in deep shit.

In the end it was a mixed result. I let her go, and she landed on the deck after her head hit the gunwale with an almighty thump. I threw the remaining plastic sheeting aboard, quickly closed the van doors, climbed in and reversed off the quay, parking in the car park behind the harbour office.

I ran back to the boat, jumped aboard and dragged Millie inside the wheelhouse. I'd planned to sail at first light, so in the meantime I set about completing the package with the bags of stones I'd loaded aboard a few days earlier. Each bag contained loose gravel and weighed twenty-five kilos. I lashed one to the top end, at Millie's head, one to her middle and one to her lower legs. Finally, I wrapped the second sheet of polythene around her, taped it closed and then tied it off with three metres of nylon rope. I hoped that would be enough to see poor Millie to the bottom of the Irish Sea.

I spent the next few days waiting for news. Couldn't help running things over and over in my head. Had anyone seen me? Shoving her into the van? Dropping her onto the boat? Did I leave anything lying around that could be traced back to me? The van wasn't registered in my name so that was OK. I'd thrown away my clothes and Millie's, promising myself that next time everything would go with the body to the bottom of the sea. I'd cleaned out the van as best I could, but already I was thinking of selling it on or burning it out. Seemed to me that the more clues I destroyed the less chance I had of getting caught.

A week went by before reports began appearing in the news about a nineteen-year-old girl who'd gone missing from her home in East Belfast. But these things happened every day. Millie was an outgoing teenager. She could be off somewhere with friends. She might have a secret lover. I could just imagine Joe Public thinking there's nothing strange about a girl like that going missing for a few days. Police explained they had no leads regarding the whereabouts of the girl. A few weeks later they staged a reconstruction of Millie's last known movements. Her visit to the gym was the last time anyone had set eyes on her, except for me, of course. A month after that, Millie's name dropped out of the papers, and I was in the clear.

During those weeks of lying low I went over everything in my head. How could I improve things? Killing and dumping at sea, I'd decided, was the best approach; it meant there was nothing left for a pathologist to drool over, no crime scene to be scoured by a hundred peelers and, although death was involved, the police would never know for sure. Each of my girls would simply become a statistic on the missing persons list.

I realised I would have to experiment on the best method of knocking the girls out. I had to be slicker. I investigated the easiest way of gaining control and came across a technique of applying pressure to the temporomandibular joint, the TMJ. Take a firm grip of a girl under her jaw, and she won't put up much of a fight. I checked the most effective drugs for doping and the best for inducing the final sleep. Using a van was the best thing in terms of taking the girl, doing my thing and transporting her to Mother Freedom, but I decided it was best to rid myself of the present van and buy a new one for the next girl. As for Mother Freedom, I would simply have to make sure I did a good job at washing her down.

Stuck-up Gemma was next. She went like a dream, and just before I did my thing, I saw the realisation in her dopey face that we had met before. Too bloody late, sweetheart.

I will give her that, Gemma was one of the best I ever had. Maybe I was more relaxed with her, confident in what I was doing. A little too confident as it turned out. I was sailing Mother Freedom out from Groomsport, I hadn't yet decided it was a good idea to vary the harbour where I kept the boat. Just off the Copeland Islands where the swell began to rise, I happened to notice the bundle of plastic and stones with Gemma inside was moving. At first, I thought it was the roll of the boat, but the lower part of the bundle began to move more urgently than the rest. Gemma wasn't dead; she was waking up. I panicked.

What I should have done was toss the bitch overboard and let her drown, but I wasn't thinking straight. Instead, I unwrapped the plastic sheeting, undid the ropes, removed the bags of stones and pulled her free. Her naked body was clammy and cold to the touch. She wasn't completely conscious; her eyes rolled in her head, and she moaned and puffed, like someone in a dreamy sleep.

I slowed the engine right down and let the boat drift on the current. It was a clear day, but no other boats were around. I dragged Gemma into the cabin and hauled her onto the bunk where I usually slept. I needed time to think. I was no cold-blooded killer. I hadn't the nerve to strangle her or to stab her. All I could do was stand by the hatch and watch her slowly come back to life. For the first time since all this caper began, I was shit-scared.

CHAPTER 10

Tara

She should have known better than to make plans, even to arrange a night out with the girls. Aisling and Kate knew quite well that Tara was never on time. And tonight was supposed to be catch-up night. They'd already switched venues to Aisling's flat, because Tara had texted both girls earlier in the afternoon to say she was already running late, and she wouldn't have time to do shopping for tea.

Aisling, tall, stunning, with a cheeky manner, swung open the door to her apartment, situated on the first floor in one of the restored buildings close to the Albert Dock.

'Don't you dare say it, Tara,' she said, wagging a finger.

'I know, but I really am sorry. We had another case this morning.' Tara plodded in, dropping her coat over an armchair. 'I hope you have wine in the fridge, Aisling. I'm dying for a good drink.'

'Lucky for you I stopped Kate from downing the lot.'

'Don't listen to her.' Kate laughed. 'I've only had one glass.' She rose from the sofa and went to the kitchen to fetch a drink for Tara.

'You look worn out, Tara love,' said Aisling, ushering her into an armchair.

Aisling always appeared ready for a night on the town: perfect make-up, big eager eyes and a smile capable of great pulling power or the biggest put-down imaginable. Tara didn't know of anyone else who ran around the house in heels and a mini dress as if waiting for a date to arrive. Kate reappeared from the kitchen carrying a large glass of chardy for Tara.

'Thanks, love,' said Tara.

The last thing she wanted to do when the three of them got together was to burden her friends with stories of her tiresome day even though both Kate and Aisling regarded her as the one with the exciting job. She was well aware that Kate, despite her zany fashion taste and magenta hair, was a dedicated nurse on a cardiology ward at the Royal. Her days could be just as tough. Both Tara and Kate envied Aisling who worked in promotions and on occasions rubbed shoulders with celebs, sports stars and those rich men she was holding out for. But Tara knew that Aisling would have it out of her before they'd even had time to eat supper. It had been like that since school days. Aisling was their guardian, their mentor, their patrol leader. She liked to think that she looked after them both.

'So, what's the story?' she asked.

'Morning glory,' said Tara, recalling Murray's quip, although she hadn't found it funny.

'Yeah, yeah, I know, bloody Noel Gallagher,' said Aisling with a frown.

'Don't you like Oasis?'

'Not since Noel blanked her at a party,' said Kate, kicking off her trainers and falling into the sofa.

'When?'

'Never mind that,' said Aisling. 'Are you going to tell us why you had a rough day so that I can tell you again to get the hell out of that job?'

Tara was well into her glass of wine, the relief instant.

'Been up since six, spent the morning with a body on Crosby Beach.'

'Anyone we know?' Aisling tittered before realising Tara was talking about a dead body and not a one-night stand.

'We believe it was Terry Lawler.'

'No.' Kate bolted forward in her seat. 'He's dead?'

Tara nodded.

'What happened?'

She explained a little of the murder scene then noticed that Aisling had gone quiet and slightly pale.

'Are you all right, Aisling?'

Head bowed, her long black curls obscuring her face, Aisling nodded slowly.

'He asked me out once,' she said.

'When?' Tara asked.

'Years ago. I wasn't interested; I knew he was married. Told him he was a useless bastard. That he should be at home with his wife instead of trying to hit on good girls like me.' She smiled sardonically at her own wit then rose and went to the kitchen.

Kate grimaced at Tara.

'Awkward moment,' she said.

Tara smiled weakly, and was about to go after Aisling, when she reappeared with a tray of finger food, sausage rolls, prawn toasts, chicken satays and pizza slices.

'There are nachos, sour cream and salsa in the kitchen,' she said to Tara.

Once the wine glasses had been refilled, they tucked into the food. Despite the woeful day, Tara was suddenly ravenous.

'Any idea what happened to him?' Aisling asked, breaking the silence.

'Definitely murdered, and the list of possibilities as to the killer is growing. Do you know much about him?'

She shrugged her shoulders.

'Same as everyone else. He was a thorn in the side of politicians and celebrities, and he cheated on his wife.'

'That would be Gwen Thomas, now Blackley.'

'That's right, poor girl went from one prick to another.'

'Do you know anything about Evan Blackley?'

'Steer well clear of him. I would say he's up to all sorts, but nowadays he's careful, not likely to get caught by the bizzies.'

'Shall we open another bottle?' Kate asked. 'I think I'll need more if you two are going to natter all night about crooks and murders. You know, we really need to get out more.'

CHAPTER 11

Guy

I sailed into quiet water on the north side of Lighthouse Island and dropped anchor. Thankfully, the sea was flat calm. Gemma wasn't fully conscious, but her arms and legs twitched periodically. I took off my jumper and jeans and lay down in the bunk beside her, pulling a blanket over us both. Her perfume still clung to her hair, and I nuzzled my face into the back of her head. In time, I felt her body grow warm against my own. Didn't take long to get in the mood again. I had a second helping of Gemma, and when I'd finished, I reckoned she was never going to fully come round. The guilt and fear left me, and when I'd dressed, I dragged her outside and wrapped her once more in the plastic sheeting. This time I also packed the blanket and mattress from the bunk. Satisfied that she was secure, I weighed anchor and powered the boat way out into the channel as far as I dared. I convinced myself that there was little movement from the bundle now, slowed the engine and quickly tumbled Gemma into the drink. Then I threw up.

In the days that followed, while I waited for the news to break on another disappearance, I promised myself not to mess up like that ever again. There would be no more mistakes. I would make sure the drugs were enough to do the job; I wouldn't mess about with plastic sheeting and ropes; I wouldn't do anything with girls on the boat and risk their DNA being found and, most importantly, I wouldn't do any more girls in Belfast. Too small a town. More than two disappearances and the peelers would definitely put together a connection. They're not as stupid as they look.

It was time to move on.

CHAPTER 12

Tara

Superintendent Tweedy closed his Bible, returning it to its usual place at the left-hand corner of his desk as his team of detectives filed into his office. By the time Murray, Wilson and Tara were seated, Tweedy was standing by his whiteboard at the ready.

'Good morning, folks,' he said in his familiar sedate tone, more counsellor than policeman. 'I hope you have had some time to put together the main facts in this very deplorable case. I'll start us off by running through the early findings from the post-mortem.' He lifted two pages of A4 from his desk and glanced down the text. 'We still await official identification, although I gather Mrs Blackley, his ex-wife, will be doing that this morning, Tara?'

'That's correct, sir, eleven-thirty.'

'We are fairly certain that the victim was Terry Lawler, a freelance journalist and well known in these parts. Findings from the PM indicate he had been dead for at least five hours. Multiple bruising and contusions to head, neck, face and abdomen. It is likely that he was unconscious when buried in the sand; there were no signs of sand or salt water in his stomach or lungs. Safe to assume also that at least he was unconscious by the time he was castrated. Any suggestions so far from this MO, on motive or suspects?'

'Had to be more than one person involved,' said Murray. 'Can't have been easy for one bloke getting the body into that position on the beach.'

'Any ideas about the castration?' Tweedy asked.

'Has the hallmarks of a gang-style murder,' said Wilson.

'Do you know of any gang that does the likes of this, John?' Tweedy replied.

'No, sir. But it seems to me that the killer was trying to make a statement of some kind. A warning to others, maybe.'

'What are your feelings so far, Tara?' Tweedy asked.

'I tend to agree with John at the moment. Someone is making a statement all right, but I wonder if their intention is to mislead, an attempt to hide the truth.'

If she was honest, Tara had no real basis for making such a remark. It was merely her gut instinct. The vision of a naked body castrated and buried head first on a beach puzzled her. She was not so much focused on the details of the murder scene but more on potential suspects. She and Murray had already stepped into a veritable quagmire of possibilities. According to family and friends, Lawler had, over the years, annoyed a lot of people. Those with an axe to grind against Terry Lawler might well have been queuing up to put an end to the journalist.

Tara reported on the events of the previous day, the conversations with Paul Macklin, Gwen Blackley, Lynsey

Yeats, and she told them about the trip they'd made to Terry Lawler's flat and what they had found on his bedroom wall.

'Do you think these photographs may have some relevance, Tara?' Tweedy asked.

'I think it's possible. But we need to look at all the investigations that Lawler has reported in his career. It may be that someone has held a grudge for some time and finally found a way to get back at him.'

'He certainly unchained a few beasts in his time,' said Murray. 'More enemies than friends, I'd say.'

'Anything on his last known whereabouts?'

'He had lunch with his friend Paul Macklin, about a week ago,' Tara replied. 'He spoke to his ex-wife on the phone around the same time. We have nothing more recent than that.'

Tweedy looked despondent at the news. He was a man well accustomed to investigating violent murders, but his mood always tended toward pensive when there didn't seem to be a clear direction ahead. He dismissed his officers with their list of tasks to improve matters in finding the killer of Terry Lawler.

Following the investigation of Lawler's flat by a team of forensics, all of the paperwork, news stories and files had been delivered to the operations room at St Anne Street station. Tara set Wilson, along with two other junior officers, the task of putting the relevant files and folders together. She and Murray, after attending the official identification of Lawler's body by his ex-wife, spent the remainder of the day, and into the evening, going over the writings of the journalist. Somewhere amongst it all, Tara hoped to find at least the next step to take in this case.

Around seven o'clock, Murray brought sandwiches and coffee for both of them. Even while they ate, they continued to read in silence on opposite sides of the room. Tara had decided simply to create a pile of those items that were worth following up. Most of them would probably never amount to anything, and it was wishful thinking to believe any patterns would emerge from their search.

It would be a gross understatement to say that during his time as a reporter for a Liverpool daily paper, Lawler had taken a slight interest in the workings of the City Council. It seemed that over a five-year period very few councillors escaped his wrath. For the more prominent, it was their decision-making he'd targeted, in some cases the lack of it, and in others it was, he alleged, their activities that were tantamount to corruption. For a few he dug deep into their details of expense accounts, foreign trips and wining and dining at the city's expense.

Lawler was not a man to let things go. Once he had his teeth into a story, he'd shaken it violently until things began to fall out. His paper had been sued seven times in five years over his stories, although it was interesting to note that only one ended in the court deciding for the plaintiff. Tara jotted down the name of the councillor involved. Matt Sullivan, now chairman of the city council planning committee, was at the time of the court case merely a committee member. She noted with interest that the allegations made by Lawler against Councillor Sullivan concerned his dealings with a company called EB Property Management. Lawler's paper had to fork out a five-figure sum to Sullivan for what the judge described as 'reckless story-making' by one of its top journalists.

For Tara, this was perhaps one of the leads she'd been hoping for. It was a link between Terry Lawler, his work and someone who might hold a grudge. It could be that Matt Sullivan still had issues with Lawler, enough to have him killed perhaps, but Tara was more interested in Sullivan's connection to the property company and its director Evan Blackley, husband to Lawler's ex-wife Gwen.

'Thought this might be worth looking into,' said Murray, his voice sounding weary, not his upbeat self.

He stood over her, shirt open at the neck, tie long since discarded, odour not pleasant.

'I think it's possibly Lawler's last published article,' he said and dropped the typed pages onto her desk. 'Dated three weeks ago. I have Wilson searching for the actual newsprint, if it got that far.'

Tara sat back in her chair to read. She'd kicked off her shoes hours ago, and Murray looked bemused to see her stockinged feet now resting on her desk. They were having a productive evening.

Murray had unearthed a story pointing to Lawler's investigation of local drug dealing. It was clear from what he had written that Lawler was not frightened of getting into the centre of the action. He claimed to have been witness to street-level dealing, a local lad supplying kids with tabs and speed, then moving further up the chain, he had observed a major delivery of cannabis and its distribution across Merseyside. The only problem with this particular story was that it lacked names, real names. But had Lawler done enough to expose the people involved in trafficking drugs across Liverpool? Had he gone too far? Had he put his own life on the line? And why had the killer chosen to place his body, in such a bizarre configuration, on Crosby Beach?

CHAPTER 13

Guy

Ecstasy: Mandy, MDMA, 3,4-methylenedioxy-methamphetamine. A psychoactive drug that causes hypothermia, dehydration and insomnia. No bloody use to me.

Ketamine hydrochloride: an anaesthetic; numbs the body; comes in powder form to snort, to mix with drinks or to smoke with marijuana. A standard date-rape drug.

Rohypnol: Roofies, seven times more potent than Valium.

GHB: gamma hydroxybutyrate, a depressant of the central nervous system. Known as Grievous Bodily Harm or Liquid Ecstasy. Causes drowsiness, dizziness and unconsciousness; an overdose can be fatal.

Chloral hydrate: Mickey Finn, good for slipping into drinks.

Oxycodone: Hillbilly Heroin. Very addictive, induces extreme relaxation, slurred speech, respiratory depression. Can be injected by needle.

Fentanyl: China Girl, China White, TNT and Murder 8. More potent than heroin. The lethal dose in humans is 2 milligrams.

In the beginning I used anything I could lay my hands on: Roofies, Valium, GHB, Mickey Finns and even bog standard sleeping pills. Later, when I got nice and settled in Liverpool, set up a few contacts, fentanyl became my drug of choice. I'll never know how I managed to see off Millie and Gemma without it. Before leaving Belfast, I promised myself that I wouldn't mess about with sub-standard gear. Everything had to be slick. I couldn't face another episode like the one with Gemma waking up on the boat.

When I'd secured a supply of the right stuff, I checked out the correct dosage to induce sleep or drowsiness. I would give my girls just enough to stop them from putting up a fight but leave them so they could see what I was doing with them. Then I had to get the right lethal dose. Easy done, you might say; just pump them full of the stuff. But the drugs cost money, you know. I didn't want to waste a drop. Get the dose right and I wouldn't have a problem.

In Liverpool, I got a couple of jobs, one delivering medical supplies, the other working at a burger bar. With shift work, both gave me the chance to indulge my hobby. I had enough money to rent a one-bedroom flat in Toxteth, a bit of a dive, but I didn't need much. Once I got settled, I made the journey home one weekend in May to collect Mother Freedom. I sailed her across the shuck, stopping off at Ramsey on the Isle of Man, then on to the Liverpool Marina. I'd already arranged a berth there that hopefully could serve as my home port, so to speak. Next, I sussed out some of the local car auctions, where I could easily buy or sell a van when I needed to.

The whole time, while I got set up in Liverpool, I kept an eye on events at home. I was still nervous that somehow the body of Gemma or Millie might be found washed up on the beach, that someone would remember seeing me hanging around by Millie's house, or following Gemma as she arrived each morning at Queen's for a lecture, that somehow the peelers had me captured on CCTV taking Gemma, shoving her into the van and driving off, that some nosey git walking late at night by the harbour had seen me dropping a heavy package onto Mother Freedom. But there was nothing. Not a damn thing. Appeals from the police for information came and went. Both girls had nice wee pictures on the UK missing persons website, but there were thousands of similar pictures of people from all over the country. Eventually, I came to realise that Millie and Gemma were nothing but statistics; only their families and close friends missed them.

I won't bore you with the details of every score. Like I said already, I never made a list of them, I didn't keep souvenirs and I didn't leave any clues. I just enjoyed myself. Didn't see the time going in. Five years after leaving Belfast, I'd done girls in all the major cities. Liverpool was first, then Manchester, Bristol, Brighton, a couple in London, it's so easy down there, like a pick 'n' mix. Then I scored in Leeds, Glasgow and Birmingham.

Of course, I keep a mental note of all my girls. I remember the first one who was married, Hetty, I called her, came from Altrincham. Then my first Black girl. I named her Donna, beautiful little thing squeezed into the tightest white jeans you've ever seen. I picked her up in Woolwich.

In the summer, I would sail Mother Freedom around the coast. Sometimes I couldn't find what I was looking for. I remember getting bored to tears in Ramsgate, and so angry I sailed all the way back to Penrhyn having wasted a week's holiday. I suppose I was getting fussy. Having notched up more than a dozen girls, I found I was needing more of a challenge. I'd always told myself that I'd cornered the market. I knew the best way of doing things, of getting it right so that I didn't get caught. I needed the thrill of lying beside a beautiful girl, doing what I enjoyed most; I didn't need to make things more difficult. I didn't need to stretch myself. I was doing just fine. No need to change.

But once you start thinking this way, you're beat. One of those bloody criminal psychologists would probably suggest that I did need to challenge myself, that I had a built-in desire to boast of my conquests. I needed more coal in my boiler; like a wino, the more I drank the more drink it took to get the buzz. But I had the perfect ruse. No one, barring a disaster on my part, was ever going to catch me. I didn't need to play games with the peelers. But in the end, I guess those shrinks were right. I did seek a bigger thrill. What worried me most was that having conquered this bigger challenge, I would have to keep moving upwards, raising the bar every time. What would happen if I set it too high?

CHAPTER 14

Tara

Smart grey suit, silk tie, expensive cufflinks, Tara couldn't decide if Evan Blackley was the real deal or a man who wanted people to think he was. She found it hard to believe also, that the fifty-year-old with sagging flesh around his face and bulging stomach had once graced some of the world's most famous football stadiums.

Murray had described him as the greatest poacher of all time; he'd scored goals not so much by his skill but more by getting himself in the right place at the right time. Several England managers, however, had seen through this lack of talent, despite the goals, and he never quite made his full England cap. After his move to Italy, he was largely forgotten at home until news broke of his alleged involvement in a match-fixing scam. Nothing ever proven, of course.

Tara discussed this football history with Murray as they drove from Liverpool to the offices of EB Property Management in Sankey Street, Warrington. They parked directly outside a two-storey building, fronted entirely by plate glass. Inside, the ground-floor reception and open-plan office had an airy clinical feel with light-coloured paintwork, polished floor and clean-lined furniture with no clutter.

Blackley had charm but few natural manners. When Tara and Murray were shown into his office by the secretary, he neither stood to greet them nor did he invite them to sit. This room also had that feeling of space and tidiness. His desk was a heavy-duty affair of dark oak, and

Blackley was seated behind it in a high-back padded chair. Two black leather sofas, either side of a glass coffee table, were set perpendicular to the large window overlooking the street.

'And what can I do for Merseyside's finest?' he said, his accent as rough-cut Scouse as the day he first ran out at Anfield.

His grin appeared as one of bemused curiosity; his dark eyes sparkled, darting back and forth from Tara to Murray. Shifty. Tara, by now, was well used to smug reactions. Most people she interviewed expected Murray to be the officer in charge.

'We've already spoken with your wife, Mr Blackley, regarding the death of her ex-husband, Terry Lawler.'

He nodded with an expression suggesting he was already tired of hearing about the dead journalist. He swivelled gently from side to side in his chair, fiddling with a pen, saying nothing. Tara thought it strange that he hadn't at least added a note of concern or regret that his wife's ex-husband had been murdered.

'We were wondering if you could tell us something of your relationship with Mr Lawler?' she said.

'Huh! Didn't have one, simple as that.'

'Your wife suggested that you and Mr Lawler didn't get along.'

'Didn't have to, more like. I had no dealings with him. Gwen had to speak with him from time to time about their daughter Maisie. I stayed out of it. I'm just the guy who pays for her schooling.'

'What did you think of Terry Lawler, the journalist?' said Murray.

If the intention had been to shake Blackley from his nonchalance, it didn't work. The smile stayed firmly in place. He began his reply with a shrug.

'Didn't take much interest in what he got up to.'

'Not even when Lawler's paper was sued by Councillor Sullivan?' said Murray.

'Oh, here we go. You think because Lawler tried to upset things once, I held a grudge? Sullivan won his case, remember?'

'And did you hold a grudge?' said Tara.

'Look, Inspector, I don't know what you're trying to cook up here, but I had nothing to do with Terry's death. Yes, I didn't much like the guy. He treated Gwen badly when they were married, he was a crap father to Maisie and yes, he tried to interfere in a perfectly legitimate business arrangement between the council and my company, but I had no reason to go after him. Like I said, I didn't care about him enough to have him sorted.'

'When did you see him last?' said Tara, piqued by Blackley's choice of the word 'sorted'.

It was the question to finally provoke a reaction in Blackley. He got to his feet, and tall as he was, at six-two, he bent forward and faced Tara across the desk. She didn't flinch.

'Gwen spoke to him last week about some concert at Maisie's school.'

'And when did *you* last see him, Mr Blackley?'

He turned away from Tara and gazed out the window, his hands thrust into his trouser pockets. Tara waited patiently for his reply. She could wait all day. Perhaps it was her silence that prompted him to relent, but finally he puffed air through pursed lips.

'OK. I suppose you lot won't let it drop until you get what you want. I spoke to Terry four days ago.'

'By phone, or did you meet?' said Tara.

'We met in a pub, his idea not mine. Can't think of anyone worse to have a drink with.'

'Which pub?' said Murray, his notebook out, preparing to jot down the name.

'Four Archers, near Southport.'

'Why there?'

Blackley shrugged.

'His choice.'

'And what did you talk about?' said Tara.

'He was stirring it again. Another story. Load of bollocks, more like.'

'You'll need to be more specific, Mr Blackley,' said Tara. 'It'll help us and will save you time in the long run.'

More air squeezed through his lips, and he dumped himself back in his chair.

'Lawler got wind of a council proposal to sell off land for development. When he discovered that I was interested in buying, he did his usual put two and two together and weighed in with both feet.'

'What was the problem with the council selling off land?' said Murray.

'Look, I've told you all I know. Terry got wind of the plan and decided it would make a story. He met me to get my side of things. I told him it was all perfectly straight but Terry being Terry—'

'You haven't answered the question,' said Tara. 'What was the problem with selling the land?'

'There was no problem except in Terry's mind.'

From ten hours of studying Lawler's work the previous day, Tara and Murray already knew what the alleged problem was with the sale of land. But Tara wanted to hear Blackley say it.

'What was Terry intending to do with his information?'

'Publish, of course. Another swipe at the council and my business.'

'And you didn't want that to happen?'

'I didn't kill him. He was trying to prevent the building project, but he didn't deserve to die for it.'

'Again, Mr Blackley,' said Tara. 'I would appreciate you telling me why he wanted to stop the sale.'

'I wanted to buy the land for a housing project. Terry was going to stop it by revealing that the planners were willing to overlook something to allow that to happen. He claimed the land was poisoned, contaminated with factory waste from years back. He said that it was never to be used for housing.'

'And is that true?'

'Course not. What do you take me for?'

'What did you say to Mr Lawler?'

'I told him his information was wrong. He could go ahead and publish, but the council had already made their decision. I had already started building on the site.'

'And what did he say to that?'

'Didn't like it much, said he was meeting with Matt Sullivan and reckoned that he would take it more seriously.'

'Anything else?'

'He left shortly after I told him to go fuck himself.'

'And was that the last time you saw him?'

Blackley clasped his hands behind his head and gazed to the ceiling.

'No. He came to the house, the following night. Told me it was my last chance. Sullivan had threatened to sue him again, and that seemed to get under his skin. He said if I didn't agree to drop the project straightaway, the story would go to print. I refused, obviously, and he left.'

'Was your wife at home at that time?' said Murray.

'Yes. She pleaded with Terry to drop the whole thing. She told him that hurting me would hurt Maisie and her. He didn't seem that bothered.'

'Why didn't your wife mention to us that Mr Lawler had visited your home the night before he was killed?' said Tara.

'I suppose she was trying to protect me, Inspector.'

'Do you need protecting?'

He shrugged.

'What were you doing last Tuesday evening?'

'Left here at six, home by seven with me feet up. Are you finished? I have a business to run.'

'For now,' said Tara. 'Don't plan any trips for the next few weeks, Mr Blackley.'

CHAPTER 15

Guy

Cindy was my next girl. I didn't set out looking for someone to be a bigger challenge, thought I would give myself time to think about it, to plan it right. In the end, though, Cindy turned out to be the most exciting and most difficult girl I had to deal with since leaving Belfast. Nearly three years had passed since I last picked a girl from Liverpool. By now I reckoned no one would ever establish a pattern between the girls I had taken. For a while afterwards, though, it seemed that Cindy was my biggest mistake, the girl who might cost me everything.

Shouldn't have to state the bloody obvious, but Cindy was gorgeous. The type of girl I could easily have settled down with and married. Friendly, straight-talker, funny, streetwise, the kind of girl who should never have got into the situation where a bloke like me could take her.

I got a job at the Royal Hospital as a porter. It paid better than the driving and the burger bar, and the shifts still allowed me to work at my obsession. Cindy was a staff nurse on a medical ward, and all the porters looked to flirt with any pretty nurse they could find. Cindy was easy; she could take stick and dish it out in equal measure. Sometimes we had longer conversations, for instance, when we were transferring a patient to another ward, or when I called by to collect the meal trolley. I teased her about her pouty wee mouth. She raked me about my dumb Belfast accent. Once I brought her a Twix and a bottle of water on my way past the vending machines. She accepted them as a peace offering, after I'd told her that her bum did look big in jeans. I asked her out. She said no. Told me she had a boyfriend. And that was that. Cindy was chosen.

Wasn't hard to figure out her work routine. I managed the odd glimpse of the nurses' rota for her ward. Soon, I knew her start time, her quitting time and her days off. I know this is a departure from my tried and trusted method, but I stayed friendly with her. The whole time I was sussing out her life, I still took her the odd Twix, still joked about her arse, which wasn't big at all, else I wouldn't have been chasing after her. I even asked her out a second time.

'Go on,' I said, one lunchtime on the ward. 'Where's the harm in going for a drink, maybe a bite to eat? Tell Gary you're working.'

Cindy had short dark hair cut in a bowl style, large grey eyes and clear skin to go with the pouty mouth. I swear she was going to say yes until I suggested she lie to her boyfriend.

'I don't keep secrets from Gary,' she said. 'He trusts me. Besides, I don't get to see him that often. When I'm not working, I'm at home looking after my sister.'

'Your sister? What's the matter with her?' For a second I pictured an equally delightful sibling who might fit the bill instead of Cindy.

'She has learning difficulties. Can't be left on her own for too long.'

'Can't someone else take care of her?'

I was beginning to sound desperate. It felt so weird. It was like I wanted to go out with Cindy so badly, because I didn't want to resort to taking her for good, and yet I knew that I could never walk away. It was either a date or I snatched her.

'My brother helps out when he can, but he has to work all hours.'

She looked as though she was weary of our conversation, and I let the subject drop. I felt strange about her having a sister who depended on her, but it made Cindy all the more of a challenge. Don't expect me to feel guilty about it.

We didn't say much to each other after that conversation, just 'hello' and 'big arse' to which she would reply, 'fucking Paddy.' She lived in a semi-detached council house in Speke with her big sister, Beth. Opposite ends of the beauty spectrum, they were. Cindy, small and perfectly formed, Beth, big and bug ugly. I drove down to the house a few times when I knew Cindy was working to have a look at Beth, to see what she got up to without her sister. Most weekdays, a bus collected her about nine in the morning and drove her to a day centre, where I assume she met with more of her kind. I spoke to her once when she arrived home in the afternoon.

'Hiya, Beth,' I said as she stepped from the bus. 'How was your day?'

'No ice-cream at lunch,' she said, barging past me into the garden and up to her door.

'Right.'

That was it. She slammed the door behind her.

I soon realised it was going to be easier to lift Cindy from somewhere near the hospital. Things were too unpredictable closer to home. Big Beth could complicate matters. Before I set it all up, I gave Cindy another chance to go out with me.

'How's Gary doing?' I said as we descended in the lift with an elderly patient minus his dentures.

'He's fine, I suppose. We're still friends, but we don't get much time together these days.'

'Which is why you should go out with me. I'm always here. We can have lunch together, go out to the pictures after work. I can help you with Beth on my days off when you're working. What do you say? Give it a go, eh?'

She smiled with that tiny mouth of hers. Lovely white teeth, she had. I saw a twinkle in those eyes. I could feel her about to say yes, and my wee heart skipped a beat. Then she cocked her head to the side.

'How did you know my sister's name?'

Felt like a stab in my throat. How could I have been so careless?

'You told me,' I said.

'Don't think so.'

I shrugged.

'Must have heard you talking to somebody about her.'

She didn't respond, and we left the lift in silence. I didn't get an answer to my invite. She wouldn't get another chance.

Within two weeks I'd done all the preparation I needed to do. I had a hell of a good time with Cindy, and she was soon at rest under the Irish Sea. I did the usual thing afterwards, covered my tracks, got rid of the van and kept an eye out for the news of her disappearance. All was normal, no problem. A couple of months passed, and then I heard Cindy's name – her real name – mentioned on a late-night news programme. Her brother was being interviewed about his sister's disappearance. Turns out he was an investigative journalist, and he was determined to find out what had happened to his sister. Fuck.

CHAPTER 16

Tara

Lynsey Yeats' house on the Treadwater Estate was, Tara considered, a reasonable point to begin searching for a link between Terry Lawler and Liverpool's finest drug dealers. The very name Treadwater sent waves of dread, sickening doubts and sorrow coursing through her. How could she ever learn to even cope with entering this estate? No memories of the place were pleasant.

Tara wondered if Lawler had used the house and his time spent with Lynsey Yeats to suss out information on the drug problems on the council estate. He had certainly written plenty on the subject. She thought, too, that perhaps Lynsey had a drug habit and either it had spurred Lawler on in his attempt to expose the dealers, or it had been the issue which caused the break in the relationship.

From her first impressions of Yeats, and what she had learned so far on Lawler, she thought it an odd pairing. Lynsey was little more than a teenager, and Lawler was thirty-six. Information gleaned from criminal records and social services had revealed Yeats' turbulent past, including expulsion from several schools for aggressive behaviour, two arrests for possession of drugs and a childhood with more years spent in care than with her neglectful mother and alcoholic father. Seemed more likely that Lawler had simply used the girl to help him get his story on local drug culture.

There was a greater reluctance from Yeats, on this occasion, to allow the police into her home. The reason, Tara quickly surmised, was the visitor sprawled on the brown faux-velour sofa, seemingly engrossed in a daytime helping of *Judge Rinder*. Shaven head, thin face, tapered chin, and a mouth too full of poorly arranged teeth, the youth didn't budge when Murray entered the room ahead of Tara.

'Who are you?' Murray asked.

'What's it to you?'

'They're bizzies, Danny,' said Lynsey, her arms folded in defence. She acted nervously, glaring at her friend who glared back.

Seldom had Tara seen two people who looked as worried and guilty as this pair. Tara had already noticed the marks on the girl's left forearm, something she'd missed on their last visit. Her suspicions had been right; Lynsey was a user of something.

'Who gives a shit?' The youth had suddenly found his bluster.

'We're investigating a murder, sunshine,' said Murray, towering above the teenager who'd remained seated.

'I've told you all I know about Terry,' said Lynsey. 'So, what do you want?'

'I want you to tell me what Terry got up to while he lived here with you,' said Tara.

She watched as Danny smirked. Lynsey shrugged dismissively.

'Used this place as a doss-house, he did.'

'You tell 'em, Lynsey,' said Danny.

'Thought he owned the place; didn't pay no rent, never took me out, never bought me anything nice. Used me, he did.'

'What about your drugs? Did he pay for those?'

'Don't know what you're on about. I don't do drugs.'

'I saw your arm, Lynsey.'

'Tell them nothin', Lynsey,' Danny said. 'You ain't done nothin'. Why don't you leave her alone?'

'And what's it got to do with you, sunshine?' Murray asked. 'You her dealer? Is that it?'

'Fuck off, cop. I'm not in that game.'

'Then what exactly is your game, eh? Chief interrupting gobshite? Or maybe you pimp for the girls round here?'

'I'm clean, all right?' said Lynsey, her voice shaky and losing its aggression. 'Terry helped me to get off them.'

'Was Terry investigating what goes on around here?' Tara said.

Tara saw Lynsey's momentary glance at her friend.

Lynsey shook her head. 'No. He never told me what he got up to with his job.'

'Ever visit his flat?'

'A couple of times. Terry didn't like us staying there; that's why he moved in here.'

'How well did you know Terry Lawler, Danny?' Tara asked.

'Tell the inspector your full name, there's a good boy,' said Murray, plonking himself on the sofa up close and tight against the youth.

'Danny Ross.'

'Well, Danny Ross, you tell us how well you knew Terry Lawler, and I won't come back here in an hour with a warrant to search this house and wherever it is you live.'

Murray grinned at Ross, shifting his full weight closer to the slight body in blue jeans and white T-shirt.

'Didn't know him,' said Ross.

'So, Mr Lawler never had cause to write about you in the papers?' Tara asked.

'Why should he?'

'I was thinking maybe that Terry knew you were dealing round here, that you were supplying his girlfriend Lynsey, and he decided to do something about it. And now here we are investigating his murder.'

'Piss off.'

'Don't speak like that to a lady,' said Murray jerking his elbow into the ribs of the youth.

'Danny's my boyfriend, that's all,' said Lynsey. 'He never met Terry. So why don't you get out and leave us alone?'

'Has he been your boyfriend for long?' Tara asked.

'What do you mean?' Lynsey replied.

'She means were you shaggin' me before Terry?' said Ross.

'It was never serious with Terry. He lived here for a while, but I wasn't sleeping with him all the time. He just wanted the company and a place to stay, that's all.'

Murray took note of Ross's address, although it did appear that he was seldom away from Lynsey's house.

'I don't believe a word that girl says,' said Murray as he drove them from Treadwater back to the station.

'Me neither. Clearly, she is, or was, a drug user and that has to be connected to Lawler's articles in the press. If Ross isn't involved in supplying, I'm sure he knows those who are. Plenty of motive there to have Lawler silenced. I think we'll have the house searched, see if we can find any trace of Lawler having lived and worked there.'

CHAPTER 17

Guy

I tried my best to keep an eye on that brother of Cindy's, but it was difficult. From watching the house in Speke, I knew that he spent some time there for a while then it seemed that Cindy's sister Beth moved away. I reckoned she was put in a home of some kind. Didn't think it was likely the brother would look after her. Didn't strike me as the type.

I caught a lucky break one day and spied him leaving a pub in the city. I had time to spare, my day off, so I followed him. He wasn't in any particular hurry, he climbed on a bus and I managed to get on, too. Easy. He got off in Bootle, and all I had to do was apply my skills, honed in trailing girls, to follow him. A couple of streets away from where he got off the bus, he opened the door of a flat with a key and went inside. From the outside the place looked pretty run-down, worse than my place in Toxteth, but he never reappeared the rest of that day. I assumed he was living there, and I went by a couple times after that, but I never saw him again nor did I see any life about the place. A month or so later, hearing nothing more about Cindy or her brother on the news, I felt the urge to start planning again.

Liverpool was definitely out of the equation for a while. I'd overstepped the mark with Cindy. I'd got too close to her. We worked together, we flirted; I'd asked her out a couple of times. She could easily have told other people about me. Her boyfriend, for instance, or that journalist brother. I'd been slack. I needed to get back to basics. To do what I was really good at doing. Taking a sweet girl, having a great time and leaving no trace. I was horny as fuck; I needed a confidence booster. I had to know that I wasn't losing my touch. I needed a challenge, something or someone that allowed me to put all my tried and trusted methods to their proper use. I headed to London.

I'd already bagged a couple down there a few years back. It was no more difficult than anywhere else except that I was further from Mother Freedom. That meant a longer journey in the van before I could get the girl out to sea. Strangely, with London, I imagined that you could go missing for a longer time before anyone started looking, before any alarm was raised. Maybe people are busier down there, or there are more distractions and more places for a body to go than in any other city. Maybe people don't care as much. Anyway, what I'm saying is that I had no problems taking a girl from London. My challenge, though, was to lift someone closer to the top of the food chain, someone famous, perhaps, or someone with money or a bit of class. I had to prove to myself that I could have any girl I wanted. Stuck-up Gemma had first prompted me to take what wasn't mine, and now I really had to prove it to myself all over again. I had to re-create that buzz I felt the first time with Millie. Cindy had been a mistake. I'd grown too fond of her; I should have walked away. Taking a girl from the place where you work was far too stupid. You don't piss in your own pen. Yet now I found myself having to go bigger to get the spark.

I took two weeks off work on the sick, said I hurt my back moving a patient. They wouldn't come after me for that, too scared of me putting in a claim. I stayed in a Travelodge in Paddington with free parking for the van. I'd brought everything I needed. There was no time for research, returning to Liverpool and then coming back to do the business. I wanted this to be the quickest and slickest job ever.

Like I've said before, it's all in the planning.

Before leaving Toxteth I'd sussed a few possibilities, managed to find addresses or the names of places where certain girls were known to be working, studios, the offices of showbiz agents, clubs they frequented. First up on my radar was a girl called Lucy. If I told you her real name you would recognise her from one of those medical dramas on TV, where she played the poison teenager with a penchant for rich and married men. I spotted her leaving her gym in Islington. Short legs, sailing blonde hair, wide mouth and full lips, Lucy ticked all the boxes as she sallied, dressed in pink leggings, baggy sweatshirt and white trainers to her Mini. I stood amongst the parked cars in the car park and watched as she drove away. Tomorrow, I thought.

The same day I hung around in New Bond Street where Victoria, daughter of a duke, who shall remain nameless, was working in the prestigious store of one of Britain's top fashion designers. When she left work, alone, inconspicuous, you'd never have known she was almost royalty. She toddled along the street in black jeans, multi-coloured jumper and black pumps, a woollen scarf draped around her neck. Fair hair snipped short, from a distance she looked ordinary, but from what I'd seen in her photographs in one of those *Hello*-type magazines, Victoria had class written all over her face.

Lying in my room at the hotel, I imagined me taking them both, Lucy and Victoria. A threesome, if you like. It would mean some careful planning, and I dropped off to sleep with the idea swirling in my head. When I awoke and got myself out among the throng of people in Oxford Street, I told myself that I should at least take a look at my third possibility.

Eve was a weather girl, mostly on national radio, but on occasion she appeared on TV. She looked foreign, that is, she looked of Asian or Middle Eastern descent. Dusky skin, shining black hair in a wispy style around her face and absolutely no meat on her bones. I'd never seen her from the waist down but, from her personal website, I noted that she was merely five foot three and single. Bless her.

Took me three days of my two weeks in London before I spied her leaving Broadcasting House. It was getting on for seven in the evening, raining and a wind getting up. Just the way I liked it, except I hadn't planned on taking her so soon. She walked right by me on the pavement as I pretended to cross the road. She glanced at me, and I tried a smile, but instantly her gaze from almond eyes dropped to the ground with the spots of rain. I decided there and then. It had to be her, and it had to be tonight, if I could manage it. Visions of Lucy and Victoria were greatly suppressed.

When she was twenty yards or so along the street, I turned and began to follow. She rounded a corner, and I ran to catch up. Fast walker. I hurried after her. In this weather she wouldn't twig to me following. No one was hanging about in the rain. My head was thumping, a pulsing in my temples. So many questions and doubts were surfacing. How did I take her? How did I get her to the van? It was nearly a mile away. This was stupid, and yet on I went. I tried telling myself that it was a dry run. Once I knew her route home, I'd take her on another night. I was so messed up.

I charged on and nearly collided with her as she stopped to cross the road. She seemed to be aware of me standing close behind her. She turned briefly, forced a quick smile, and before I had the chance to do anything, she hurried across the road, now clear of traffic. I didn't move. Without her even being aware of what I was up to she'd got the better of me. A silver Mercedes swerved to a halt on the other side of the street. A man, foreign-looking like Eve but much older, was at the wheel. Eve climbed in beside him, and the car roared away. That was the last I saw of her. I'd wasted three days on her, and in a few minutes had thrown all my experience and good practice in the bin once again. I was losing it, big time. May as well head back to Liverpool.

Instead, I had a restless night. I needed to score. Nearly five months since Cindy. Still, I was drawn to a more challenging subject. Eve, I decided, would be too difficult in a short time, and so my attention returned to Victoria and Lucy. I promised myself not to foul it up.

For a week Lucy followed the same routine, a mid-morning session at her gym then off somewhere in her Mini. Never had the chance to follow her in my van. Traffic was lousy. If I wanted her, I was going to have to take her in broad daylight. Too risky.

Victoria left her store each night between five-fifteen and five forty-five. Alone. She took the same route to Bond Street tube station. A couple of times I followed her onto a train and continued to trail her when she got off at Holland Park. From there she walked a quarter of a mile to a street lined on both sides with elegant three-storey houses. About halfway along, she descended some steps and went inside what I assumed to be her basement flat. I spent an evening pacing up and down the street keeping watch in case she reappeared. I decided then and there that I had two choices. Either I lifted her before she got to the tube station at Bond Street, or I waited until just before she arrived at her flat. Game on.

CHAPTER 18

Tara

'I would like you to sit in with me at the press conference, Tara,' said Tweedy from across his desk. He nursed his

Bible in his hand, looked preoccupied and clearly had moved on from his request. Tara's reply startled him.

'Yes, sir.'

It wasn't her first press conference, but she hated doing them. She felt uneasy sitting in front of dozens of reporters, photographers and television news teams.

At ten-fifteen they entered a ground floor meeting room at the station. Cameras flashed immediately, the huddles of conversations petering out with journalists ready to hang on Tweedy's every word. Interest was all the more heightened among the pack because Terry Lawler had been one of them.

'Good morning, ladies and gentlemen. I am Detective Superintendent Harold Tweedy, and this is my colleague Detective Inspector Tara Grogan. The purpose of our meeting this morning is to appeal to the public for information in connection with the death of Mr Terry Lawler.'

Cameras flashed again and several questions were shouted out by reporters, all ignored at this point by Tweedy. He proceeded to outline the details of the case, explaining where and when Lawler's body had been found, appealing for anyone who may have seen anything unusual in the vicinity of Crosby Beach on the night Lawler was killed. He also asked for any information regarding Lawler's activities on the days leading up to his murder, anyone who may have seen him or met with him.

Tara stared impassively at the men and women, holding out microphones and mobiles, wondering if she would get any leads from this exercise. Although she had her own ideas on who was responsible, so far, she had no proof that Blackley, Danny Ross or his drug-dealing buddies were murderers. A minute later, Tweedy ceded to the floor for questions. The first one was tame enough.

'Are you looking for anyone in particular?' a journalist from *The Echo* called out.

'Not at present,' Tweedy replied. 'We have several lines of inquiry running at the moment.'

'Is it a revenge attack by someone who got burned by one of Terry's stories?'

'As I have said, we are following several lines of inquiry.'

'And is that one of the lines?' the reporter tried again.

'We are considering it as a possibility.'

'Is the murder connected to the disappearance of Terry's sister, Ruth?'

'We are also considering that avenue of inquiry.'

Then came a question that Tara had not expected, never mind Tweedy.

'Is there any truth in the rumour that Terry Lawler was connected to the disappearance of several women, including his sister, on Merseyside in the last few years?'

Tara suddenly wished the room would swallow her whole. Tweedy glanced at her. She felt her face flush red. The pictures on the wall of Lawler's flat. She'd done nothing more about them. Hadn't followed it up. She glared at the young reporter who'd blurted the question. Another local. Maybe he knew Lawler, maybe he'd seen those pictures for himself. Is that what he was suggesting? That Lawler had murdered all of those women? But there were dozens of them. She became aware of Tweedy staring at her, waiting for her to answer the question.

'At the moment we have no reason to believe that is so,' she replied.

Her face expressed an entirely different answer as the cameras whirred and volleys of questions continued. Finally, Tweedy cut them off by repeating his appeal for information and then calling a halt to the proceedings.

Tara drew a sigh of relief as she reached the relative quiet of the corridor. Tweedy strode on by. She realised, of course, he'd want to discuss the matter that she had failed to act upon. She'd skipped over the subject at the second briefing. She'd set Wilson the task of collating the photographs of the women and trying to identify them. Macklin had told her that Lawler's sister was missing. Aside from that, she and Murray had chased after leads from ex-wives to ex-girlfriends to disgruntled businessmen. Why had she not thought that a collection of photographs of young women on the wall of the deceased's flat could be central to his murder? Her first thoughts on the subject had been to wonder what Lawler was investigating. Surely, he was trying to find out what had happened to his sister? She had not imagined that he may have been responsible for the disappearance of more than twenty women.

CHAPTER 19

Guy

A duke's daughter. Me and bloody royalty, who'd have thought it? In the end she was so easy. Picked her up on her own street. A firm grip of her soft neck, her eyes bulging in fright, I backed her inside the van and had the gaffer tape across her mouth before she could even whimper, dear love her. If I'd been into kidnapping instead of lovemaking, I could have made a pretty penny out of Lady Victoria. The fentanyl hit her fast, and within a minute she was out cold. I secured her hands and feet in the usual way and drove off, pleased as Punch. I was going to enjoy this expensive piece of totty.

After driving for half an hour, I finally pulled onto some waste ground on the edge of an industrial estate in North London. I could see the arch of Wembley Stadium in the distance. It wasn't exactly your romantic sea view but needs must.

Victoria writhed on the mattress on the floor of the van, her eyes still closed but she was slowly regaining some consciousness. I didn't waste any time. I did what I liked doing most. I stripped her naked and made love to her immediately. I didn't want it to end, and yet as I lay on top of her warm body, peering into her sweet face, I couldn't help thinking about Eve and Lucy. When I'd finished, I rolled off her and rested beside her, a blanket over both of us. After half an hour or so, Victoria woke up, groggy but awake. I'd removed the tape from her mouth, but when she began to moan and make attempts to call out, I replaced it. I made love to her once more, stroking her hair, placing tender kisses on her eyes. Great, I felt great, and yet somehow, I felt I needed more. I suppose I could have managed a third go with Victoria, but instead I gave her the lethal dose and watched as she fell into her final sleep. I realised then that I wanted Lucy, the wee soap star.

I must have dozed off, which was careless; I hadn't yet put Victoria into her bag. Anyone could have come along, although if they'd seen us both they probably would have thought we were lovers sharing a secret session. Before it was daylight, I checked Victoria was definitely gone, folded the body head to feet in the usual way, and placed her into the holdall. My clothes and the blanket usually would go with the deceased, but this morning I had some more business to attend to.

It took me a while to get my bearings, to find my way back to the gym where, hopefully, Lucy would spend yet another morning. On the way, I pulled into a retail park that had one of those sports superstores, and I bought another large kitbag on wheels. Cash only, can't be leaving a trail of me using a credit card all over the country.

The gym was one of those purpose-built things, basically a fancy shed with lots of smoked glass, sliding doors at the entrance and, thankfully, its own car park. As I pulled in, I noticed the pink Mini parked forty yards from the gym doors. I rolled past and found a space for the van well away from the entrance and as far away from any other cars as I could manage.

I sat for a while watching all who came and went, particularly the women. Some very tasty merchandise, I thought, information that I would store for future reference. I checked my watch and reckoned that Lucy, going by previous days, was about halfway through her session. Enough time for me to set my plan in motion. I climbed from the van and walked purposefully across the car park towards the gym. As I drew close to the steps, I veered away to make it look more as if I were leaving rather than entering the building. Now I was walking toward Lucy's car. I slipped between the Mini and the grey four-by-four parked beside it and, crouching down, I rammed the blade of a screwdriver deep into the wall of the Mini's rear tyre. Springing upwards in no time at all, I kept going into the next aisle of parked cars, eventually turning back on myself to head for the safety of my van. I just had to wait for young Lucy to emerge, all fit and healthy from her exercise session.

When she finally appeared on the steps above the car park, I started up the van and stuck a baseball cap on my head. I watched as she made her way to the Mini, and then I saw her go behind the four-by-four. I guessed she'd spotted the slashed tyre. I rolled forward slowly in the van, and when I reached her car, I stopped to see Lucy crouched down at the stricken wheel. I rolled down the window on the passenger side.

'Need a hand, darling?' I said in my best Cockney accent.

She glanced at me, looking a bit reluctant to even reply. She stood up straight, very pretty in pink sweatpants and grey hoodie. Her hair was still wet at the ends. I reckoned she must have been in a hurry.

'Flat tyre,' she said. 'It was fine this morning.'

I jumped from the van and came around to face her.

'Got a spare?'

She shrugged.

'I think so.'

'In your boot most likely.'

As she turned to open her boot, I slid open the side door of the van. Young Victoria, all cosy in her kitbag was in plain sight.

'I should have a jack in here,' I said.

Her head was buried somewhere inside the boot of her car. She didn't answer. Good a time as any, I thought.

I came and stood behind her as she fumbled beneath the carpet of the boot.

'Can I get that spare wheel for you? It's heavier than you think.'

When she straightened and turned, I smiled as broadly as I could manage.

'Don't I know you?' I asked.

She smiled weakly and shook her head. Modesty, eh?

'You're off the telly, aren't you? You're that girl who plays the doctor's daughter.'

'That's me,' she said. I could tell she was relaxing, her eyes widened, her ego tickled slightly. 'Are you sure I'm not giving you any trouble?'

'No trouble, darling. My pleasure.' I pulled a pair of latex gloves from my jacket pocket, slipped them on and got to work. I didn't want to leave any prints on her nice pink motor.

At first, she was content to watch me work, but as I slipped the spare wheel onto the hub, I noticed her busily texting on her mobile. Didn't like that much. No doubt she was telling somebody she was running late. I finished tightening the nuts in place and released my jack. Deliberately, I ignored her as I carried the jack to the side door of the van. This time, as luck would have it, she came up behind me. I pretended not to notice at first and set the jack into the van.

'Thanks very much,' she said friendly enough.

I swung round, gloves off, and rammed my hand tight against her neck, squeezing hard. Nothing but a gurgle from her throat and even that, I squeezed away. With my other hand, I pricked her side with my screwdriver. She nearly fell into the van all by herself. I slid the door closed behind us and quickly I did what I do brilliantly. Had her trussed in seconds, tape on her mouth and a needle jabbed into her arm. Game over.

CHAPTER 20

Tara

Murray wasn't the type to do sympathy, but he had at least managed a look of understanding as Tara took her seat next to him in Tweedy's office. She was still seething with herself.

'Well, Tara,' said Tweedy, seated behind his desk. 'It might be a good idea for us to consider some of the points raised by the press.'

Tweedy was a master at removing the heat from a situation. She'd never witnessed his calm demeanour slip, and yet she'd learned to read between his lines. She knew he was not happy to have been put on the spot by a journalist, who apparently knew more about the Lawler case than Merseyside Police. Yet Tweedy was not given to loud reprimand. Tara recognised his tone when he was making his point, and after noting the failure he always swayed it towards moving on.

'I'm sorry, sir. We had considered the women in the photographs at the outset, but our time was more taken with interviewing the immediate suspects in the case.'

Tweedy nodded acknowledgement, his hands pressed together as if in prayer.

'From what you've learned so far,' he said, 'do you believe that Mr Lawler was responsible for the disappearances of several women?'

Tara glanced at Murray, who didn't look keen to contribute. At this stage, she knew they couldn't rule out the possibility.

'I would be inclined to believe the women in the photographs were part of an investigation by Lawler,' Tara said. 'He was trying to find his sister. We need to identify the women in the photographs, learn whether they're missing, alive or dead, and it might tell us what Lawler was up to.'

Murray spoke up at last.

'Do you think it's possible that Lawler was killed by someone to avenge the deaths of the women? A relative of one of them, maybe?'

'We have yet to establish whether any of the women from those photographs are actually missing or dead,' said Tweedy. 'Perhaps that should be your starting point, Alan.'

After a brief lunch, all too brief these days, Tara gathered a small team of four officers, including Wilson, to help her sift through the photographs taken from the wall of Lawler's flat. The objective was to identify the women and then confirm whether they were listed as missing, or already known to be deceased. As they worked, she remained irked by the question of how the press found out about Lawler's connection to these women.

'Do you think that someone we've already interviewed told the press about the pictures?' she asked Murray as he scrolled through a screen of missing person details.

'Yeats seems the most likely. She did tell us that she'd visited Lawler's flat. Probably saw the pictures on the wall. Lawler may have even told her what they were doing there.'

'Something we should ask her. I wondered too about the solicitor, Macklin. He was reasonably close to Lawler. Maybe he knows what the story is behind all the pictures.'

'Why don't we get Wilson to go through Lawler's published stories again? See if he had anything to say about missing women.'

'If that's what they are,' Tara said. 'They might just be a photographic record of all Lawler's conquests.'

'Do you know something about him that I don't?'

Tara blushed. She recognised Murray's attempt at innuendo.

'Heard a few stories about him, that's all,' she said.

'Such as?'

'Well, let's just say I don't think he was the most faithful of partners.'

'Another motive for dumping him on Crosby Beach. And if you don't mind me saying it, a plausible reason for a spurned lover to cut off his privates.'

Murray was right. She'd tended to ignore the MO on the victim as if it bore no relation to why the killer did what they did. And if it were true, who could have filled the role of spurned lover? Gwen Blackley or Lynsey Yeats? For that matter, it might well have been any of the women whose pictures were stuck to Lawler's bedroom wall.

She left her team to continue their search and told Murray to drive them out to Lymm.

They found Gwen Blackley at home, although she was not alone. When she guided Tara and Murray into her plush lounge, she was about to introduce her visitor when Tara saved her the bother.

'It's all right, Mrs Blackley, we have already met Mr Macklin.'

The crumpled-looking solicitor in a grey suit and white shirt, minus tie, sat up straight in an armchair. He looked embarrassingly at Gwen Blackley. Tara saved him any further anguish.

'Nice to see you again, Mr Macklin. And thank you for the information the other day; it was very helpful.'

'No problem,' he croaked. 'I just called to see if Gwen was all right. You know, after Terry and that. I should get going.'

'Don't leave on our account,' said Tara. 'In fact, you may be able to help us a little further.'

Macklin's bony face paled, and again he glanced at Gwen as if in need of protection. She didn't take him under her notice.

'Just one question for you, Mrs Blackley, before I move on to other matters.'

Gwen Blackley slunk into her sofa and stared tentatively at Tara.

'Can you explain why you failed to mention at our first meeting that Terry was here on the night before he died?'

'Evan said you'd probably ask me that.'

Tara didn't respond, remaining stern-faced.

'He came to cause trouble for Evan. I pleaded with him to ditch the story about the council and Evan's building project. Evan was stressed out, and I didn't want Maisie to be reading anything unsavoury about her stepdad in the papers.'

'You could have told me that, Mrs Blackley.'

'I know, I'm sorry, but I didn't want Evan dragged into this mess. He has enough problems with his business.' The woman glared at Macklin, but he seemed unmoved.

Setting her handbag on her lap, Tara removed a photograph and passed it to Gwen Blackley.

'Do you know this woman?'

Blackley took one glance at the small photo that Tara had kept from Lawler's wallet.

'It's Ruth, Terry's sister.'

Tara glanced at Murray who was pursing his lips. She now had a good idea why this woman had also appeared on the wall at Lawler's flat.

'This is his sister who went missing?' Murray asked.

Gwen nodded then dropped her gaze. She removed a tissue from a box on the coffee table and dabbed at her eyes.

'It's been more than five months, Inspector,' said Macklin. 'No one's heard a thing from her.'

'What do you think happened to her?'

'Your lot were supposed to be working on it,' said Gwen rather curtly. 'She wouldn't have just taken off somewhere without a word. She looked after Beth, her older sister. She wouldn't have left her. Beth has a mental disability. Terry had to put her in a home when Ruth disappeared.'

'Did Terry ever mention trying to find Ruth?'

'All the friggin' time,' said Macklin. 'He was obsessed about finding her.'

The mystery of the photos on the wall of Lawler's flat began to make sense to Tara. Terry Lawler had put all his investigative experience into finding his sister. In doing so, had he unearthed connections to the disappearances of other women? Maybe the team at the station had already discovered a link between the women in the photos. Had Lawler's search led him to find a killer, a serial killer, and had this killer seen to it that Lawler should get no further with his investigation?

CHAPTER 21

Guy

I tucked into a full English at a service area on the M1. I was famished. It had been a busy yet productive night, made extra special by collecting my second girl in twenty-four hours. I'd never done that before. And what made it doubly satisfying was that Victoria and Lucy were two of the very best I'd ever had. Still had to pinch myself at the thought of snatching an upper-class specimen and then a TV star for dessert. It would be hard to top that. I realised that much already.

I'd chosen a table situated below a television, and fortunately it was tuned to Sky News. Early days yet, but I wondered if Victoria or Lucy's disappearance had been discovered and made public. Their bodies were still in the back of my van. With a bit of luck, my snatches had not yet triggered any alarm, and I would have time to get them out to sea before any searches got underway. I hoped also that there would not be any connection made between the two girls disappearing. London is a big place, no real reason why they should. I guessed that I had at least another day before I saw any pictures on the news. The girls would be long gone by then.

I sat back in the chair to let my breakfast go down, and I began to relax slightly as I sipped on my mug of piping hot tea. Even for a pro like me, you still get a big rush of adrenalin when you kill someone, and on every occasion my body shakes and tingles in a nervy way when I put a beautiful creature to sleep. Like I said before, I'm not a natural killer; it's just a necessary part of the job so I don't get caught. Funny thing is that it's never got any easier with time and experience. I get by, because I've learned to divorce myself from the killing part. Once I've had my fun, I try my best not to think of the girls as the warm soft beauties they were before I gave them the needle. It helps me deal with disposing of the body. I'm just tidying up after myself like I'm doing the washing up.

Satisfied that nothing was going to flash on the TV, I finished my tea and thought it best to get back on the road. I'd moored Mother Freedom in Whitehaven, quite a distance north of Liverpool, and I needed to sail before dawn the next morning. As I got to my feet, I noticed something appear on the news and, suddenly, I felt the need to sit back down.

There was a report on a press conference given by Merseyside Police. A caption at the bottom of the screen indicated that it had taken place the day before. A middle-aged, thin-faced officer was talking, and I heard him mention the name Lawler. A young-looking girl was seated next to the man, but she wasn't saying anything, and I didn't reckon on her being a policewoman anyway. Looked no more than eighteen.

I had to watch for several minutes before I deduced that they were talking about the murder of this Lawler bloke. I knew exactly who he was, of course. The prick brother of Cindy, the journalist who was investigating the disappearance of his sister. And now, what do you know? He's turned up dead. Serves the bastard right for sticking his nose in where it wasn't wanted. I wondered how far his wee investigation had gone. At least now the death of Cindy – or Ruth, may as well use her real name – was no different from any of the others. Nobody was searching for her, and I was in the clear.

The thin cop was now answering questions from reporters. It was difficult to hear what the press guys were saying, but the cop seemed to be repeating his appeal for information on Lawler's last movements. Then suddenly he turns and stares at this wee girl beside him. Could have knocked me down with a feather. She *was* a bloody cop, a detective inspector. I thought, I must be getting old if that wee slip of a thing was a police detective. Some journalist had asked if Lawler was connected to the disappearance of young women on Merseyside in the last few years. I nearly burst out laughing. Instead of Lawler being hailed as the investigator of Ruth's disappearance, here they were trying to pin what were probably my kills on him. Fills you with confidence for the police in this country. The poor wee thing, Tara was her name, didn't seem sure of what to say, but it seemed obvious to me they hadn't a clue what was going on.

My attention remained fixed now on Detective Inspector Tara Grogan of the Merseyside Police. I wasn't worried in the slightest that she might be coming after me. Just the opposite. She was certainly a tasty wee thing. Blonde hair, tied back, nice big fiery eyes and a pout that would put any Hollywood great to shame. Sky News, as they do, tend to dwell on a story for prolonged periods. I suppose they have airtime to fill like any other channel. I didn't mind. I was happy to gaze on the cute face of Tara Grogan. Now, right in front of me on the TV, I saw my next big challenge. A cop, they don't come any harder than that. Didn't even see the point in giving her another name. Here's to meeting you, young Tara.

CHAPTER 22

Tara

Matt Sullivan was not quite the man Tara had been expecting to meet. She'd imagined a middle-aged, pot-bellied Labour councillor with a gift for presenting himself as a man of the people, a grafter like the dockers of old, a man who fought tirelessly for the social rights of the working classes. She couldn't yet decide upon his politics or his motives, but in appearance she couldn't have been more wrong about Councillor Sullivan. Barely thirty, a wad of thick black curls, trim, athletic, a cheeky smile and a trendy suit, Matt Sullivan led Tara and Murray into his office.

As she placed herself upon a battered wooden chair, long since past the point of merely requiring reupholstering, she glanced about the hovel Sullivan used as an office in his role as manager in his father's haulage firm. Murray had to remain standing as Sullivan gathered files from his chair behind a bombsite of a desk.

'And what can I do for you, Inspector?' he said in a more refined accent than Tara had expected.

She noticed that his eyes were firmly set upon her breasts. Even when he dared glance at Murray, his eyes returned not to her face but to the opening in her blouse. Trying to ignore his sexual proclivity, she didn't believe for a second that Sullivan hadn't been warned of her coming by his friend Evan Blackley.

'I'm sure you're aware, Councillor, that we are investigating the murder of Terry Lawler, and since you had cause to run up against him in the past, I wondered if you had seen him in the days leading up to his death.'

'And when was that exactly?'

'Last Tuesday evening into the early hours of Wednesday.'

'You certainly get straight to the point, Inspector. But what you really want to know is, did I kill Terry Lawler? And the answer to that question is no. I didn't like him much, and he crossed me more than once, but I never wished him dead.'

'Can you please tell us when you last saw him?' Murray said with a trace of impatience in his voice.

Sullivan had to remove his eyes from Tara's chest to look up at Murray. As he did so the cheeky smile vanished.

'You know, Inspector, there is nothing illegal or improper in my dealings with Evan Blackley. He is a successful property developer, and I am simply doing what I can to get the best deal for the council. After all, it's public money I'm dealing with.'

'If you wouldn't mind telling us when you last saw Mr Lawler?' said Tara.

'Lawler was a bully. Did you know that, Inspector? He might not have used his fists or threatened violence, but he had the power to destroy reputations simply by writing some tosh in a newspaper. He did it once before as I'm sure you know. But when he came to Evan this time, and then he came to me, neither one of us was going to cave in.'

'Very convenient for you both that he ended up dead on Crosby Beach,' said Murray.

'Like I said, Inspector, we had nothing to hide, everything was above board. We had no reason to kill Lawler.'

'You said that he came to see you after he met with Mr Blackley. When exactly was that?' Tara asked. She noticed already that Sullivan possessed that remarkable politician's trait of never answering the question that was put to him.

'I threatened him with court again. Told him he could print what he liked, but he'd pay for it, just as he did before.'

'Mr Sullivan,' said Tara. 'It is our belief that Evan Blackley, his wife and you were probably the last people to see Terry Lawler alive. That makes you a suspect in his murder. Please take time to consider that before I ask you once again to tell me exactly when you last saw Mr Lawler.'

'This is ridiculous. I'm an elected official on the council–'

'When did you last see him, Councillor?' Tara's face coloured as her voice hardened. 'I can always bring you along to the station if you'd prefer.'

Sullivan stared blankly, yet still at Tara's breasts. He scratched his head, wrung his hands, glanced at his watch then rubbed a hand across his mouth. Tara could see he was fighting a battle of conscience, but she wasn't sure if he was about to land himself or someone else in trouble.

'OK. I saw him the night before he died.'

'We've already deduced that much,' said Murray. 'Exactly when and where, please?'

'How confidential is this, Inspector?'

'Depends on what you have to tell us.'

He resumed the fidgeting and the preoccupation with Tara's chest.

'He came to my home, late on Tuesday night.'

'What time?'

'Close to midnight. He'd just left Blackley's, and I suppose he came to warn me that the story was going ahead.'

'Seems very decent of him considering that he'd told Blackley the same thing before calling on you.'

Sullivan had taken to chewing his nails, and tiny beads of sweat emerged on his cheeks.

'Did Mr Lawler have another reason for dropping by so late?'

Sullivan nodded several times before he spoke. It seemed he'd finally succumbed to the pressure he was feeling in being interviewed by the police.

'He guessed that I'd have company, Inspector.'

'And was he correct?'

'I'm having an affair with Councillor Doreen Leitch. She's married, in case you don't know. Lawler saw us together in a restaurant a few weeks ago. He called last Tuesday to tell me that if he didn't get anywhere with the housing story, he would certainly have fun revealing my affair with Doreen.'

'What happened when he called at your house?'

'Told me he'd seen Doreen arrive. He'd been watching us through the window. By the time he rang the doorbell, Doreen was naked and so was I. He stood at my front door laughing. He knew he'd got me by the balls.'

'And then?'

'He backed away, and I slammed the door. I know how it looks, Inspector, but that's it. That's the last time I saw him.'

'And Councillor Leitch?'

'She went home in a bit of a state.'

'So, you have no alibi for the remainder of that night?'

They left Councillor Sullivan to his personal battle of fear. If they didn't charge him with murder, the papers were likely to uncover his affair or at least his unpopular dealings with Evan Blackley.

Tara feared the case was growing very messy. People with motive for killing Lawler were popping up from all corners. She worried also that Tweedy would be thinking she was out of her depth, unable to cope. Strange how quickly stress can bring on a headache. She lay reclined in the front seat as Murray drove them back to the station. It had been a gruesome killing, and yet somehow, she struggled to sympathise with the plight of Terry Lawler. She couldn't help wondering, though, about his sister Ruth, the one who disappeared. And now it seemed she had another suspect to query. Councillor Doreen Leitch.

CHAPTER 23

Guy

My head was buzzing. Couldn't settle myself. Awake half the night. I had visions of all my girls, all mixed together, like they'd formed a gang in the afterlife, and they were coming to get me. During the day I drank heavily, vodka mostly. I hadn't been to work in two weeks, and I thought maybe it was time to move on. To a new job, a new town, a new country even. France or Spain, Canada maybe. I'd just done the best two fillies I'd ever had. Nothing to beat them. And here I was going over and over in my head, the time I did wee Millie and then stuck-up Gemma, and how she came round on the boat and I had to do her again. Was I beginning to feel guilty? Who knows?

And then all the messed-up pictures I was seeing switched off in my head, and all I could think about was this wee cop, Tara Grogan. It had to mean something. Was it a warning from my subconscious, telling me to leave off, that taking a peeler was a step too far? I just kept drinking and passing out. I hadn't eaten a decent meal for days. My guts were full of cramps; I couldn't take a shite. I didn't shave or wash, and my clothes were stinking. She must be a hell of a woman to have that effect on me.

The first thing to bring me round a bit, to sober me up, was the story on the news about the disappearance of a young soap star in London. Lucy had been at the bottom of the Irish Sea for a week, lying right beside Lady Victoria. No news of her so far. Didn't matter, I was in the clear. Looking forward to watching it all re-created on *Crimewatch*. Brilliant programme, the way they do those reconstructions.

I wondered how much they'd managed to piece together on Lucy. The television news mentioned her car abandoned outside her gym. Her colleagues on the daytime TV series told the press they were unaware of anything troubling the young actress. Her boyfriend, an up-and-coming footballer, had been interviewed, but all family were at a loss to explain Lucy's disappearance. That's the way I liked it. Straight out of my textbook. No clues, no CCTV, no reasons for Lucy to scarper. And then a couple of nights later, on the six o'clock news, they said that a friend had received a text message from Lucy on the day she disappeared, stating that she had a flat tyre, that a man was helping her, and she was going to be late for an audition. So, this Good Samaritan was the number one suspect. Not great news, but considering the way I had to work down in London, I reckoned I got off with it all right. It was time I pulled myself together.

My first shift back at the hospital was a Saturday night. Worst shift of the week. Drunks, muckers from Anfield and Goodison punching each other out, blood and broken noses everywhere, and we porters had to wheel the bastards all over the show. Down to X-ray, back to A&E, up to a ward if there was, miracle of all miracles, a bed available. The whole time those poor innocent people, sick kids, disabled, pensioners, had to wait quietly for their turn while these useless twats jumped the queue because they managed to kick up a row. Not much chat between the staff on a Saturday night. Nurses too busy and not enough doctors. It makes me so mad when government ministers tell us the health service is running efficiently, that everything is being done to improve the system. I'd like to bring one of them down here at two o'clock on a Sunday morning and get them to deal with one of those football louts. See how they take that.

The one thing about all the chaos in a hospital, though, for me, is that life moves at a tremendous pace. Shifts change, staff change. No time to dwell much on the past. What I'm thinking about here is that Cindy's, or Ruth's, name never gets mentioned now. It's only been five months. No one has ever spoken to me about her. Somebody must have noticed us chatting, heard us flirting. Maybe another nurse was well aware that I had asked Cindy out on a date. Nothing. And then her brother ends up dead on a beach. Some things are just meant to be. Sweet.

I thought it a bit strange how news of Lady Victoria sort of gradually crept into the news. Maybe at first the family were trying to avoid publicity. Maybe they didn't want a fuss. Maybe they reckoned on their daughter having gone off somewhere with a lover, someone not entirely in keeping with the family's standing in polite society. Sounds like the early 1900s doesn't it? But maybe Victoria was prone to spontaneous disappearance. Nothing strange in her escaping for a while. This time, though, the family were in for a shock. Victoria wouldn't be coming home to a parental scolding or a family lecture. They would live in hope on their country estate, for years perhaps, but she was never going to turn up living in a kibbutz or sharing an artist's studio in Corsica. I felt sorry, in a way, that I could never tell her family that Victoria was the tastiest bit of skirt I'd ever had. Maybe there is something in the breeding.

After a couple of days of the story loitering in the side columns of the daily papers, someone at ITN thought it worthy of broadcast news. They described it on the evening bulletin as a baffling mystery with no clues to Victoria's whereabouts and no evidence that she had been snatched. But the best bit for me was that no one proposed a link to the missing soap star Lucy. How good am I? It's just like in football when a team begins to build a run of victories, the confidence levels rise and suddenly they're unstoppable. That's how I felt. Tara Grogan was my next target, and I had every confidence of success.

CHAPTER 24

Tara

Tara considered herself fortunate that she still had friends. Good friends. But every now and then she had to remember that fact and make an effort to spend some time with them. Kate had a busy job at the hospital; she had a partner and an infant daughter. Aisling worked odd times, late into the night, early mornings; her work and social life were almost indistinguishable. She worked big events, like fashion shows, celebrity appearances, film and music promotions, all that promotional stuff, where she might be required to stand around making a room look beautiful.

Her friends led hectic lives, and at times Tara felt guilty being the one to raise excuses when she couldn't make it to dinner, or to the cinema, or even a night at home with the girls. It felt lame to say, I can't make it; I'm working late; I'm on a case. She didn't want to sound as if her job mattered more than Kate's or even Aisling's, but most of the time she did feel that way. Her job came with her everywhere. So much thinking to be done. She couldn't switch off at the end of a shift. Some nights she woke up in a sweat, petrified of failure, of missing a lead or a link, of the guilty being passed over. At least she slept alone. How could she ever share her bed with someone when she couldn't share her worries, her problems? At times she felt so alone.

She sneaked a glance at her watch. Ten past seven. Should be on her way to Kate's by now. At best she was late, at worst she was about to cry off. Tweedy wanted things straightened out. In his own measured style, he told her that the case was becoming cluttered with suspects, with too much speculation and not enough concrete facts. Tara didn't take it well. Although Murray and Wilson were also seated in Tweedy's office, she was responsible, she was the failure so far in this case. They'd gathered a mountain of information but hadn't yet figured out anything to indicate a logical next step. Then Tweedy noticed her checking her watch. She flushed, knowing that he would make no comment, but still it was noted.

Tweedy had done some rearranging upon his whiteboard of important points from the case.

'And who is this latest suspect you mentioned, Tara?'

'Councillor Doreen Leitch, sir.'

'You have yet to interview her?'

'Sir. According to Councillor Sullivan, the two of them have been having an affair. Terry Lawler was aware of this; he saw them both on the night before he died. Both of them therefore have motive.'

Tweedy stood back from the board, replacing the top on his marker.

'It's all a bit of a mess,' he said with a sigh.

Tara felt it like a punch in her stomach. Despite none of them holding any firm views on the potential killer, she took it personally. It was her case, she should have one eye on the killer by now. Silence in the office made her feel worse.

'Answers on a postcard?' said Murray.

Tara seldom appreciated his wit. He had such poor timing.

'I want to concentrate on the missing women theory,' she said. Tweedy raised an eyebrow. She wasn't to be put off. 'Lawler was obsessed with finding his sister. He seems to have linked her disappearance with the cases of other women.'

'But they're spread all over the country,' said Murray.

'They don't all have to be linked to Lawler's sister, but if we find that some of them are, it might give us an indication of what Terry Lawler had uncovered. If he stumbled upon the killer of one or more of these women, and the killer became aware of him, then I think it's likely that Terry became the next victim.'

'What about Councillor Leitch?' said Tweedy.

'It's still worth speaking to her, but I don't believe the MO is right for one or both councillors. Burying Lawler in the sand and then castration, I don't think Leitch or Sullivan would have wanted to make that kind of statement.'

Tweedy nodded his agreement, and Tara relaxed slightly.

'We don't know what Leitch is capable of; we haven't met her yet,' said Murray.

Tara fixed a cold stare in his direction, but she realised he was right. They knew nothing of Councillor Leitch so far except that she was capable of an extra-marital affair.

'What about Evan and Gwen Blackley?' said Wilson, in rather the same tone used by Tweedy.

'The same applies,' said Tara, looking at Tweedy, ignoring Wilson. 'Neither couple would want to draw more attention by killing Lawler in that manner.'

'Is it possible,' said Wilson, 'that the killer was trying to make it look like something it wasn't? A gang killing linked to drugs, for instance, who knows what those nutters would do?'

'A fair point, John,' said Tweedy.

'It might be connected to a drug gang,' said Tara. 'We know that Lawler had also been investigating the drug trade on Treadwater Estate.'

'You mean that guy, Danny Ross?' said Murray.

'Okay,' said Tweedy. 'It's getting late. We're all in need of a break. I think it's best not to rule out any of these scenarios just yet. Some, I know, are more plausible than others. Tara, I want you to catch up with that Leitch woman, and for now you may continue to examine the missing women theory.'

Eyes closed, she breathed in the cool air of the station yard, a welcome relief to the stuffy atmosphere that had developed in Tweedy's office. She thought she was alone until a voice startled her.

'I hope I haven't spoiled your plans for this evening, Tara?'

'No, sir. Nothing special planned. Just have to call with a friend on the way home.'

She knew he'd noticed her clock-watching, and he had that subtle way of making her aware that he knew. He was a nice man, a gentleman, but his years as a detective meant that there wasn't much that got by him. He was her boss, not really a friend although she reckoned, in times of trouble, he would be a good person to have on her side. She wondered how he spent his evenings. A Bible study class, most likely.

Kate had already put Adele down to sleep. Tara had hoped to see her goddaughter before bedtime, but it wasn't to be. She told herself not to make a big song and dance about being late, expecting her friends to understand how important a case she was working. Instead, she offered nothing by way of apology.

Aisling was halfway down a bottle of Prosecco, already her jolly self. When Kate entered the open-plan kitchen living space in the flat, she clapped both hands together.

'Right, who's up first?'

'Do Aisling, I need a drink,' said Tara.

'That doesn't sound good, is everything all right, love?'

Didn't last long, did it? Her trying not to go off on one about her job.

'I'm fine; just thirsty, that's all.'

'Come on, Aisling, into the bathroom.'

While Kate went to wash and dye Aisling's hair, Tara poured some of the wine and sank into an armchair in front of the TV. She was only faintly aware of *Holby City* as her mind clung to theories for murder, for the reasons why people disappeared and, uppermost, the vision of a body poking out of the sand on Crosby Beach. It wasn't just a change of hair colour she needed. At times she craved a better life. And all around this flat there were reminders that, like Kate, she should be caring for a child. Would the pain and horror of that day ever leave her?

Some lasagne and much wine later, the girls, in the final throes of new hairstyles, sat around the TV in Kate's lounge, curlers in Aisling's hair and Tara wielding a pair of straighteners over Kate's head. Not for the first time, the girls had swapped colours. At school they'd done it regularly every month, but time was more precious nowadays, and the occasions when they would cast off all inhibition and revisit the craziness of their youth were becoming rare. Aisling's long wavy locks of jet black were now more of a chestnut brown; she couldn't go directly to Tara's golden blonde in a single session. Kate, on the other hand, had no difficulty in taking on the shining black usually worn by Aisling, while Tara wondered already what her boss would say when he saw her orange bob. For now, though, the wine did its work brilliantly.

'We should go on the pull right now,' said Aisling, swinging her glass in the air as she spoke. 'No man could resist hair like that,' she said, giggling at Tara's glowing head.

'Thanks, Aisling. You don't look so bad yourself.'

'Oh, get a room, you two,' said Kate. 'What's my Adam going to say when he sees my hair?'

'Come off it, Kate,' said Aisling. 'You change your hair colour more often than you have a period.'

'That's just lovely. Thanks, Aisling.'

'It's all right for you two,' said Tara, following it with a hiccup. 'I have to conduct a murder enquiry with a bright orange head. What's my super going to say?'

All three laughed, and more wine was passed around.

'Don't you dare wash that out, Tara,' said Kate. 'We have to have at least one night out before we change back.'

'No, no, you're right. Besides, I might just keep it like this.'

Aisling sprayed a mouthful of wine trying to stifle her laughter. And for a few hours Tara had managed to put her case, her worries and fears to the back of her mind. She had always been happiest in the company of Kate and Aisling. Kate was now sharing her life once again with Adele's father Adam. Tara missed the times she and Kate shared her flat. Tonight, she wondered what Tweedy would say when he saw the colour of her hair.

CHAPTER 25

Guy

Took the whole day just to catch a glimpse of her. I couldn't hang around outside a bloody cop shop. How suspicious would that be? Instead, I wandered slowly by in one direction, lingered at the end of the road and went back the opposite way. Nothing. Not a sign of a policewoman, although I could never get a decent peek inside a police car as they came and went from the station. I was fairly certain that a cop, a detective, wouldn't keep regular hours anyway. Just had to hope that I might see her going off her shift, maybe catch sight of her driving her own car home.

Sometimes I'm the luckiest bastard to ever walk the earth. I'd given up for the day, headed to a chip shop for my dinner, because I still had a nine-hour shift to face at the hospital. After I filled up on cod and chips and mushy peas, I thought I'd stroll past the station one last time. And there she was, getting into a blue Ford Focus in the station car park. I waited by the roadside for her to drive away. If I'd had my car close by, I would have followed her. At least I'd learned what type of motor she drove. It was a start.

The following evening, I parked in a visitor space in the station car park. The blue Focus sat close to the building, no more than twenty yards away. Crouching down in my seat, a baseball cap on my head, I watched and waited, squeezing on my rubber ball. I studied the clock on the dash. After seven and still no show. She was out by six the day before. But you have to be patient in this game. I reminded myself that this was all part of the fun. This was how it all started for me. Doing the research, gathering the facts, laying down plans, all the while your mouth salivating at the prospect of taking a girl.

Seven-thirty when she stepped outside. Only out the door and she stopped in the middle of the yard. I thought she'd noticed me, but she raised her head and peered into the sky, her arms hanging loosely by her sides. Then a tall man, much older, came out behind her, and she spun round to speak to him. Could have been the bloke who was with her on the press conference I'd seen on TV. They didn't speak for long, and then they headed off in opposite directions. The man climbed into a silver Beamer, and Tara started up her car and raced to the exit. I gunned my engine and followed.

Certainly wasn't like those Yank cop shows on TV. She didn't have a notion that I was following her. I could feel the flutter in my stomach, the sort of feeling I usually get when I'm just about to grab somebody. This Tara had me all excited already, and I'd hardly got to know her.

There wasn't much traffic, and nothing came between us as she made her way across the city. I followed her into Canning Street, and she pulled into a parking space as I drove on by. I slowed down and pretended to make a hash of parallel parking while glimpsing her in the mirror. By the time I'd got out of the car, she'd flitted across the street and up to the door of a large cream-painted house. A few seconds later the door opened, and I heard the voice of a woman with short orange hair saying 'Hiya, Tara.' She went in, and I was left to pace another street for several hours.

Bloody midnight and the wee bitch never came out. I'd assumed the house wasn't her home because of the way the orange head welcomed her in. I'd missed the start of my shift at the hospital, waiting for her to leave. I took more chances than I should have done, walking past the window of the house, the curtains open, me chancing a glimpse inside. A late-night jogger ran past, scared the shit out of me. I slowed my pace as I strolled by the house for one last look before calling it a night. There were three of them, including Tara. A little gang of three. By one o'clock, the lights went out downstairs, and still no one appeared at the front door. Seemed like she was staying the night with her two friends. Sod it. I went to work. It was going to be difficult establishing her routine. Tara was going to be a hard graft, but I was up for it.

When I came off my shift the next morning, I felt like shit warmed up. All I wanted was to get home to bed. There'd be hell to pay if I was late for my next shift. Cranley, my supervisor, was a right Hitler when he wanted to be. Letting me know who was boss, telling me I was lucky to have the job. I knew he was on the verge of saying that I should fuck off home to Ireland where I belonged and let some poor Scouse lad do my job. But he didn't. He was smarter than that. Knew I'd have him for discrimination. Either that or I'd break his nose as quick as look at him. I wondered if he had a pretty daughter that might be of interest, and then I realised he would have needed a pretty wife first, and I'd seen his other half. Face like a slapped arse. Not likely she would ever have given birth to a princess. Maybe an ugly sister. Anyway, from now on, I knew I had to be on time for work.

I realised when I reached my car that if I didn't attempt a sighting of Tara this morning, I would lose a whole day. Once I got home, I'd sleep for hours, and then it would be time for work again. I drove from the hospital to the police station on St Anne Street. Driving into the car park, turning around and then straight out again, I noticed her blue Ford in the same spot as the day before. I took a guess as to which direction she would go when she eventually left the station, pulled into a lay-by a hundred yards down the road and waited for her to drive past. Wasn't long before I nodded off, the noise and vibration of a passing lorry jerking me awake an hour later. I drove back to the station, saw her car still in its place and returned to the lay-by.

I'd had nothing to eat or drink since my break during work at six in the morning, but I wanted to see Tara more than I wanted to stuff my face. Already this was a challenge that I was determined would not beat me. I would win. I wanted Tara, and she would be mine even if it took me a year.

Sometimes the gods, whoever they are, are rooting for you. Might be luck, but I liked to think it was destiny. I was meant to have all the women I'd had. And now I was meant to have Tara. It was half past four; traffic was building and beginning to queue. There, rolling to a halt behind a black van on the far side of the road was the blue Ford Focus. I tried to get a good look at Tara, but she wasn't driving. The licence plate was definitely hers, but it didn't look like Tara sitting behind the wheel.

I gunned the engine and pulled a U-ey into the traffic, a couple of cars down from the Focus. Some smart-arse in a people carrier blared his horn because I'd pulled across him. I just ignored him; I didn't want to attract attention from whoever was driving the Focus. When the lights changed up ahead, I followed the car easily in the queue, and when traffic gained speed, I moved to the outside lane, cutting back in again directly behind her. If it wasn't Tara driving, I'd just wasted my whole day.

She drove along Islington, then Churchill Way and onto the Strand. I began to wonder that maybe she lived miles out of town or on the far side of the river, but then she hadn't followed the signs for the tunnel. Nearly missed her when she turned right onto Queen's Wharf and, following her, I soon realised I would get no further. The residents' car park at Wapping Dock had a barrier; no way could I follow her through. Even if I piggy-backed, she would notice and get suspicious. Instead, I abandoned my car on double yellows and walked to the car park gate, stealing a glimpse of the woman getting out of the Focus.

Certainly, she had the same build as Tara and wore similar dark clothes, trousers and jacket. It was the hair. She wasn't blonde. She was a redhead. For a second I wondered if I'd got the wrong girl. Was it that redhead girl who invited Tara into the house on Canning Street? Was she a cop, too? Then I saw her as she turned and walked towards the entrance. I knew the face. It was Tara. So, what about the hair? Bit of a surprise, but I wasn't that fussy. It all added to the excitement. What an incredible girl. Tara was going to be so good. And now I reckoned I knew where she lived. We were practically neighbours.

CHAPTER 26

Tara

Closing the door of her flat, she hurried downstairs. Late. She'd told Murray she would pick him up from home by eight-thirty. Quarter to nine already, and she had yet to suffer the slow crawl of city traffic in trying to get to his flat near Liverpool University. There was a man standing at the corner, looking as though he was waiting for someone, his lift perhaps. He dropped his gaze when hers lingered on him for a second. A gap in the traffic and she was away.

She'd wanted to wash some of that damned orange from her hair before work. What an embarrassment, walking into the station, people she'd known for years asking if they could help her, thinking she was a visitor. Tweedy just looked confused, uncertain if it was actually her. Worst of all, was the smirking Murray, laughing with Wilson behind her back. What the hell was wrong with people? All she'd done was dye her hair, for goodness' sake. It wasn't as if she was a natural blonde in the first place.

'I was thinking of the best way to play this,' she said to Murray on the drive to Bootle.

'Do you think she'll deny the affair?'

'Wouldn't you? Politicians usually deny everything at first. Gives them time to make up their response, to assess the possible fallout.'

'Very cynical.'

'Come on. You see it all the time. An MP denies his affair, threatens to sue the papers, and the next thing he's making a public apology about his lapse and how he and his wife still love each other and are working to save their marriage, bla-bla-bla.'

'This time the politician is a woman.'

'And that makes a difference? I think Doreen Leitch will fight just as hard to save her reputation, her job and her marriage.'

The day before, Tara had made an appointment in order to interview Councillor Doreen Leitch. That gave the woman nearly twenty-four hours to get her story straight. There was no doubt in Tara's mind that Sullivan would have told her everything. Tara had no reason to believe at this point that the affair had ended. Sullivan hadn't said so.

The venue for the appointment, Tara wondered, may have been chosen deliberately to show Councillor Leitch in the best light. She was volunteering at a drug rehabilitation centre in Bootle. The building was formerly a Methodist church hall, a bit run-down, green stains of moss on the grey stone walls and a battered wooden door in need of some paint.

Tara and Murray entered the main hall through the open door to be greeted with suspicious looks from three young men and two women who, presumably, were drug users, seated around a trestle table and sipping tea from white mugs. A bald-headed man holding a teapot directed them to a door at the far end of the hall. It led to a dim corridor and a kitchen, where two women were washing dishes and chatting. One of them in black leggings and a green T-shirt stopped talking immediately when she noticed Tara and Murray. She smiled weakly and asked if she could help them.

'We're here to see Councillor Leitch?' said Tara.

The woman looked at her companion, who grimaced at the two police officers.

'Can you give us a moment, Sandra?' said Leitch.

The woman set her tea towel on a table and left the room.

'I'm Detective Inspector Grogan, Councillor Leitch, and this is Detective Sergeant Murray.'

'Yes, Inspector, how can I help you?'

Leitch was not at all the kind of woman Tara had been expecting to see. She'd imagined a fairly attractive thirty-something, closer in age to Matt Sullivan than the woman of fifty-nine who stood before her. She was, of course, remarkably well kept, glamorous even, with shoulder-length dark brown hair and large dark eyes. It seemed to Tara that Leitch could have Matt Sullivan for breakfast.

'I gather you are in a relationship with Councillor Matt Sullivan?'

The woman's pleasant smile dropped from her face. Clearly, she hadn't expected Tara to be quite so blunt.

'I believe you already know the answer to that question, Inspector. I didn't think my private life warranted attention from the police.'

'We're investigating the murder of Mr Terry Lawler, and I understand both you and Mr Sullivan were perhaps the last people to see him alive.'

'And?'

'Can you tell me what happened the night Terry Lawler came to see you at Mr Sullivan's house?'

'Matt and Lawler had a row. It had nothing to do with me.'

'What was the row about?'

'Lawler was threatening to expose Matt's connections to Evan Blackley and his building projects.'

'That was all?'

'As far as I know.' Leitch took to placing washed cups and saucers into a cupboard below the workbench.

'Did Lawler threaten also to expose your affair?'

'No, he did not. If Matt has told you otherwise, I can assure you that our affair was not the subject of the row.'

'Why, then, do you think Matt Sullivan would tell us that Lawler was intending to publish a story about your affair?'

'I really don't know, Inspector. Perhaps he wished to deflect attention from his dealings with Evan Blackley.'

'Do you think he had a reason to do that?'

'I don't know. You really should have asked him that question.'

'Where did you go when you left Mr Sullivan's house last Tuesday night?'

'I went home to a gin and tonic and then to bed.'

'Did you see or speak to anyone else after leaving?'

'No, I'm afraid not. My husband is abroad on business. My children live and work in London. I hope you are not suggesting that I had anything to do with Terry Lawler's death?'

'If you can account for your whereabouts after leaving Mr Sullivan's home, then I guess not.'

'Will that be all, Inspector? I have only a little time to spend here before my next appointment.'

'For now, Mrs Leitch, thank you.'

As they turned to leave, Doreen Leitch spoke in a softer, much friendlier tone.

'I would appreciate your discretion, Inspector, with regard to my relationship with Matt Sullivan. I have two children, both in their twenties now, but I don't wish to inflict any pain or scandal upon them.'

Tara gave a single nod, and she and Murray retraced their steps through the church hall and into the street.

She felt like discussing things with Murray. Despite her reservations about his personality and his attitude toward her at times, she did trust him as an excellent detective. She stopped at a Costa in St Paul's Square, and they both had coffee. Murray was unable to resist a blueberry muffin.

'A very complex woman, that Doreen Leitch,' he said with his mouth full of food.

'Certainly sure of herself.'

'Has to be, I suppose. I was reading last night that she is tipped to run for Parliament at the next election. If her affair comes to light, then I reckon that ends her chances of becoming an MP.'

'A motive to murder, do you think?'

'The woman is also a lay preacher at her local church, and she's been on radio several times heralding family values, talking about the tragedy of broken homes, single-parent families, couples living in sin, drugs, the dangers of the internet and children playing violent games. The proper upright citizen, she is.'

'Except for her extra-marital activities with a man nearly half her age.'

'Now, Tara, what does age matter when you're in love?'

He laughed at his own quip, but she was more niggled by his over-familiarity in once again calling her by her first name. Her problem with Murray in a nutshell, he had a tendency to overstep the mark with her.

'Seems to me,' she said, 'that Doreen's secret would have a much greater impact if it got out than Evan Blackley's property ambitions. That woman has as strong a motive to murder as anyone I've ever come across.'

'Where do we go from here?'

Tara couldn't manage the rest of her latte. It had only been an excuse to chat with Murray outside of the station.

'It's time we chased up Wilson to see what he's found on all those women whose pictures were stuck on Lawler's bedroom wall.'

'You still think there's a connection?'

'Lawler's murdered while he's investigating his sister's disappearance, what do you think?'

CHAPTER 27

Guy

So, some smart-arse saw a white van in the car park of the gym before Lucy disappeared. Big deal. No way could they trace it to me. The van was never registered in my name. I bought it the week before going down to London. It was gone two days after Lucy and Victoria went to the bottom of the sea. Besides, they didn't have the licence plate number. It's just some clever person dug it from the back of his mind, that a white van had been sitting in the car park before Lucy disappeared. Nothing to worry about. But it was careless of me. I've never left a trace of evidence before. That was me being greedy, taking two birds inside a day, one of them in broad daylight. I won't be that stupid where Tara is concerned. Everything will be perfect before I even lay a finger on her.

I switched off my TV, nothing but bad news on nowadays. What is the world coming to? An end, probably.

I tried not to let my flat get me down. Hadn't put much effort into sprucing the place up. How could I ever bring a girl here for the night? Filthy curtains, brown with grime but actually cream in colour. Bare floorboards, the varnish long since scuffed away. One rug, well-worn and stained with beer and Chinese takeaways. I hadn't washed my dishes for weeks. I just reused the same dirty plate and mug. My granny would have turned in her grave if she knew I was living like that. I needed to make an effort. What was I supposed to do if I managed a date with Tara? There's no excuse for untidiness. After all, I was so meticulous when it came to dispensing with girls, why shouldn't I apply myself to cleaning my flat?

All this bloody thinking was getting me frustrated. I needed to get a move on with Tara or else I was going to take another girl in the meantime. I wondered that if I were to follow one of Tara's friends, the redhead who lived in Canning Street, maybe she would have a more predictable routine, one that would lead me eventually to Tara. I was finding it difficult keeping tabs on her. One morning she leaves her place around eight, the next she either doesn't go out at all or she's gone before I get there. When I do track her to the police station I never know when she will make a rapid exit in the course of the day or whether she's likely to return. I'm used to establishing a girl's routine. Sometimes I can even figure out when it's their time of the month. But with Tara, she doesn't have any sort of routine that I can understand. I'm lucky to catch sight of her at all.

It took me three days to discover that the girl I'd first seen at the house in Canning Street was no longer a redhead. Now she had dark hair. It seemed like her friends were as mixed up as Tara. This friend also had a kid, a toddler. I didn't much like that. It was a complication, especially if I decided that after Tara I would go for her mates. As far as I knew, I'd never done a mother. Didn't seem right to deny a child one of its parents.

I sat in my car one morning, across the road from the house. Must have been around ten when she came out with the kid by the hand. They walked down the street, and I couldn't help noticing the lovely arse in tight blue jeans, and for some reason it made me want to hurry things along with Tara. Less than an hour later, mother and daughter returned to the house with a couple of shopping bags.

My big breakthrough came a few days later when this friend of Tara's left her house wearing a nurse's uniform, blue tunic and trousers, climbed into her car and drove away. When I followed, I couldn't believe my luck. She worked at the Royal, and I'd never noticed her before. Now it was going to be so easy keeping up with her. During my next shift I was able to figure out where in the hospital she worked, and within a day or so I knew her work pattern and her name. All I had to do now was decide whether to befriend her in the hope she would lead me to Tara or just track her movements.

CHAPTER 28

Tara

DC Wilson had done a remarkable job. Of the twenty-nine pictures of women taken from the bedroom wall of Terry Lawler's flat, Wilson had identified twenty-three and had provided case references for each woman. Tara was shocked by the scale of the investigation upon which she might now be embarked. Twenty-three women: all cases of disappearance, no clues to their whereabouts and no evidence to confirm that any of them were alive or dead. She wondered how and why Lawler had chosen them. Had he believed that each of their cases were similar to the disappearance of his sister Ruth? Of even greater mystery was that the disappearances were not confined to one city, to one county or even a region of the country. They were spread over the whole of the British Isles. What had

Lawler seen that connected them, perhaps to a single killer?

She kicked off her shoes, slid her chair under the desk and leaned over the files. The room was quiet, but not yet deserted. Tweedy was still working in his office. Murray had kindly brought her a large coffee and a cheese salad sandwich before leaving, rather nervous at the prospect of facing his first real date since his divorce.

Wilson had arranged the files on the women in chronological order of their disappearance. In each buff folder was the picture taken from Lawler's flat, an official police photograph used on the missing persons website, personal information on the woman, the details of her disappearance and any follow-up news and progress in the case. Tara began reading from the first case file, a disappearance that had been reported more than six years ago.

Eighteen-year-old Diane McCartney, a student of English at Queen's University, Belfast went missing six years and seven months ago. Tara studied the photograph of a broadly smiling face with blue eyes and flowing locks of blonde hair. Diane was last seen leaving the university library around eight in the evening. As far as police were aware, she never made it back to her room at the Queen's Elms Village student accommodation. Nothing had been heard from her since. Her family had said that there was no reason for her to disappear, and police were convinced that it was a case of abduction.

Tara read each case in the order set out by Wilson. The names of the women, their ages and the locations changed but, in every case, nothing more had ever been heard or found relating to any of the disappearances. It seemed that all these women had simply vanished from the face of the earth. She was well aware of the statistics: in Britain, every two minutes someone goes missing. Most turn up within forty-eight hours, but over two thousand people go missing every year and no trace of them is ever found.

Lorna Campbell was twenty-three, from Glasgow – disappeared after late night shopping in the city centre, never heard of again. Carol Rose, twenty-one from Northolt, London, worked in a call centre – disappeared on her way home from a late shift.

Each woman was undeniably pretty, but there were no other apparent similarities. They weren't all blondes or brunettes, they weren't all white or all Asian, they weren't prostitutes, some were married, some had partners, but Tara couldn't see anything to link the circumstances of any of the women to a single killer who may have had a specific reason for taking them.

She lingered for a while longer on the photograph of Ruth Lawler, sister of Terry, and she pondered how Terry could have made the connection between Ruth and the others. All of them had disappeared without trace, but what was it about Ruth that had been of interest to this killer, if indeed there was only one killer?

She examined the cases that had arisen on Merseyside. There were three of them, including Ruth, who had been the latest girl in this collection to vanish from Liverpool.

Even if one person was responsible for killing all twenty-three women, or more, it was impossible to conclude where they were based given the information she had.

The girl from Northern Ireland was the earliest. Did that mean the killer had simply begun to kill in Belfast and then moved across to England and Scotland? There were three cases in Greater Manchester and as many in Greater London. Who could say where this person came from or where they now lived? If Terry Lawler had really been onto something, had he in some way alerted the killer to what he knew? Had Lawler managed to identify them? Is that why he ended up buried on Crosby Beach?

'Putting in a late night, Tara?' said Tweedy, dressed in his black overcoat, ready for home.

Tara, bleary-eyed, gazed up from her desk.

'Trying to make sense of what Terry Lawler was doing with the pictures of all these young women who have disappeared.'

'Do you think he may have been involved with these women in some way? At least one member of the press thought so.'

'I did wonder, sir, until I discovered that one of the women was Terry's sister and that he was obsessed with finding out what happened to her. I think someone who didn't like Lawler very much thought they could muddy the water by trying to suggest that he was a serial killer.'

'Have you any idea who that might be?'

'I do, but at the moment I can't prove it, nor can I say they are responsible for Lawler's death.'

When Tweedy had departed, she spent another half hour going through the files again, trying to discover what Lawler may have seen and whether that led him to identify the person responsible for all these disappearances.

Finally, returning the files to a cabinet next to Wilson's desk, she realised she'd learned next to nothing about the cases of the women and why they were taken. The only thing that they had in common, it appeared, was that they were all quite petite, no more than five foot three. The photos of the six unidentified women, she held back. They would go home with her. Was it simply that these women had no connection to the others, or was it that there was no information available in police or missing persons files?

Sitting in her car, about to drive home, she looked once more at the pictures of the unidentified women. One intrigued her more than the others. A faded colour snap of a woman, mid-twenties probably, a hairdo reminiscent of the eighties, blonde highlights swept back and high, long dangling earrings and shoulder pads. A girl with no name. A girl who may not have disappeared. A shiver ran down her back. So many women all gone. What was she getting into?

CHAPTER 29

Guy

Another smart journalist managed to suggest a link between the disappearance of actress Lucy and Lady Victoria. Sells papers, doesn't it? Don't have to be true for them tossers to write about it.

I was sitting in the hospital dining room, on my evening break, just finished some breaded plaice and chips and reading the paper, while I drank my tea. Just so happened that Kate, Tara's friend, was seated only three tables away chatting with another nurse and a man I assumed was a doctor. Reading about my conquests was not something I'd planned on, not when I was keeping tabs on Kate. But I couldn't help searching the paper to see what facts they had on my girls. Nothing, as it turned out, except that they disappeared within twelve hours of each other.

I read an interview with the ninth Duke of Berkeley, father of Lady Victoria as I had named her. Turns out her real name was Tamsin, and she was twenty-two, lived in a flat in Holland Park. Of course, I knew that cos that's where I snatched her. She was a promising fashion designer and an excellent pianist, apparently. So said her da. She had two younger sisters and an older brother, and the entire family were devastated by Tamsin's disappearance. There was no mention of a boyfriend, which I found a bit irritating. Always good that the girls I take have a boyfriend or a husband. They make such good suspects. Keeps the peelers busy.

It was a two-page spread in *The Mirror*, pictures of Tamsin as a child and a recent shot for the public to study in case someone noticed her wandering the streets. There was a timeline of her last known movements which, thanks to my good work, didn't amount to shit squared. Basically, young Tamsin left work, rode home on the tube and was never seen again. Incidentally, the family home was in Worcestershire, a big country estate, the place where Tamsin was most happy. Dear, dear, should have stayed there, much safer.

As for Lucy, there was little reported in the paper except to say that she disappeared the morning after Tamsin, a little over three miles from where the duke's daughter vanished. Police so far had no clues as to the whereabouts of either woman. That's what I liked to hear.

Kate and friends got up from their table and placed their food trays in the collection trolley. I didn't feel the need to follow her everywhere. As luck would have it, Kate's shift on that particular evening was similar to mine. We both knocked off at nine-fifteen. I could follow her home, check a few details, such as, was anyone else in her house when she got home? Where was her child while she was working? Most important of all, was there any chance that she would be meeting up with Tara?

Once I was certain she was headed for home, I didn't have to follow so close behind her car. She found a parking space a couple of doors down from her own. I drove on by without even glancing at her. Better for now if she didn't recognise me from work. I parked in the next road and walked back to Canning Street. Lights were on in the front room, but the blinds were drawn, and I walked on by.

A few minutes later I'd turned around and was walking back slowly, in the hope of some action from the house, when I saw a man approaching from the opposite direction. I couldn't make out much detail of his face, but he had thick curly hair and glasses and wasn't very tall.

About five-seven, I guessed. Jangling his car keys and carrying what looked like a takeaway meal in a brown bag, he looked towards me then immediately turned to his left and was inside Kate's house before I reached it.

So, she had a fella. He looked a bit plain and ordinary for the colourful Kate. A live-in fella? Husband? Father to her kid? It didn't really interest me. Kate was just my road to Tara, and tonight, it seemed she wouldn't be coming out to play again.

I drove to Albert Dock, parked the car and walked around by the Echo Arena to Tara's apartment block at Wapping Dock. I still had to figure out which number she lived in, because there was nothing to identify her by name on the nameplates at the building's entrance. It wasn't a wise thing to hang around outside, that's when you draw attention to yourself, and I couldn't see inside the private car park, so I didn't know if Tara was out or at home. She was going to be the hardest target I'd ever set myself. The longer it went on, I knew, the more frustrated I would get.

CHAPTER 30

Tara

'Where to first, ma'am?'

'Birkenhead. Marlene Nolan's mother has agreed to speak with us.'

Murray negotiated the traffic and made for the Kingsway Tunnel. Tara sat with the files and pictures of Marlene Nolan, Judith Braithwaite and Ruth Lawler on her lap. All three women had featured on the bedroom wall of Terry Lawler's flat. All three had disappeared without trace. All three had lived on Merseyside. If Terry Lawler had established a link between the women he had posted on his wall, then there had to be a link between those who had lived on Merseyside.

She read through the scant notes DC Wilson had prepared on Marlene Nolan. She was a twenty-year-old supermarket check-out girl, lived at home with her mother and younger sister, and was of mixed race. Tara couldn't tell if the mother or the father was of Afro-Caribbean origin. Marlene had disappeared on her way home from work in Birkenhead nearly four years ago. The police investigation was now dormant, and what perturbed Tara on the drive over to the family home was that the mother might now be expecting to get some positive news on the whereabouts of her daughter.

Murray turned into a street off Downham Road, opposite an entrance to Mersey Park. Halfway down the street, he pulled over outside a terraced house with bay windows and hanging baskets of primula on either side of the front door. When a woman answered the chime of the doorbell, Tara saw that the mixed-race issue was a little more complex than first thought, because Mrs Nolan also appeared to be a woman of mixed race.

She smiled weakly, a woman in her mid-forties, a thin face, high cheekbones, smooth skin, long hair in a ponytail, a red checked shirt open over a white T-shirt and baggy blue jeans.

'Mrs Nolan? I'm Detective Inspector Tara Grogan and this is Detective Sergeant Murray. Thank you for agreeing to speak with us this morning.'

'It's about Marlene, right? You better come in.'

They were led through to a lounge, clean and tidy, with a sofa that was rather too large for the room, as was the television, but there was nothing out of place here, including the collection of four framed pictures of the missing daughter Marlene. Mrs Nolan invited them to sit.

'Can I get you some tea or coffee?'

'No thanks. We'll try to keep this as brief as possible, Mrs Nolan. I realise this must be terribly painful for you.'

The woman sat on the arm of a chair. Her hands were trembling, and she looked eagerly at Tara.

'Do you have news about Marlene?'

'Not exactly. We're investigating the murder of Mr Terry Lawler, a journalist. He had pictures of women who have disappeared over the last few years, including one of Marlene.' Tara handed the photograph to the woman. 'Did Mr Lawler have any contact with you?'

'Yes, he came to see me about three months ago.' She handed back the photograph and reached across to the small table that held the pictures of her daughter. She lifted the largest frame and passed it to Tara. 'That is the last good picture I have of her.'

Tara examined the coloured photograph of a beaming young woman, smooth skin, brown eyes and glossy black hair resting on her shoulders. It was a head and shoulders shot, but the delicate straps of the dress suggested Marlene had been at a party or a formal evening, or perhaps a wedding.

'Lovely girl,' said Murray. 'And I see she got her looks from her mother.'

Mrs Nolan smiled thinly at Murray then took the frame back, returning it to the exact spot from where she'd lifted it.

'Did he have anything to tell you about Marlene?' Tara asked.

'No. He said he was searching for his sister and had come across Marlene's name on the missing persons register. He was just checking out as many cases of missing women as he could find.'

'Did he say if he had discovered any connection between Marlene and his sister's disappearance?'

Mrs Nolan shook her head.

* * *

Just off the M62 in Huyton, they pulled up outside a modern semi-detached chalet bungalow, the home of Mark Braithwaite, husband of Judith who had disappeared two and a half years ago.

'Can you tell me the circumstances of Judith's disappearance?' Tara asked the clean-shaven, fair-haired man in his thirties.

He was smartly dressed in white shirt and striped tie, grey trousers and black slip-on shoes. They stood on the doorstep; Braithwaite had not invited them inside.

'She never came home from work. Taught primary school in Knowsley. No one saw her after leaving school on a Wednesday. Why are you asking me this? I thought you people would have had this information already?'

His tone was dry, although Tara could understand his frustration. Judith's case, like Marlene's, was dormant. The only person actively searching for these women in recent months had been Terry Lawler, and now he was dead. She asked Mark Braithwaite if he had met with Lawler.

'I met him, yes. Seemed to me like another journalist on the sniff for a story. It really pisses me off. I'd had enough of the police investigating me after Judith went missing; I didn't like the idea of the press trying to make up stories about me.'

'Did he give you any information on Judith's disappearance?'

'He reckoned that one man was responsible for a whole list of girls going missing, but he couldn't prove anything. Said his own sister was missing. I didn't believe a word.'

'Did he give a name? The person he thought was responsible?'

Braithwaite laughed.

'He didn't have a clue, Inspector. I knew he was making the whole thing up. Now, if you're finished, I have a business to run.'

'Thank you, Mr Braithwaite. Just before you rush off, you might be interested to know that Mr Lawler did indeed have a sister missing, and currently we are investigating Mr Lawler's murder.'

The man's face reddened, he dropped his head and closed the door behind them.

'Nought out of two,' said Murray with a sigh. 'Where next?'

'I want to speak again with Gwen Blackley.'

* * *

They were invited into the kitchen of the Blackley home in Lymm. Gwen Blackley had her daughter Maisie home for half-term.

'I want to ask you some questions about Terry's sister, Ruth?'

'Maisie, can you leave us for a while, darling?'

The fourteen-year-old, long fair hair, dressed and very convincing as an adult, strode across the open space of the kitchen smiling amorously at Murray. He couldn't help his amusement, but Tara cut him off with a cold stare.

'What do you want to know, Inspector?'

'Did Terry mention anything to you on how his search for Ruth was going?'

Gwen continued her preparations for coffee, placing some chocolate cookies on a plate in front of Murray and Tara who were seated around an island bench. She, like daughter Maisie, was well-dressed and made-up, as if ready for an outing.

'The last few times I saw him he spoke of little else except to throw in digs about Evan's business. Although he was searching for her, he'd already accepted that she was dead.'

'Why did he believe that?'

'He told me that the circumstances of her disappearing, knowing her and how she cared for Beth, there was no way she would just take off somewhere, somebody had to have taken her. He blamed himself. Thought that somebody was trying to get back at him for something he'd written in the papers.'

'Did he mention that he had any proof of her being taken? Any suspects?'

Gwen shook her head as she poured coffee into three mugs and set a small jug of milk and a bowl of brown sugar in front of them.

'He'd gathered information on other women who'd gone missing. He had this theory that one killer was responsible for all of them, but it didn't seem likely; the women came from so many different places around the country.'

'In what way did he connect these disappearances?'

Gwen shrugged then took a seat next to Murray, who was tucking into the biscuits.

'Terry was obsessed with finding her, Inspector. I think he was prepared to believe anything.'

'But Terry had specifically chosen twenty-nine women who had gone missing,' said Murray. 'Thousands of women would have disappeared in that period. He must have had a reason for choosing those particular girls.'

'I can't help you, Sergeant. All I know is that Terry was going off around the country interviewing relatives of missing women. I don't know why he chose them, and I don't know what he found out.'

'He travelled around the country?' said Tara.

'Yes, he got it into his head that the killer, if there was just one, began his killing in Northern Ireland then moved to England. He reckoned, going by the dates of the disappearances, that he came to Liverpool more than once. Terry went to Belfast and spoke with the family of a girl who had disappeared in much the same way as Ruth. But they couldn't help him.'

'Do you think his sister Beth could help us with these questions?'

'I doubt it, Inspector. Beth has learning difficulties. She doesn't know that Ruth is missing, Terry had told her she was travelling round the world. And right now, she is struggling with the news that Terry is dead. She would never be able to handle questions from the police.'

'Do you keep in touch with her?'

'Yes, she has no one else now. We were a close family once, despite what you might think about Terry and me. I still cared for him. He was a lovable bastard, you might say. That's why I find it so upsetting to be labelled a suspect for his murder.'

'I would say you are more of a point of reference than a suspect, Mrs Blackley. We had to begin our investigation somewhere.'

'And what about Evan? Is he still a suspect? I know the pair of them never got on, not since Terry tried to connect him with the match-fixing scandal in Italy. That's how I met Evan, you know, through Terry. We were on the verge of separating when I went to a party with Terry. It was hosted by Evan. Of course, Terry, being Terry, only went to cause trouble. In the end he got more than he bargained for.'

'One last question, Mrs Blackley, did Terry ever mention his relationship with Lynsey Yeats?'

'Not really. He said he was staying over at hers while he worked on a story. To me, when Terry said he was staying over it meant he was sleeping with her. It wasn't the first time he'd used the phrase, Inspector.'

On the drive back to Liverpool, Tara reluctantly slipped the photographs and notes on the three missing women back into the files. That line of inquiry had already run out of steam. Lawler had no real method to his inquiries, he'd found nothing except for his hunch that a single killer, if one existed, had begun his work in Belfast, moved to England, and continued from there. Beyond that Lawler had nothing or, if he did, he took it to his grave. Unlikely then that this phantom killer had sought out Terry Lawler and killed him on Crosby Beach.

If she'd learned anything from a day's work, it was that Evan Blackley had yet another reason to murder Lawler. Blackley's football career had been cut short in Italy by allegations of match-fixing. For Lawler to have satisfied his journalistic appetite on the story, damaging a career in the process, then Blackley, in the face of further trouble from Lawler in disrupting his building plans, might well have resorted to a final solution where this journalist was concerned.

CHAPTER 31

Guy

Kate turned out to be a star. Took a few days though, but she did it in the end. I overheard her, at work, talking to someone on her mobile.

'See you tonight,' she said. I had to hope it was Tara she was speaking to, or maybe the other one. Nevertheless, I got myself all sorted with my shift, so that I could knock off before Kate, wait for her to leave work and then follow from there.

She drove home to Canning Street first, and as I waited, and an hour went by and then another, I thought I'd got it wrong. She was going nowhere; just sitting with her child waiting for Mr Plain to come home and do whatever it was that satisfied her. Then I thought, maybe Tara and the other girl would be calling by for another sleepover. But nobody called. I'd managed step by step to get my car parked opposite the house, and I could see perfectly if anyone were to slip in or out. I'd got myself neatly dressed, freshly shaven, my best clothes and shoes on, and as I slid further into my seat, I couldn't help wondering about Tara. What was she up to right now? Had she found out stuff about that journalist who got himself killed? Had she discovered something about me? It would be useful for me to know how the peelers worked on searching for missing girls. Then I'd be able to keep a step ahead of them, refine my technique, and maybe try something new.

Darkness had descended; it was well past eight when a mini cab stopped in the middle of the road alongside my car. The driver glanced at me but didn't seem bothered by me sitting there. I squeezed tight on my rubber ball. Seconds later, the front door of the house opened and out stepped a lovely Kate in a short light blue dress and leather biker-style jacket. She climbed into the back of the taxi, and the car rushed off down the street. She didn't seem to notice me. I was slow to get started, but I saw the direction they turned, and in a minute or so I was tailing them from about fifty yards.

When they eventually turned into Dawson Street, I slowed and waited for the cab to stop. At the junction with a narrow lane, the taxi pulled to the side, and Kate climbed out in her high heels. She hurried into a bar on the corner, so I quickly found a place to leave my car and went inside after her.

It was a lively place, loud and filling up with punters. Kate was already seated with a girl I assumed to be the other member of the gang of three I'd first noticed in Kate's house. She also was a tasty bit of skirt, long hair, confident face, not the type of woman I could ever have picked up on my own, and not the kind of woman I would ever consider taking. She was a real picture, definitely, but she had a bigger build than Kate or Tara. She would have strength in her favour if anyone ever tried to snatch her.

Kate or Tara: that sounded like a match to me, and for a moment I wondered if it were possible. A good follow up to Lucy and Lady Victoria down in London.

The bar was one of those retro-rustic places, bare brick walls, wooden panels, partitioned booths, ceiling fans and tiled floors. Pictures of the fab four, Gerry and the Pacemakers, the Merseybeats, Cilla, Herman's Hermits, and The Swinging Blue Jeans, were scattered about the walls between posters advertising cheap shots, cocktails and karaoke nights, while some Indie rock band blared from a powerful sound system.

I watched the two women, unnoticed for a few seconds, then as the big one glanced in my direction, I looked away and wandered to the bar, gazing about me as if waiting for someone. If only she knew for whom I was waiting, she might not look so happy.

At the bar I bought a sparkling mineral water and stayed put, feigning interest in the television, high in the corner, while scanning the room for what I hoped would be Tara's arrival.

Another ten minutes went by, no Tara. I kept an eye on Kate and her friend, they were looking less happy than when they'd first come in. The big one kept looking at her watch then texting on her mobile. Then Kate looked in my direction and caught my eye. I smiled and proffered a 'cheers' with my glass. She smiled back, looking puzzled, then turned to her friend. I ordered a pint of lager; couldn't be drinking water all night. A few minutes later Kate rose from her seat and walked towards the ladies. I gave her another minute or so and made for the gents, hopefully timing it just right that I could meet her as she emerged from the toilets. Bloody perfect. She almost collided with me in what was a crowded corner of the room.

'Hi there,' I said, smiling broadly. 'Kate, isn't it?'

'Do I know you?'

God, she was pretty close up. A few freckles on her nose and bare shoulders, having shed her jacket. Her short hair was still black, her eyes blue.

'Hospital. I work at the Royal.'

'Oh, right,' she said. 'Sorry, I didn't recognise you.'

And why would you, I thought.

'It's OK, lots of people work there.'

I remained on the spot waiting to see if she would come back with anything. She had to squeeze between two young lads and me to head for her table. Her arms brushed mine and I glimpsed her cleavage.

'Well, enjoy your night,' she said with a faint smile.

I smiled back and watched her go. I realised I'd just done a very dangerous thing. I was breaking my own rules again.

After visiting the toilets, I fought my way back to a place at the bar and ordered another pint. When I turned to survey the people in the room, I saw the door pushed open and in hurried a serious-looking Tara, surveying the place, looking for her mates. BINGO.

Smiles and hugs all round when she met them. The tall one went to the bar, and Tara sat down beside Kate. She wasn't turned-out like her friends; still in her work clothes, I reckoned. Her dark jacket was soon discarded to reveal a white blouse. Her hair was loose from the ponytail I'd only ever seen her wear, but she had retained that bright orange dye job. At that moment, I could easily have ignored her and focussed all my desire on Kate, but she was no real challenge. Tara, a cleaned-up and presentable Tara, would be my ultimate achievement. A nice wee cop.

I must have been staring vacantly at them for some time, because when I sort of came to my senses, Kate was looking right at me. I smiled and saluted her with my glass. Immediately, she whispered something to Tara who, I could tell, was doing her best not to look in my direction. The tall one, returning with drinks, wasn't so coy about staring. I cheered her also, and she sort of frowned then sat down with her back to me.

I was feeling cocky as hell. I had three women, acquainted with each other, all aware of my presence, of my existence. Right then, I felt I could take any one of them. I nabbed a waitress walking past collecting empties and asked her to take a drinks order from the girls' table.

A few minutes later, I watched as Tara, Kate and their leggy companion smiled mischievously at me. The waitress appeared to have successfully taken a list of drinks, and when she had placed the order at the bar, she presented me with the bill. Expensive tastes, those girls, although I got the impression they'd done it deliberately. I gave them a few minutes to enjoy their cocktails then wandered over.

'Would you mind if I joined in, ladies? I've been stood up again.'

Kate smiled at her tall friend.

'What do you think, Aisling? Has he paid enough to deserve a seat at our table?'

'Don't know about that, love. I'm only getting started.'

I was already pulling up a stool to sit between Tara and this Aisling girl.

'I'm James.' Had to give them a name, any name.

'James No-Mates, more like,' said Aisling, taking a healthy mouthful of her Manhattan.

'Who stood you up?' Tara asked.

'Just my mates. One of them is married, he wasn't allowed out to play, and the other one had to work at the last minute.'

'I know what that's like,' said Aisling. 'This one here' – she pointed to Kate – 'has a fella and a daughter, and this one works all the hours God sends.'

'That's not true,' said Tara. 'You work nights lots of times.'

I laughed and Aisling thumped my arm.

'Not that kind of work, sunshine. You men are all the same.'

Kate and Tara both laughed, and I reckoned I had it cracked.

'Let me guess then,' I said, smiling at Aisling. Close up, she was a real honey, big eyes, full of fun and life, a large mouth and a body like one of them catwalk models. 'I would say you are a self-made woman, you have your own business, like a beauty parlour or maybe one of those on-line mail order companies selling lingerie.'

All three laughed and Aisling said, 'A man with imagination or a dirty mind. And completely wrong. OK, smarty-pants, what about our Kate and Tara?'

It was brilliant. Kate seemed happy to play along, knowing, of course, that I knew exactly where she worked. I took my time examining her face, moving right up close, breathing her scent, feeling her breath on my face. Her eyes studied me, too, as if she wished she could place me, figure out what it was I did at the hospital.

'Kate is a professional, a nurse or maybe a dentist or even a doctor.'

'Wow,' said Aisling. 'Not bad for a man with no friends.' I know my smile dropped, but I didn't appreciate Aisling repeating the no mates theme. 'And what about Tara?'

I leaned toward Tara, trying to do the same thing I'd done with Kate, get close to her face, but she wasn't for joining in. She stared at me, all right, but she was keeping her distance. For the first time, though, I was able to appreciate what I'd noticed when I saw her on TV at the press conference. She had the most seductive little pout I'd ever seen. I wanted to put my lips on hers right then and there. Her eyes looked stern, however, as if she had already figured me out. She was sucking the confidence out of me. I decided not to be accurate about her job.

'I would say Tara is a private secretary of some kind, maybe for a big boss who always keeps her working late. Maybe he has a secret longing for her?'

Aisling laughed, as did Kate. Tara just continued to stare at me.

'Way off, love,' said Aisling. 'Although you were close with Kate.'

'Our James works at the Royal, too,' said Kate, laughing.

'You know each other?' Tara asked.

'No, not really,' I said. 'I saw her here tonight and realised the face was familiar; that she works at the Royal.'

Kate said nothing to this, but I saw her making eyes at Aisling. I offered to buy another round, and they agreed. I was having a ball.

'Right,' said Aisling, 'while drinks are coming, I'm away to powder me nose.'

'I'll come too,' said Kate, and now I was alone with Tara.

CHAPTER 32

Tara

Tara and Murray discussed with Wilson the lack of progress from the day's interviews. On the drive back to the station from Lymm, Tara had convinced herself it was now better to follow other leads in the case, such as Lawler's feud with Councillor Sullivan or his interest in the drug scene up on the Treadwater Estate. Wilson, however, had gathered more information on the missing women front. He passed a printed list of names to Tara. It ran to several sheets of A4.

'All the listed missing females in the UK from the last ten years.'

'There are hundreds if not thousands of them,' said Tara.

Wilson handed her another list.

'I've taken out all those who were found eventually, dead or alive. Most people who go missing are found within forty-eight hours, and they disappear for a whole variety of reasons: family quarrels, depression, stress, taking off to have fun, lovers, and the list goes on. Some of the dead were declared as suicides, some as misadventure, the rest are classed as unlawful killings.' He indicated on the sheets of paper, where he'd highlighted in green, the females who had been murdered, their bodies having been found. 'Of those murders, the ones marked in blue have had successful convictions.'

'Leaves quite a lot unsolved,' said Murray.

'Yes, it does, but on this list all the bodies have been recovered,' said Wilson. He turned to his desk and lifted yet another set of papers. 'Here we have all the females listed as missing, and we don't know if they're alive or dead. No trace has ever been found.'

'There are still hundreds of them, John,' said Tara.

'Think again about the pictures found in Lawler's flat. We've identified all of them except six, and their names are on this list, and they have never been found. Why?'

'Are you suggesting that Lawler did know something about these women?'

'Why else would he choose only those cases where not a trace of the victims has ever been found? What's so different about these women from those whose bodies were recovered?'

'What did Lawler find out that we haven't?' said Murray.

'And another thing,' said Wilson. 'If you look at the profiles of each woman, they're quite distinct. Some were married, some were Black or Asian, some were office workers; there was a teacher, a student, some were blonde and some brunette. All different, except for one thing.'

'Which is?' said Tara.

'Their weight, or more accurately, their build. Not one of those women from Lawler's collection is more than a size eight, five foot to five-three, shoe size three to five. All petites you might say.'

'The same build as Lawler's sister, Ruth. Would have made it easier to snatch them,' said Murray.

'There must be more than that for Lawler to have selected them,' said Tara. 'Trawl through his files again, Alan, see if you can find anything that would have given Lawler reason for researching these particular women.'

'Unless he was actually the man responsible for their disappearances,' said Murray.

'But his sister is among them,' said Tara.

Murray shrugged. 'It can happen.'

She hurried from the station, already late. There was no time to get home and change. Yet again she would turn up in front of Kate and Aisling in drab clothes, while they were dressed for a night on the town. All she had to contribute this week was an orange hairdo. After tonight, though, she could return to her normal self, as would Aisling. Kate's normal self was a different colour every month.

The pub on Dawson Street was crammed, stuffy and noisy. She found Kate and Aisling at a small table in a corner to the left of the bar and, determined to be upbeat, she negotiated her way through the throng with a happy face complete with apology. Aisling went to fetch her a drink. Tara settled down beside them and immediately began to relax. But it wasn't long before they were interrupted. A man who'd been standing at the bar had bought them a round of drinks. Aisling insisted they choose the most expensive cocktails just to see if he was 'worth his salt' as she put it. Shortly after the drinks arrived, the man wandered over and introduced himself as James. He joined their company, not Tara's idea of a relaxing evening, but she was carried along by Kate and Aisling who loved to flirt. When the pair suddenly made a dash to the ladies, Tara realised she'd been set up.

'So how close was I to guessing what you do?' he said.

Tara took a sip of her drink, stalling for time. She hated telling people, men in particular, what she did for a living. It never made for light-hearted conversation. She could throttle Kate and Aisling for clearing off.

'I'm a police officer,' she said, watching intently for his reaction.

'Mm… I would never have guessed that.'

She was intrigued by the lack of shock or even surprise on his face, and he didn't crack some silly joke about her going to arrest him, or that he'll come quietly. He simply smiled and looked into her eyes. Her friends hadn't left her with an unattractive man. Quite the opposite; she found him very handsome. She was disconcerted, however, by the resemblance he bore to the last man she'd loved. Sparkling dark eyes, black hair and a killer of a smile, although she didn't take much to his accent. Too much of a coincidence that he should not only resemble Callum but sound like him, too. She'd loved Callum for only a matter of days; he died leaving her expecting his child, a son who didn't survive beyond her sixteen hours of labour. It wasn't an experience that you get over easily. The pain and heartache still poked to the surface. Kate and Aisling were always on a crusade to see her married off even though Aisling, for herself, was determined to hold out for a millionaire.

'What do you do at the hospital?' she asked him.

'This and that, nothing special.'

'You're a doctor?'

'I'm a porter. I wheel things about on trolleys.'

She could tell now that he was looking for her reaction to him. She found him strange, as if he was out of his time, like he belonged somewhere in the sixties. His Belfast cheek would have sat well with the Liverpool wit of the time – if John, Paul, George and Ringo were anything to go by.

'How long have you been in Liverpool?'

'About six years.'

'Why here?'

He shrugged.

'It's somewhere that isn't Belfast. Good a place as any, I suppose.'

She was conscious of sounding like she was working, conducting an interview. He was quick to cut across her.

'So how does a young girl like you end up in the police?'

'Good a place as any, I suppose.'

They both smiled, and then he leaned a little closer.

'Do you fancy getting out of here, going somewhere quieter?'

'I'm here with my friends.'

'Considering how quickly they got offside, I don't think they'll mind.'

'No thanks, not tonight.'

'Does that mean that you'll come out with me some other time?'

He peered into her eyes; she felt as though he was boring into her very soul. But his face had a warm glow, he seemed easy-going, as if, despite his bravado, he was quite shy and he *would* take no for an answer.

'I'll go out with you on one condition,' she said, moving a little closer so that she caught his breath.

'Which is?'

'You leave us girls to ourselves this evening.'

With a smile, he dropped his head.

'Give me your number and I'll call you,' he said rising from the stool.

'You give me yours.'

'Spoken like a true officer of the law.'

He hadn't been gone for long when Kate and Aisling came back, as if Tara was supposed to believe they'd been in the bathroom all that time.

'Well?' said Aisling. 'How did you get on?'

'You two are really cruel to me, do you know that?'

'So, you sent him on his way?' said Kate.

'Yep.' She couldn't hide her smirk.

'But you're going out with him sometime?'

'Might be.'

CHAPTER 33

'Good afternoon, Councillor, have you got something for me?'

Sullivan stopped in his tracks in the leafy car park behind the city council offices and examined the man who was leaning against the wing of his Mercedes. He wore a scruffy grey suit, white shirt and flowery tie, his face thin and bony, narrow eyes, a slightly twisted mouth and his hair greasy, in need of combing. His arms were folded, and he held a lit cigarette in his right hand.

Sullivan couldn't summon words to address him. Bending over, he extracted an A4-size envelope, well packed, from his briefcase. For a moment, he held the stare of a man who had no trouble smiling as if proud of his day's work. Then he stepped forward and passed him the envelope.

'You're playing a dangerous game.'

'Is that a threat, Councillor, or have you been watching too many old gangster movies?' He dropped his cigarette on the ground and stamped it out with his shoe. He began to open the envelope.

'Don't do that out here,' said Sullivan. 'It's all there.'

'OK, take your word for it.'

'You're just like Lawler. Must have had the same low-life mother.'

'Now, now, let's not get personal. It's purely business, Councillor. Besides, Terry and I are quite different. He was happy just to rubbish your lot in the papers. I'm much more practically minded. When Terry told me what was going on, I just couldn't pass up the opportunity to make a few bob.'

'Like I said, you need to be careful. Terry is dead now, remember?'

'No, no, I think that's where *you* need to be careful. How much do you think it's worth me not telling the bizzies what you know about Terry's murder?'

Sullivan cracked a smile.

'You know nothing because there is nothing to tell.'

'Glad to hear you're confident on that point. How about your friends?'

'This is between me and whatever's in your sick head. And it's the only time I'm paying up. Don't be thinking you can come back for more. Now piss off.'

Sullivan pressed his key to unlock his car. The man smirked and looked on as the councillor set his briefcase on the back seat and went to sit behind the wheel.

'Tell Doreen I was asking for her. Nice woman, that. Getting on a bit, though, but she must still have it, eh, Councillor?'

Sullivan gunned his engine, and the silver Mercedes roared from its space toward the exit. The man watched it go, and when he turned to head in the opposite direction, he saw Doreen Leitch watching him from the top of the steps leading into the building. He waved, but it was not returned, and with a shrug of his shoulders he set off with his earnings.

CHAPTER 34

Tara

Next morning, having had the best night's sleep in a while, thanks to a cocktail, several glasses of wine, although no one was counting, and a good laugh with her mates, Tara strolled almost carefree into the office. Wilson and Murray were both eager to see her. She hadn't sat down at her desk before the pair of them closed in.

'You two are keen, anything new?'

Wilson was about to let Murray, his superior, speak first when Murray nudged him forward.

'You first, John.'

Wilson proceeded to place a bundle of files on the desk in front of Tara.

'I picked up a few more common threads between the women who've disappeared,' he said.

'Let's hear them.'

'I went through the police case notes for each woman. Took a long time because they're from seven different police authorities around the country. What I mean is there is a different emphasis from one case to another. Some concentrate on the woman's background as the main reason for the disappearance, a couple attempt to establish the last place a woman was seen before disappearing, some on the time of day, the weather, and it goes on, but no one, I think, has brought all these files together in one place before. No one, other than Lawler, tried to establish connections or common factors between each one.'

'We realise that, John. If it hadn't been for our investigation of Lawler's murder, we wouldn't be doing this either.'

'Of course, ma'am, it's just my way of explaining that there are several common factors running through these cases. It isn't simply a matter of the women never having been traced. It's got more to do with how they disappeared.'

Wilson opened several of the buff folders in front of Tara.

'These are a couple of files I've chosen at random. One woman comes from Glasgow, one from Manchester.' He began indicating the relevant notes in the file on each woman. 'See here, the woman in Glasgow, investigations by Strathclyde Police suggest she disappeared from a lay-by in a narrow street in the city's west end. Probably late at night, after ten o'clock. No CCTV in the immediate vicinity, no apparent witnesses. Same thing in Manchester, girl last seen about nine, leaving work at a city centre store. Doesn't make it as far as her regular bus stop where there is CCTV. Probably taken before that. Exactly the same in every case, no matter the region of the country. Woman disappears in dark city centre street or quiet residential area. No CCTV recordings for any of them. No personal belongings retrieved from the possible site of abduction. You'd think one of them would have lost a shoe, a handbag, shopping – nothing. All very tidy. And in every case, in every police investigation, beyond the initial inquiries there have never been viable suspects identified. No scene identified; no mobile phone messages sent by any of the women.'

'Has to be the work of one person,' said Murray. 'Too much of a coincidence.'

'And that's why Lawler selected them,' said Tara. 'Because he worked out the connections. I wonder about the women we haven't yet identified.'

'Could be several too many. Maybe Lawler realised they didn't fit the pattern,' said Wilson.

'What have you got, Alan?'

'Well, if this is true' – he waved a folder before them – 'it probably eliminates Lawler as a suspect in these disappearances. This has happened since Lawler's death.'

He tossed the file on top of those Wilson had displayed.

'Two recent missing women cases. You probably heard about them on the news. Both down in London, one is an actress, the other is the daughter of the Duke of Berkeley.'

'Same pattern?' Tara asked.

Murray grimaced slightly.

'Not quite. The women disappeared within twenty-four hours of each other. The duke's daughter, Tamsin, it is believed did not return to her flat in Holland Park after her day's work. Nothing found on CCTV after she left the underground station half a mile from her home. The situation for the actress is a bit different. Disappeared in broad daylight from outside her gym. Her car had been abandoned, and witnesses report seeing a man, driving a white van, stop to help the girl change a flat tyre. Again, no CCTV covering that area of the gym's car park.'

'So, this girl's disappearance doesn't fit the pattern,' said Wilson.

Tara, who had been browsing the file, leaned back in her chair and looked up at her colleagues.

'Interesting work,' she said, 'but it hasn't got us any closer to the killer of Terry Lawler. All it has done is remove him as a suspect for these women going missing.'

'But what if Lawler actually identified the person responsible for taking all these women?' said Murray. 'The killer realises they've been sussed out and decides to eliminate Lawler?'

'I don't disagree that it's possible, Alan,' said Tara. 'But we are no closer to identifying them if they are the killer.'

'We'll have to go through Lawler's papers again. If he identified the killer, the name must be there.'

Her beleaguered colleagues returned to their desks on the far side of the office. Tara, before she had a second chance to tackle her work, was interrupted by her phone signalling a text. She opened the message.

Have you phoned him yet?

It was Aisling, impatient as ever. Obviously with nothing more important to occupy her morning than to wind up her friend. Tara quickly responded before getting back to her work.

Not yet.

She'd only just managed to read one email on her computer when her phone went again.

Don't you dare chicken out Tara.

Of course, it wasn't long before Kate, probably goaded by Aisling, was sending texts on the same subject. Tara refused to indulge either one any further in the matter, although somewhere in her subconscious she felt that she was actually toying with the idea of calling this man. Before falling into a sleep the night before, she'd been determined not to pursue the matter. This morning, she wondered if it was worth giving him a try. One date wouldn't hurt, and at least it would get Kate and Aisling off her back.

When she'd dealt with her mundane stream of emails, she turned her attention to some research on Councillor Doreen Leitch. Reading from the council's website, she learned that Leitch had been a councillor for more than fifteen years, had served on numerous committees, including the Select Committee on Housing, and the Finance and Resources Select Committee. She had also served on scrutiny panels for Neighbourhood and for Shadow Health and Wellbeing. What stood out most, however, was that Leitch had been a member of the Planning Committee and a former secretary of the Environment Regulatory Committee. Tara wondered then if she had connections in the past with Evan Blackley, and thought it might be a rather convenient arrangement arising from her current clandestine relationship with Matt Sullivan. She came across several press releases in relation to Leitch's involvement in various neighbourhood schemes in the city, one concerning drinking alcohol in public, another on neighbourhood watch and one reporting her close involvement with a city centre drop-in facility for drug abuse.

On the face of it, Doreen Leitch was a hard-working elected official, keen on social issues and, whether intentional or otherwise, on getting her name in the papers. As Tara had already learned, several local journalists had tipped her as a possible candidate for

Westminster in the next general election. Obviously, any journalist who outed this dedicated councillor, lay preacher, affectionate wife and devoted mother as an adulteress and perhaps a corrupt public figure would be destroying a parliamentary career in the making. Motive indeed for killing Terry Lawler.

Tara called Murray to her desk.

'I want you to look through the libel case on Sullivan versus Lawler.'

'Am I looking for anything in particular?'

'Yes, see if Doreen Leitch gets a mention.'

CHAPTER 35

Guy

I was wheeling a trolley with a stiff on board from a ward down to the mortuary when my phoned vibrated in my pocket. It was her. Could hardly believe it. When she refused to give me her number, and asked for mine instead, I thought I was already dumped. She was never going to call me. Thought I'd blown it. I'd already decided that I was going to snatch her somewhere when the time was right. And then she calls me. She sounded nervous, unsure of herself. I hadn't found her to be like that when we met.

'Hi, James,' she said. 'I bet you thought I wouldn't call?'

'I thought that it was your way of saying no when you didn't give me your number.'

'I'm a police officer, remember. Can't afford too many private calls when I'm working.'

'No, I suppose not.'

'Anyway, I was thinking that maybe we could meet for a drink?'

'Sounds good,' I said. 'I'd love to see you again. When are you free?'

'How about this evening, about seven? Same place as last time?'

'Great. I'll see you there.'

Could hardly believe it. A woman, a fabulous-looking woman asking me out. There's hope for true love yet, I thought, patting the sadly departed on the head as I entered the lift.

Felt like my first ever date. My tummy jingling, my head racing, wondering exactly how to play it. Doubts creeping in, thinking that she was already onto me. That Lawler had suspected me before he snuffed it, and I was about to be trapped. But just as quickly, the doubts were swamped by my lurid thoughts of what I could do with that baby face, the sexy pout and trim little body, and this time it would all be legal and consensual.

When I finished my shift, I hurried back to my flat, took a quick dip in the bath, ironed my best shirt and trousers and was back in the city centre in good time to get to the bar ready and waiting for Tara. I had a sneaking suspicion that I'd be waiting a long time if she even turned up at all.

The bar was busy as usual. I pulled open the door and stepped inside, glancing around for a free table. Instead, I saw her. Surprise, surprise. What an eager lady. Then I saw the man sitting opposite her. What the hell was this? I could have turned around and walked out, but for some reason I moved toward them. See? All my good rules, years of experience going to waste for the sake of a pretty cop in a skirt.

Suddenly she glanced in my direction and smiled. Then she turned to her companion and said something. The big bloke was up from his seat and heading straight for me. I clenched my fists. I wasn't for giving in that easily. I'd hit the bastard and make a run for it. He was a big guy, broad shoulders, fat neck and large protruding eyes which seemed full of laughter or ridicule. I stopped, waiting for his approach, Tara looking on. At least an inch taller, studying my face, he smirked and walked on by. I dropped my guard with relief. I was sure he was a peeler, and if he worked with Tara, I was quite certain he would remember me. Already, I was past the point of no return. All my good sense had deserted me.

Tara's hair was once again blonde, falling just below her shoulders. She wore a black jacket over a blue and white top in a swirling pattern, a short black and blue checked skirt, and tights, and black shiny heels. Difficult to tell if she was dressed for work or dressed for a date.

'Hi,' she said. 'You're early.'

CHAPTER 36

Tara

'So are you,' he replied.

'Came straight from work.'

'And the fella?'

'Colleague. We took the opportunity to discuss some casework over a drink.'

She couldn't help feeling attracted to this man. Dark wavy hair, eyes just as dark, but she viewed them as sparkling pools. His skin seemed tanned and healthy, his nose thin and tapering to a point. Cheeky, if she had to describe him in a word. Cheeky and smart, a Liverpool lad but for the accent. Full of mischief, yet irresistible. He seemed at ease in a striped shirt, open at the neck, a navy sports jacket and faded blue jeans. Looked fit, too. Only one thing haunted her, made her feel uneasy. That Belfast accent cut through with Scouse. She'd experienced that before. Why had she set herself up for this?

This man, James, she had yet to learn his last name, ordered drinks for both of them and sat down on a low stool directly opposite, peering intently into her eyes. She matched his stare for a moment or two. She smelled the spice from his aftershave, and felt his minted breath wafting on her face. His skin was smooth, and he was clean-shaven, but there was sweat appearing on his cheeks. If he hadn't behaved so confidently, she'd swear he was nervous. Nervous of her? He smiled and finally pulled away. Round one to her.

'And how was work?' he asked.

'Busy, frustrating and tiring.'

He leaned toward her for a second attempt.

'Talk to me,' he said. 'Tell what you did.'

'You really want to know about my day?'

'Bound to be a cut above mine.'

'You think so?'

'I do surely. For instance, when you called me this afternoon, I was wheeling a dead body down to the morgue. Now you can hardly call that a rewarding experience.' He clinked his pint glass to hers, and they both drank.

'My day was spent trawling through files and papers looking for something that might help me with my present case. On top of that I had to deal with texts from my two girlfriends who were trying to get me to call you.'

'Glad to see you took their advice.'

'Aisling doesn't let things go without a fight. She'd be on at me for weeks if I hadn't called you.'

'Is that the only reason you did it?'

She smiled coyly, feeling herself blush.

'Might be.'

'So, tell me about this case you're working on?'

'Can't do that, I'm afraid.'

'Must be something exciting then? A robbery? A murder? I know, a serial killer?'

She smiled weakly but didn't respond. She wasn't to be drawn.

'You have an active imagination. Why don't we start by you telling me what you get up to?'

'Sounds like the sort of question a police detective would ask.'

'I thought you were interested in police work.'

'OK, you win. I work at the Royal as a porter, but you already know that.'

'What do you do when you're not working? And don't say you hang around in bars trying to pick up women.'

He laughed and took another drink of his beer.

'Shift work doesn't allow for much except sleeping and watching telly.'

'And where do you watch telly?'

'Home.'

She cocked her head suggesting he should elaborate.

'I live alone,' he said. 'A flat in Toxteth.'

She held her gaze on him and didn't speak knowing that he was the type to fill the silence.

'Not married, never have been. Not gay either, in case you're wondering.' He leaned close until only an inch separated them. 'Now it's your turn.'

She wouldn't have minded if he'd kissed her then, but she moved back anyway; didn't want to give the impression she was a push-over.

'I'm single, a police officer, and I have a flat in Wapping Dock.'

'How long have you been a peeler?'

It was the accent again, and the Belfast way of referring to the police as peelers. She felt uncomfortable. A nice-looking fella and yet she could hardly bear to hear him speak.

'Seven years.'

'Put many crooks away?'

'A few. I see we're back to my job again. Here's one for you. What does a man from Belfast think of Merseyside?'

'Merseyside? Only a peeler would call it that. There are loads of Paddies in Liverpool. Isn't that what we are?' With a wry smile he stood and went to the bar.

It had begun to feel like a tennis match, hitting a ball back and forth, trying to set up a winning stroke, trying to score points from each other. This was no romantic encounter. She didn't know what it was.

When he returned with the drinks, thankfully for Tara, the conversation developed beyond their lives into discussion on city nightlife, movies, holidays, and for a time the competition between them ebbed away. She found herself talking about Aisling and Kate, about the things the three of them got up to, now and years ago at school. He didn't say much, seemed more content to listen and to feed her the questions. By the time she managed a third glass of wine, following the first pint of beer, he caught her glancing at her watch.

'Do you have to be somewhere?'

'No, but it's late. I've an early start in the morning.'

'I can drive you home if you like?'

'That would be a no for two reasons. Firstly, I can get a taxi, and secondly you've had too much to drink and should not be driving anywhere.'

'Here's me suggesting I drink and drive to a peeler. At least let me wait with you until your taxi arrives?'

She didn't refuse, rose from her seat and gathered her jacket and bag.

'Thanks for the drinks,' she said.

'No problem. I enjoyed our wee chat.'

He followed her outside, where the cool air refreshed them after the heady atmosphere of the crowded bar.

Tara was relieved to hail a black cab right away. She was tired, weary of making conversation, especially one that for a time was so competitive. Standing next to him in the street, she only reached his shoulder.

'Thanks again for this evening,' she said, hoping to sound genuine.

Placing his hand on her arm, he smiled down at her and edged closer. She couldn't help arching her neck to return his gaze, and then he lowered his head further and placed a heavy kiss on her lips. For a second she responded, then quickly told herself this should not be going anywhere. His hands gripped her waist, and he pulled her tight against him. They kissed again, but she slipped her hands between them and pushed him away gently, the best she could manage after feeling him go hard against her.

'I have to go, James.' She freed herself from his grasp and opened the door of the cab.

'But can I see you again, Tara? We can go for dinner, maybe go to a club?'

'Thanks, James. You're very sweet, but I don't think so.'

She could see that he looked genuinely shocked by her rebuttal. He stood open-mouthed, his palms spread by his sides. She smiled briefly before the cab roared away.

CHAPTER 37

Guy

'I will see you again, Tara. You can be sure of that, love,' I said to myself as she drove away.

I saw signs of victory on her cute little face as she peered out of the cab, pleased with herself that she'd managed to dump me without a fight. Clever, too, that she gave herself to me for a few seconds, long enough for me to get excited. And I did get excited.

Here's me thinking I'd charmed her, that I was attractive to her, that maybe she was the one. This was the girl that I could love, really love. And what did she do? Pissed on that notion, didn't she? What had I done wrong? She seemed to enjoy our chat, our banter. We had a laugh. I wasn't looking to sleep with her on the first date. I'm not impatient. I could get to know her properly. She could be my fresh start. No more taking girls that I couldn't have. Loving Tara, I wouldn't need anyone else.

As the taxi disappeared from view, I wondered if she would give me a second chance. Maybe it was up to me to find her, give her a call or send her flowers. But as I dandered back to my car I thought of the things she'd said. Her mates coaxing her into going out with me. Her reluctance to tell me about her work. Asking so little about me, looking down on me, a Paddy. That's what she really thought. A fucking Paddy, slaving in a hospital, no prospects, and her a peeler. A big shot detective. She wouldn't want to be seen with the likes of me. If her peeler colleague hadn't seen me, hadn't clocked me, I could have taken her the way I've taken all my girls. One good fuck and then a lethal dose. That's what I did to stuck-up Gemma, and Tara, I reckoned, was just like her. I'd be seeing her again definitely.

My problem was what to do right now. I hadn't done a girl since Lucy and Lady Victoria, or Tamsin to use her real name. I'd broken nearly all my own rules, acquired bad habits of trying to pick up women in bars, even those I'd been trailing for days. And look where it got me. One measly date with a peeler. I needed something. I needed a girl right now to restore my faith in my own abilities. I would do what I knew best. Little did Tara know, but she had just got some wee darling killed, all because she'd turned me down. Funny how things turn out.

I had the morning off before my evening shift, and I lay on the sofa with a cup of tea pondering my next step. There was a nice wee thing doing a consumer article on breakfast TV, talking about rip-off beauty products sold on the internet. She was cute, a Geordie accent but nice with it; long fair hair to her waist, a sticky-out bum in tight trousers and platform shoes, bloody lovely. I imagined a whole list of possibilities, but vying for my attention, still, was the wee cop.

Sitting at the wheel of my car, I couldn't decide where to go for my next snatch, all I could see before me was Tara. I couldn't give up on her just yet. I just sat there tossing ideas in the air, for the first time ever trying to rid myself of a girl that I had already chosen. For my own peace of mind, I decided to go for a dual approach. Make plans to lift her, and at the same time give her another chance to go out with me. I drove off hoping to strike it lucky at St Anne Street police station.

After an hour of waiting close to the station entrance, reading my paper, I noticed a familiar figure crossing the yard and climbing into an unmarked car. It was that big bastard who'd been sitting with Tara in the pub when I arrived. The car swung toward the exit then braked to a halt by the door of the building. To my surprise, Tara hurried out and got into the passenger seat. Immediately, I prepared to follow; I'd try my best not to lose them but, more importantly, not to get noticed by them.

They headed out of the city, and soon it seemed they were going in the direction of Crosby. I remembered that the body of that journalist creep had been found out there, and I assumed they were going for another look. Maybe they'd missed something first time round. I needn't have worried about losing them or arousing their suspicion. For a copper this guy was a slow and sloppy driver. At one point I drew up behind them at traffic lights, and I swear he didn't once look in his mirror. After that I dropped back a little, even let another car come between us. Soon I realised I'd been wrong about where they were going. The black Vauxhall pulled up outside a bungalow about a mile or so before the beach. I drove on by and found a place to turn around. When I passed by again, both cops were stood by the front door of the house talking to some guy. I drove on for a mile or so assuming that when they'd finished their little chat they would return along the same road.

As I sat waiting, one thing began to irk me. The guy at the house, although I only got a brief look at him, did seem familiar. I'd never been out this way before, but I recognised that face. A friendly, untroubled face, large nose, mousey hair, skinny build. It would come to me.

CHAPTER 38

Tara

Tara studied the face of Gary Hill, former boyfriend of Ruth Lawler. He seemed a jovial character, friendly, relaxed, the sort of man you wouldn't mind spending time with. Slightly dishevelled, his wavy hair in need of combing, he bore an afternoon stubble and looked comfortable in a crumpled red sweatshirt and faded jeans. She and Murray were seated in the front sitting room of the bungalow, Gary Hill nursing a young baby girl of no more than a year on his lap.

'When did you last speak with Mr Lawler?'

Gary Hill tried his best to conjure up his daughter's interest in the rattle he shook in front of her. His efforts forced a smile from Tara.

'Couple of months ago. He came to speak to me about Ruth. I knew he was trying his best to find her. I'd asked him to keep me informed.'

'You're in another relationship now, I take it?'

'Yes, married. Ruth and I had split a year before she disappeared.'

'Do you think,' said Murray, 'that your break-up may have caused her to run away?'

'My first thought when I heard she'd disappeared, to be honest.'

'But now you don't think so?' Tara asked.

'Terry came to see me. He said there was no way Ruth would just up and leave; she wouldn't have left her sister Beth to fend for herself. He was certain she'd been taken. I reckon he was trying to suss me out, since Ruth and I had broken up, but I wasn't about to take his accusations and let him off with it. You see, it didn't end particularly well between Ruth and me. She found out that I'd been seeing Alice, who is now my wife. She was already pregnant with Amy when I finished with Ruth. Terry suggested that I might know where she'd gone, since I was responsible for breaking her heart. I told him when I'd last seen her, when we'd last communicated, what was said, and he seemed to accept that I was telling the truth.'

'Did he pass on anything that he'd discovered about Ruth's disappearance?'

Hill shook his head.

'He'd found nothing, Inspector. All he had was some way-out theory that Ruth was one of dozens of women who'd all disappeared in the same manner, but he had nothing to back it up. Since you're here, I take it that you are still looking for Ruth?'

'Not directly,' Tara replied. 'We're investigating Mr Lawler's murder, and we came across his attempts at trying to find his sister.'

'Of course. Do you think Terry's death is linked to Ruth's disappearance?'

Hill's attention remained on his daughter, her tiny hand gripping his little finger.

'We're considering that possibility.'

Hardly a word was spoken on the journey back to St Anne Street, but Tara, deep in thought, was gradually coming to realise that they were wasting time in chasing a lead which so far had served only to drag them further from the central themes of the case.

'I think we should put this idea of taking up Lawler's search for missing women on the shelf for now,' she said. 'We've found nothing so far, and if what Gary Hill says is true, then Lawler didn't get anywhere with his investigation.'

'Unless he was killed before he could pass on what he knew,' said Murray.

'Still doesn't help us. If Lawler didn't have a name, then we aren't going to find one easily.'

When she returned to her desk, she found a Post-it stuck to her screen. Written upon it was the name Blackley and a mobile number. Unsure whether it was the male or female of the couple, she dialled the number and waited for a voice to answer.

'Evan Blackley,' was stated abruptly.

'Detective Inspector Grogan returning your call, Mr Blackley.'

'Ah yes, Inspector,' came a more jovial reply. 'Something you can do for me and may also be of interest to the police. That so-called mate of Terry's, Paul Macklin, has taken over where Terry left off.'

'You'll have to explain, Mr Blackley.'

'Threatening my business, just like his mate. Says he'll take Lawler's story to the press if I don't pay up.'

'Do you mean he's blackmailing you?'

'Damn right he's blackmailing me. Didn't have the balls to meet me face to face. Went crawling to our Gwen. The lowlife. I want to know what the bizzies are going to do about it.'

'Perhaps we should meet first, get some more details from you and then I can take it up with Mr Macklin.'

'You need to get to him before I do, cos if I set eyes on him, I'll ring his bloody neck.'

'Making threats of your own won't help the situation, Mr Blackley.'

'Then the police better get off their arses and do something.'

CHAPTER 39

He thought it strange. The location. But he came anyway. Couldn't pass up on the opportunity to make a few more quid. These guys were easy pickings. Terry had been in the wrong business. Instead of writing a few harsh words in the papers, thinking he was cleaning up the world, ridding Liverpool of all the lowlife trash, Terry could have been milking it in. These people were only too willing to cough up just to keep their reputations.

Smoking a fag didn't do much for his nerves. He hadn't got used to the meetings yet. It would take a while. But he was in the right business to learn the secrets of others, and besides he had many secrets gathered by Terry to use for a long time to come.

Unable to bear his discomfort behind the wheel, he climbed out of the car and paced up and down on the lane overlooking the playing fields. He should be here any minute. If the bastard had thought he could palm him off with a few measly quid that he'd given him that last time, then he had better think again. If the money wasn't right this time, he would send his information to the papers and they would just have to face the music.

His suit jacket did little to keep him warm, yet his shirt was soaked with sweat. The lights of a car moved along the perimeter of the park, and he prepared himself for the arrival. But then he saw the lights swing in the opposite direction, and soon they were lost amongst the houses. Why had the bugger chosen this place? Gave him the creeps. He didn't know this part of the city. He'd grown up in Speke, for God's sake. Terry, Ruth and him. He couldn't believe it when she disappeared. Terry was a mess, and now he was gone.

He felt the cold rip through him, his heart thumping in his chest, his head pulsing. Maybe he wasn't cut out for this underhand business. Maybe the sod knew what he was doing, choosing this spot. The bastard could tell that underneath all the smart talk he was just an amateur. They had him sussed. The bastard wasn't scared; he wasn't for turning up with more cash. Maybe he should go, clear off now. Then he heard a voice from behind.

'Hiya, Paul, mate.'

He spun round, eyes darting as he peered into the darkness.

'Who's there?'

CHAPTER 40

Guy

Modesty, I called this one. Don't ask me why. Just seemed right. Appropriate. She was probably the plainest girl I've ever gone for, and that's the best I can say about her. I was desperate, what do you want me to do? I couldn't wait around for Tara. It was taking too bloody long. I needed to pop me cork or I would've cracked open. Modesty was there for the taking, didn't need a lot of planning. A girl, and I use that term loosely, living alone, in her late thirties, early forties I'd guess, not married, divorced possibly and didn't seem to have a job. She wasn't pretty, slim or curvy, and definitely not a looker. The only thing in her favour, or mine, depending on how you look at it, was that she dressed nice. Probably spent all her benefits on clothes, bright, colourful clothes.

The evening after I'd followed Tara out to Crosby, I spotted Modesty coming out of a pub on Anfield Road. I was wound up to the neck, and there she was just walking down the street. Sounds like a bloody pop song, but I was drawn to the high heel boots, her bright pink jeans and wee matching jacket. Only took me two days to suss her out.

Like I said, she was hardly a stunner, but as we used to say in Belfast, you don't look at the clock on the mantelpiece when you're poking the fire. I did my stuff with Modesty, using my tried and trusted method and felt the better for it. A day out to sea on Mother Freedom helped to clear my head. I was back in my natural habitat, in control, I went through my routine: body in the holdall, bag of stones along with her, forty minutes south-west of Anglesey and I tipped her in the drink. Sweet. I did everything the way I always had. The boat was hosed down, mattress from the van dumped at the civic amenity site in Llandudno, van power-hosed, and I was home by midnight and checking the local news for anything on a missing girl from Anfield. I hoped, though, that taking Modesty would tide me over until the time was right for Tara.

CHAPTER 41

Tara

The face of Gwen Blackley was strained and very pale. Tara had grown accustomed to seeing the woman immaculately dressed, with full make-up and carefully tended hair. Not this morning. The collar of her long navy raincoat was up around her neck, her hair unbrushed and floundering in the breeze. She seemed cold, her body trembling as she stood next to her husband, he with hands in the pockets of his overcoat, looking concerned as he listened to Murray speak. Tara had just arrived on the scene and was content for Murray to finish his conversation. But when Evan Blackley noticed her approach he wasn't prepared to wait.

'I hope you don't think I had anything to do with this,' he said, stepping toward her.

'If you don't mind, Mr Blackley, I'd like to find out exactly what's happened before I speak to you.'

Gwen Blackley suddenly looked alarmed as Tara walked past them and made for the incident tent by the wire fence that enclosed the building site. DC Wilson stood outside, scribbling in his notebook.

'Morning, ma'am.'

'What have we got, John?'

'Another gruesome one: male, late thirties, we think it's Paul Macklin. Found a wallet in that car.' He nodded toward a black Volkswagen Golf sitting on the lane and now bracketed by two police cars. 'Had a driving licence inside.'

'I'll know if it's him.'

'It'll be hard to tell, ma'am. There's not much left of the face.'

The compulsion to shiver at the thought wasn't far away as she stepped into the tent. Brian Witney was busy with his examination of the victim. Tara's hand shot immediately to her mouth at the sight before her. There was a body, sagging but upright, held in place against the mesh fence with cable ties, one at each outstretched wrist. That was all she could tell. Everything beyond that observation was a bloodied mess.

'Multiple slash wounds, Tara,' said Witney, turning to face her. 'Bled to death within a few minutes. Quite a sharp knife, not such a long blade, none of the cuts are deep, just delivered to the right places. His neck in particular.'

Tara now had both hands held over her mouth and nose. She recognised nothing of Paul Macklin in the figure. There were gashes to the head, neck and ears. The flesh on either side of the mouth had been slit open causing the lower jaw to drop, and copious amounts of deep red blood had flowed from the lacerated tongue. The man's clothes, jacket, shirt and trousers had been partially ripped away, hanging ribbons of deep red. The torso had a dozen or more cuts, several of which ran from the neck and shoulders to the lower abdomen. Intestines were visible in several places. Thighs were sliced open with vertical cuts and criss-crossed by smaller gashes all the way to the knees. Even the shins and ankles had been cut. Only the feet, still in shoes, had been spared.

'Killer didn't know where to stop, or else didn't want to,' said Witney.

'Any idea of time?'

'Ten hours, roughly.'

'Thanks, Brian.' She emerged from the tent reeling from the horror she'd witnessed. She felt nauseous but had to try hard to hold it together. She just wanted to go home, curl up in bed and forget she had a life as a police officer.

'You all right, ma'am?' said Wilson.

'I'll be fine, thanks.'

'Not for the faint-hearted, that one.'

She smiled acknowledgement and made her way to where the Blackleys were waiting.

'Is it Paul?' Gwen Blackley asked her.

'Difficult to say at the moment.'

'What do you mean difficult?' Evan Blackley snapped. 'Don't you recognise him? Let me have a look; I'll soon tell you.'

'It's a crime scene, Mr Blackley. You'll not be going anywhere near it.'

His wife attempted to hold him by the arm, but he shrugged her off.

'When can I get this site opened again? I have a schedule to keep.'

'Not today, sir. We are searching the area for a weapon.'

Shaking his head, he made to walk away, but Tara hadn't finished with him.

'I know this is your building site but may I ask, is there any special reason why you are here?'

'I got a call from my contractor; he found the body and we came down. Your lot were already here. Told us sweet FA so far.'

'Calm down, Evan,' said Gwen Blackley. 'Let the police do their job.'

'When did either of you last see Mr Macklin?'

'Oh, here we go. I know what you're suggesting. That because I phoned you, sounding off about Macklin sticking his nose in where it didn't belong, you think I bumped him off. Why would I phone the police if I was going to kill him?'

'I asked when you last saw him, that's all. I haven't accused you of anything.'

'He came to the house about a week ago,' said Gwen.

'Is that when he threatened to blackmail you?'

'Evan wasn't at home, but yes he told me that if Evan didn't give him a hundred thousand pounds he would go to the press with Terry's story and a lot more.'

'What did he mean by a lot more?'

Evan Blackley jumped in.

'Ancient bloody history, that's all. Lawler thought he had something on me from my time playing in Italy, betting scams and match-fixing, but he had nothing. Damn lies, nothing but lies. That scumbag Macklin must have thought he'd struck gold. What I would like to know is why Terry passed his shit on to him?'

'A good question,' said Tara. She wondered how much information Lawler had shared with his friend. Enough to get him killed? 'Did you give any money to Mr Macklin?'

'Of course not. He didn't scare me with his threats.'

From the lane entrance to the building site, where a dozen expensive-looking houses were under construction, she gazed across the expanse of playing fields, the Treadwater Estate in the distance.

She and Murray spent the late afternoon briefing Superintendent Tweedy on the murder of the man, now confirmed as Paul Macklin. After leaving the building site, they'd paid a visit to Macklin's flat in Speke. There they found all the evidence they needed to prove that the solicitor was embarked upon a series of blackmail attempts against Matt Sullivan, Evan Blackley and Doreen Leitch. He'd simply taken up where Terry Lawler had left off, except that he was intent on making money from his victims rather than seizing the moral high ground by exposing their activities.

'It's likely, then,' said Tweedy, pacing around in front of his whiteboard, 'that the same person is responsible for killing Lawler and Macklin?'

'Seems that way, sir,' Tara replied. 'The main suspects have to be the intended victims of Macklin's blackmail attempts.'

Tweedy sank into deep thought; his face lent itself well to looking contemplative.

'But they were such brutal killings,' he said. 'Macklin's, in particular, was frenzied. A very angry killer. Do any of these suspects fit that profile?'

'Blackley has a temper,' said Murray.

'Mm. And what about the lead regarding Lawler's missing sister and those other women? Is there any possibility that Macklin had also taken up that project and stumbled upon the same person as his friend, a potential serial killer?'

CHAPTER 42

Guy

Saw it on the news at lunchtime; they found the body of some bloke. Macklin, a solicitor. Turns out he was a mate of that guy Lawler; you know, the one whose sister I took? But I've never heard of him. Can't help wondering what's going on, though. Tara will be knee-deep in corpses soon. Who the hell would join the police? Nightmare.

Today, after I finished work, I went to look for a new van. I need to have one ready for when I finally get a chance to go for Tara. It's doing my bloody head in, all this waiting. I'm usually patient, but it's harder when you can't even do proper reconnaissance. Tara is so difficult to pin down. She works odd hours; she's home when you think she'd be out enjoying herself; sometimes she drives, sometimes it's that big copper who drives her. I can't be taking another girl just to fill in time. I want Tara, and I want her now.

I've bought a few vans from the auctions on West Derby Road. I've been lucky so far, getting them at the right price, few questions asked. It's better than private deals, always a chance the seller may remember me if it ever came to an investigation. And I always pay in cash at the auction. They have a note of my name, that is, the name I give them, but not much else. This time I managed a Vauxhall van with side loading doors for three grand. A bargain. When I'm done with Tara, I can easily make the money back at an auction in Manchester or Burnley.

When I'd settled me debts, I drove the van out of the city toward Netherton. It's not a place I know well, but it's easy to park on a road without restrictions and no questions asked. I can leave the van there until I need it. I didn't hang about, though, caught a bus back to the city centre. I had an appointment to keep.

His name is Janek. That's all I know. Not even sure if that's his real name. He's Estonian, and that's what's important. In Estonia they take China White like bloody Smarties. The streets of Tallinn are paved with the stuff. Anyway, Janek is my supplier. He doesn't ask questions, and I don't offer information. I reckon he assumes I pass the gear on to friends. China White's becoming very popular in the North West. Stronger than heroin, but I don't give a shit about that. I'm not trying to get high; I'm trying to get laid by the woman of my choice.

Late in the afternoon, I met up with Janek outside St Johns Shopping Centre. He prefers to meet clients in busy places, lots of people all going about their own business. But no matter how I try, I can never spot him first. He just seems to appear from thin air. I thought I was good at stealth and all that shit, but this guy is a whole level above me. I was standing by the wall a few feet from the entrance to the shopping centre and looking all around me. Sure as hell, when I glanced to my right, Janek was standing to my left when I turned around again.

He was a tall, gangly bastard, thin face, cheekbones sticking out. Looked as if he came from a labour camp in Siberia. His hair was black and greasy, he needed a shave, and his clothes were shabby and in need of a good wash. His brown leather jacket had absorbed years of grime from trawling the streets and should've been dumped. He had both hands in his jacket pockets, but a plastic carrier bag was dangling from his right wrist.

'How are you, Mr James?' he said in quite good English.

'Dead on, Janek mate, how about you?'

'Busy. Everybody wants what I have to sell.'

'I hope it's good gear this time.'

Not that he began with a smile, but he didn't look happy at my suggesting there had been anything inferior about his previous gear.

'Always good. I don't do bad drugs. Not good for business. How much do you want this time?'

'As much as you can give me.'

'You planning some big party?'

'You know me, Janek, low key.'

At that he walked away, and I knew to tag along. Always better not to loiter in one place. Keep moving through the shoppers and people hurrying home from work. No one took notice of Janek removing a small white parcel from his shopping bag. He handed it to me while looking straight ahead. I knew not to begin studying the package. I could tell how much gear was wrapped in the bag just by the weight and size. There was enough inside to do Tara and several dozen more Merseyside policewomen. I slipped him a roll of notes, four hundred quid to be exact. Before I got the chance to wish him well, he scurried off down a side street. I watched him go. You have to admire his business acumen.

The next day, which was Saturday, I was off work. It was kind of a nice day if you're into that sort of thing, admiring the weather and the like, so I drove my car down to Penrhyn harbour. I wanted to check on Mother Freedom, make sure she was seaworthy. I looked over the engine, made sure it was clean and that no water had got into it. The cabin needed a good tidying, and when I'd changed the seat covers and replaced the pillowcases with fresh ones, I decided it might be a nice idea to keep Tara alive until we were out to sea. Then I would give her the send-off she deserved. I told myself there would be nothing different about taking Tara, she was simply another conquest, but I felt on edge about something. Yes, she was a cop, yes, she was difficult to watch, but that wasn't it. Somehow, I imagined that Tara was going to be the best girl I'd ever taken, and I didn't want to mess it up. Everything would have to be perfect for Tara Grogan. I would give her the time of her life. Something worth dying for.

CHAPTER 43

Tara

Reluctantly, Tara had to endure another interview with Councillor Sullivan while he ogled her chest. And, it seemed, he didn't confine his behaviour to his office. She and Murray sat opposite the young politician in the restaurant of the council offices in Hatton Garden. Sullivan was feasting on steak pie, chips and peas accompanied by a mug of tea. Tara chose not to eat, while Murray took the opportunity to tuck into a cheeseburger and a glass of milk. It was evident that Sullivan was unnerved by their presence, but it didn't deter him from his study of Tara's breasts while he ate.

'I'm sure by now, Councillor, that you've learned of the murder of Paul Macklin?'

'Heard, yes, but if you've come to ask me about him, Inspector, I can't help you. Didn't know the guy.'

Tara cocked her head to the side in disbelief. She hadn't thought him that silly to deny knowledge of the man who had probably attempted to blackmail him. Murray, enjoying his burger, ceased eating.

'I find that hard to believe.'

'And why is that, Inspector?'

Please speak to my face, she wanted to say.

'Evan Blackley was more than happy to tell us of his association with Paul Macklin.'

Sullivan didn't reply, feigning a greater interest in the food on his plate. Tara was happy to wait, while he gathered his thoughts. Murray resumed eating.

'Have you met with Evan Blackley recently?' she said.

'Why do you ask that? You already know I have contact with Blackley's company on the council's behalf.'

'I was wondering, perhaps, if you *had* met with Blackley, whether Paul Macklin was present too.'

'Already told you. I didn't know Macklin. Are you going to waste my afternoon finding different ways to ask the same question?'

He took a mouthful of tea, and for the first time, stared Tara in the face.

Glad you've decided to join me at last, she thought.

'Tell me, Councillor, was Macklin trying to blackmail you over your dealings with Evan Blackley or did it concern your relationship with Doreen Leitch?'

Sullivan didn't even baulk at the suggestion and merely finished off the last mouthful of pie.

'Well, that was good,' he said, setting his knife and fork on the plate. 'If you're finished, Inspector, I have a meeting at two o'clock. Something to do with greater police presence in the city centre at night. Maybe you and

your mate would fancy a spot of overtime on the beat.'
Sullivan rose from his chair, smiled and walked away.

'Cheeky bugger,' said Murray.

Tara was surprised at the degree of backbone shown by the councillor. From their first meeting, she didn't think he had it in him.

'Maybe we'll do better with Councillor Leitch,' she said.

* * *

Remarkable, Tara thought, learning from Murray after he'd finished speaking to Leitch on the phone, that Doreen was enjoying a leisurely day at home. From first impressions it seemed the woman was a workaholic, dashing from council meetings to constituency gatherings to her various charitable projects, advice surgeries and drug and alcohol drop-in centres. Home for Leitch was, to Tara's surprise, quite a distance from inner city Liverpool. She may have dedicated herself to working for the people of the city, but Tara thought it telling that she hadn't chosen to live there. With the aid of sat-nav, Murray turned left off Westcliffe Road in Birkdale, and they found themselves in a neat yet spacious modern development of large, detached houses. The Leitch family home was located at the far end of a cul-de-sac.

Murray pulled up at a pair of double gates and climbed out of the car. Tara looked on as he spoke into an intercom on the right-hand gatepost, and a few seconds later the metal gates began to swing inwards. The red-brick house had three floors, windows and doors were framed in white, and a double garage was set some way off to the right. There was ample room in the drive for a couple of city buses never mind a couple of family cars. Despite the announcement at the gate that visitors had just entered, they still had to ring the doorbell which chimed merrily somewhere in the centre of the house. A full minute later, Doreen Leitch opened the half-paned door. Dressed casually in black trousers and green tunic, she didn't apologise for the delay, nor did she offer any greeting.

'This way,' she said dryly, walking briskly down the hallway.

Soon they were seated around a breakfast bar in a bright expansive kitchen. No refreshment was offered, and no offence was taken. Tara was certain that Sullivan would have briefed his lover on the reasons for another interview with the police. But the woman was set on playing her part as a mildly interested bystander.

'How may I help you today, Inspector?'

She sat opposite Tara at the bar, her hands resting one on the other. Her smile was strong, but forced, her eyes suggesting that Tara should get to the point immediately and be done with it. Murray remained standing, pacing around the kitchen, although Tara knew that he would be a keen listener.

'I want to ask you about your relationship with Paul Macklin.'

'I'm afraid I've never heard of Mr Macklin.'

'He was a friend of Terry Lawler's.'

Doreen Leitch shook her head.

'Sorry, I can't help you, Inspector. It seems you've had a wasted journey. I could have answered your query when I spoke to your colleague on the phone.'

She glared in Murray's direction, but his back was turned. Tara hadn't finished with the patronising woman.

'This is a murder inquiry, Councillor. We believe the death of Paul Macklin is connected to that of Terry Lawler.'

'And I explained when we last met that I had no dealings with Mr Lawler.'

'According to Councillor Sullivan, Lawler had threatened to expose your affair, and the following morning his body was found on Crosby Beach. I believe that Paul Macklin also threatened to expose your affair but was willing to accept payment to remain silent. We found his body tied to a fence and slashed to ribbons. Have you any comment to make about that, Councillor?'

Tara was conscious of her face warming. She didn't much care for this woman's attitude, innocent or not.

Suddenly, Doreen Leitch was on her feet and scurrying across her kitchen to an open doorway through which Murray had just disappeared.

'Where do you think you're going?' she fumed. 'I didn't give you permission to go wandering around my home.'

Tara could just about hear Leitch admonishing Murray somewhere deep within the next room. A moment later she emerged looking fraught, Murray following behind with a bemused smirk playing on his face. He raised his eyes at Tara as Leitch continued to rant.

'I don't care for the tone of your questions, Inspector, and I don't appreciate one of your officers taking liberties in my home. If you have nothing more to say, I think it's time you left.'

'I didn't get an answer to my question,' said Tara, getting to her feet. 'Did Paul Macklin attempt to blackmail you over your affair with Matt Sullivan?'

'And I have told you that I've never had any contact with this man. Now please go.'

'One more thing, Councillor. Is your affair with Matt Sullivan ongoing?'

'That's no business of yours or the Merseyside Police.'

'If Macklin was blackmailing you, and he was then killed, I rather think it is our business. You have motive to murder, and I will call again if I find you have not been forthcoming with the truth.'

* * *

On the drive back to the city, Tara pondered their next move in silence, but Murray was keen to talk.

'That didn't go too well.'

'No, and it wouldn't surprise me if that hateful woman goes complaining to the Chief Constable.'

'That'll bring Tweedy down on us.'

'Did you find anything interesting on your walkabout?'

'Found her study, but she didn't give me the chance to have a good peek. So, what do we do now?'

Tara gave a heavy sigh.

'We've spoken to all the potential suspects and got nowhere. I think it's time to lean a bit harder on the Blackleys. They know a lot more about Macklin, and I want to know why he was killed at the very place, the building site, that caused so much trouble for Lawler. Is there more to it than merely poisoned ground?'

CHAPTER 44

Tara

Tara and Murray sat across the table from Evan Blackley in an interview room at St Anne Street station. In a dark blue sweater, and matching slacks, he looked all set for a morning on the golf course. Instead, he had been requested to show up at the station to be questioned in connection with the murder of Paul Macklin. He was far from happy, tapping his fingers impatiently on the table as Tara formulated her questions.

'Tell me about the building site where Paul Macklin's body was found.'

'It's a building site; we're building houses and apartments. What else is there to say about it?'

'Why do you think Paul Macklin was killed there?'

'I have no idea.' Blackley drilled his eyes into her as if to remind her how busy he was and how utterly pointless it was to quiz him about a murder.

'Is this not the contentious site that caused so much trouble between you and Terry Lawler?'

'I don't see how that's got anything to do with it.'

Tara met his enflamed stare.

'Really? One man died after threatening to expose your project and another is found strapped to a fence and slashed to ribbons at the very site and the morning after you had informed us of his attempt to blackmail you. Have you anything to say about that, Mr Blackley?'

'I had nothing to do with these murders. I've told you before, Lawler was a pain in the ass, but Sullivan put him in his place when he took him to court. He was no longer a threat.'

'Then why did he come to see you the night before he died? He must have believed he was still a threat to you. Was it merely a rehash of his original charge about the building land being unfit for housing? Or did Lawler have something else to say?'

Blackley shook his head but offered no reply.

'Let's move on, shall we?' Tara closed the folder relating to Lawler and opened another, marked with Paul Macklin's name. 'When Macklin called to see you, and spoke to Gwen the week before he died, what specific threat did he make toward you?'

'He tried to blackmail me.'

'Over what? The building project?'

'Yes.'

'But you said that Lawler was no longer a threat with respect to your building project, so what did Macklin have to say that was different?'

Blackley rubbed his face with both hands and sighed deeply. Tara was content to wait until he'd gathered his thoughts, be they truth or lies.

'Nothing. He'd just got hold of Lawler's story and threatened to have it published in the paper.'

'Nothing? No difference?'

'Not a thing.'

'Then why did you call me about Macklin and make threats against him?'

'I don't know. I was angry at his cheek.'

'Why did you wait for almost a week before calling me?'

'Gwen spotted some guy hanging around near our house. I assumed it was Macklin looking for trouble. I was angry, so I called you.'

'Did you have anything to do with Paul Macklin's death?'

'No, of course not.'

'Did you have anything to do with placing Macklin's body at your building site?'

'No. If you have nothing further to accuse me of, I'd like to go now.'

'We're not quite finished, Mr Blackley.'

Tara glanced sideways at Murray who took it as his cue to take over the questioning. Blackley sat, arms folded, looking angry. He didn't appear the suave individual they'd first met a couple of weeks earlier.

'Tell me about the trouble with the land you're building on,' Murray began.

'This is ridiculous, it has nothing to do with these men dying.'

'How did the land become poisoned?'

'It wasn't bloody poisoned. There used to be a paints factory on the site, so the stories went round that loads of chemicals had been dumped on the land. It didn't help matters that some asbestos had to be removed from the factory building. But there's nothing odd in that. It was an old building. Once Lawler got hold of the idea, he wouldn't let it drop. Then he stumbled across the council involvement which was all above board. There were planning regulations to be followed.'

'And did you follow them?'

'Yes, of course.'

'Is that how Matt Sullivan became involved?'

'I suppose so.'

'Only suppose?'

'He was on the planning committee, and I'd dealt with him before on other projects. He helped pave the way with more senior officials.'

'Such as?'

'Well, anyone on the planning committee who might not be favourable to some building proposals.'

'Anyone in particular?'

'A couple of Lib Dems, Jack Cook, an independent, and Doreen Leitch.'

Tara suddenly sat forward at the mention of the name.

'You have an association with Doreen Leitch?' she asked.

A look of exasperation spread across Blackley's face.

'Why are you asking me all of these questions? What the hell have my contacts with councillors got to do with these killings?'

'Please answer the question, Mr Blackley.'

'No. I've had enough of this crap. If you think I've had anything to do with killing these guys, then bloody charge me. Otherwise, I'm out of here.'

He stood up, the back of his legs sliding his chair across the floor. Tara raised her eyes at his outburst, but she was content to let him go. He was not about to confess to anything.

'Just one thing before you storm out.'

'What?'

'Your whereabouts, please, two nights ago?'

'I was out to dinner with my wife and some friends.'

'And they can confirm that?'

'Yes.'

'Their names please?'

'Gwen, obviously. Matt Sullivan and Doreen Leitch.'

Blackley was already out the door. Those same names again.

CHAPTER 45

Guy

Shit. Following this wee girl is getting harder, not easier. I'm going to lose my job with all the time I'm taking off. That bastard Cranley has it in for me anyway without me giving him the bullets to fire at me. But Tara is driving me mental. This is what I've got so far after all of my surveillance.

She leaves her flat at Wapping Dock, any time between seven and eight-thirty. When she's driving, the car comes out of the private car park and she makes for that bloody cop shop on St Anne Street. Sometimes she's in there all day, then usually after five she drives home to her flat and that's her for the rest of the night. When she does leave the cop shop during the day, she is with that big gobshite I nearly ran into in the bar when I had my date with Tara. Ugly big git. I wonder if he's ever had a go at his colleague. Is he her type? I obviously wasn't. But she's definitely mine. I can tell you that for nothing. She spends her weekends either at home or else she's out with her mates, Kate and Aisling. I did track her once all the way out to Caldy; I think it was to her parents' place. She spent the entire day inside and then drove back to Wapping Dock.

For the first time in years, I don't know what to do next. How the heck am I ever going to set things up so I can snatch her? I tried snooping on her friend Kate who lives up on Canning Street, the one with the funny hair, but lately she doesn't seem to be having much face-to-face contact with Tara. I'm horny again, and it's only been a few days or so since I had Modesty.

I'd been so busy with Tara that I almost forgot to keep a check on the news and the papers for anything on a girl missing from Anfield. Not a squeak. No one to miss the poor wee thing. I think that's sad. No one seemed to care about what happened to her. At least I cared enough to show her a good time. In the past few days, I began to wonder if Modesty was actually a prostitute. A loner prostitute with no pimp. Not likely that anyone would miss her if that's what she did for a living. One of her regular customers, maybe. But I'm not too happy at the notion that I may have taken a hooker. No real need for my specialist treatment. I could have had her for a few quid instead. Waste of good China White.

I spied a lovely wee thing the other night, near the police station. Don't know if she works there, but she has walked past several times. Short blonde hair, you know the kind that's nearly white. It's cut like a boy's and she wears long dangly earrings, a leather jacket, a tartan skirt and a pair of those boots supposed to look like old army boots but aren't, because they have a bit of a heel. She's not very tall, looks about eighteen, but that's what I'm worried about. Looks eighteen but more likely is sixteen or even fourteen. Scares me that. I would never take kids. Not my bag. But if I don't make progress with Tara soon, I'll end up giving this wee girl one of my names and that means she's chosen. No going back once I've chosen them. And that's my whole problem. I've chosen Tara, and I have to see it through no matter what.

CHAPTER 46

Tara

Denim jeans, long-sleeve T-shirt and training shoes for a night out. It was only to Aisling's flat, just across the complex from her own. No one to see her, and no need to drive. She clutched a hefty glass of chardy, shoes off, her feet up on the deep-cushioned sofa. Aisling was fidgeting in the open kitchen area; she couldn't manage much else. She would claim it was cooking, but piercing the film on trays of Tesco Finest Pasta with Chicken and Rosemary, placing them on a baking tray and into the oven was hardly even a Jamie Oliver fifteen-minute special. Kate mirrored Tara's pose on the second sofa, feet up, glass of wine in hand.

'Tara, you still haven't told us all the biz on your new fella?' said Kate, mischievously glancing towards Aisling in search of a cohort for her tease.

'What fella?'

'Don't play the dumb blonde, you know who I'm talking about. That bloke Aisling and I set you up with in Dawson Street the other week.'

'I've already told you about him.'

'No, you haven't.'

'I thought I'd sent you a text.'

'That's when you were on the date, but what happened after that?'

'Kate wants to know if you've slept with him,' said Aisling.

'Only had that one date, and I told him that was enough, thanks very much.'

'But why?' said Kate. 'He looked nice.'

Tara sipped at her wine, taking her time before resuming the conversation, or the inquisition, more like. Aisling and Kate always, since they'd been kids, quizzed each other relentlessly about boyfriends, dates and, when a little older, sex. The pair were freer and easier in discussing such things. Tara was the shy one, joining in only at the insistence of the other two.

'I don't know,' she said at last. 'Didn't get a good feeling about him.'

Aisling, always the blunt one, ploughed in.

'Did he try it on with you?'

Kate laughed, and Aisling joined in, but Tara suddenly felt that now she actually wanted to discuss this man. She had felt strange in his company; maybe her friends could help her understand what had passed between her and James on that evening.

'We talked for a while in the pub, but it felt more like he was questioning me the whole time.'

'That's what you do on a first date,' said Aisling. 'You have to get to know each other, you have to ask each other questions about jobs, family, interests…'

'Jeez, Aisling,' said Kate. 'I never thought you bothered with all that. I thought if you liked the look of them, you shagged them senseless.'

'Ha-ha.'

'But this guy was strange,' said Tara. 'He asked me constantly about my job, and when I told him that there was stuff I couldn't share, he sort of changed tack and tried to get the same information by asking in another way. I didn't like it. Didn't feel comfortable. And when I asked about his job, he was so negative in his answer I didn't feel he wanted to discuss it at all. His accent bothered me, too. That Northern Irish mixed with Scouse, it reminded me of Callum. And then when I looked into his eyes for a second, I thought it was Callum. We kissed outside, but I freaked out. I had to get away. It was so weird.'

'Doesn't sound weird to me,' said Kate. 'It's natural to think of Callum. You went through a very traumatic time, losing him and then the baby.'

An awkward silence ensued, and Tara and Kate retreated to their glasses of wine, while Aisling slid a tray of pre-prepared garlic bread into the oven beside the pasta bake.

Rather than sink deeper into her lake of depressing experiences, Tara sought to lighten the mood. After all, the three of them were supposed to be having a good time, sharing a few laughs.

'Do you think it's normal for a man to get hard in the middle of the first kiss?' she asked.

Kate giggled, and Aisling, as usual, jumped in.

'Every time, if he's kissing me,' she said.

* * *

She was in the office early, before Tweedy or Murray arrived. The plan for first thing was to discuss progress in the investigation of Terry Lawler's murder. Now they had a second killing to contend with, the urgency to get a result was mounting. Tara dumped her bag on a desk, picked up a dry marker pen and marched over to a blank whiteboard. In the centre, she wrote the names of Terry Lawler and Paul Macklin, encasing each within a rectangle. At the top of the board she wrote, side by side, the names of the suspects they had so far identified: Gwen Blackley, Evan Blackley, Matt Sullivan and Doreen Leitch.

She paused for a moment, examining each name then recalled a couple of other angles she had considered previously. She added the word 'unknown,' bordering it with a rectangle. This was reserved for the possibility that Lawler had unearthed a serial killer responsible for abducting several women on Merseyside and goodness knows where else. Finally, she wrote the names Lynsey Yeats and Danny Ross, realising that she hadn't devoted much time to their involvement with Terry Lawler. She stood back from the board, pondering the connections between the suspects and the victims. At that point Superintendent Tweedy came into the room on the way to his office.

'Good morning, Tara. A new lead?'

'Morning, sir. I'm afraid not. Just going over a few things to help decide on the next step.'

She began drawing lines to represent the connections between the people in the group. She found that she was able to draw a line from each suspect to Terry Lawler. He had threatened to expose Blackley, Sullivan and Leitch. Also, he'd possibly identified a serial killer, and he seemed to have pissed off his former girlfriend Lynsey Yeats and her sidekick Danny Ross. All had a motive to murder Lawler. Paul Macklin had been a close friend of Lawler's but, realistically, she could only connect Evan Blackley and Matt Sullivan to the murdered solicitor. He had tried to blackmail them both and perhaps Doreen Leitch, although she and Sullivan denied knowing the man.

Tweedy looked on as she worked.

'Seems ominous for any of the named suspects who had associations with Lawler and Macklin,' he said.

'I agree, sir, but the Blackleys, Sullivan and Leitch all have an alibi for the night Macklin was killed. They were having dinner together.'

'Very convenient. You don't imagine there is a conspiracy?'

'Seems a bit unlikely. For instance, why kill Macklin at the building site in which Blackley and Sullivan have an interest?'

'Blackley told you that Doreen Leitch is against the building project.'

'I realise that, sir, but she is in a relationship with Sullivan. And why such brutal killings? The attack on Macklin was frenzied, and there is something very disturbing about the manner in which Lawler was killed.'

'You're right. And it must have taken more than one person to carry out the burial of Lawler on the beach.'

'Definitely a crazed attack.'

'Like someone was off their head on drugs,' said Murray, who'd just joined his colleagues.

'Could be,' Tweedy replied. 'So, any suggestions, folks, on what to do next?'

'I would like to go back to Treadwater and have another chat with Lynsey Yeats. If drugs were involved in the killings it could be linked to Lawler's investigation and his published story on the drug problems in housing estates. Yeats, if she's willing to talk this time, may be able to give a few pointers on the drug set-up Lawler studied and those involved, not least her boyfriend Danny Ross.'

CHAPTER 47

Tara

Tara and Murray wasted no time in driving out to Treadwater. A fine drizzle was falling, but the air was quite warm and still. One or two locals strolled down the street, an elderly woman pulling an old shopping bag on wheels behind her, and a heavy, slow-moving man, smoking as he went. It was pension day. No doubt they were headed for the post office.

Tara gazed at the home of Lynsey Yeats. Adjoining houses either side were quite well kept, tidy gardens, a few plant pots and PVC windows and doors. The house to the right had modern vertical blinds on the windows, the one to the left, lace curtains. The Yeats house had a battered front door in need of painting, a garden that had been paved over, weeds poking through the cracks, and neither blinds nor curtains on the windows.

'How do you want to play this?' Murray asked her.

Neither of them had made any move to get out of the car.

'Good question. Lynsey won't be terribly happy to see a couple of bizzies at the door. Best if she's on her own. Hopefully, Ross will not be with her.'

Murray kept a sharp eye, gazing around the street as Tara approached the front door and rang the bell, soon realising that it was unlikely to be working. In any case there was no reply, even to her knocks on the window.

'Here they are, ma'am,' Murray called from the pavement.

Tara turned around to see Yeats and Ross at the top of the street, both loaded with plastic carrier bags. When Tara reached Murray at the car, Ross seemed to recognise them, because he ditched his bags and made off the way he'd come. It took a second longer for Yeats to notice her visitors, but she kept hold of her bags and disappeared down an alley between the houses.

'I'll take Ross, you take Lynsey,' said Murray racing off.

Tara quickly followed, immediately regretting having chosen to wear a skirt and shoes with heels, not of great height but enough to make running awkward. Murray veered across the road but was making little progress on closing the gap to Ross, who was almost at the end of the street. By the time Tara reached the alley down which Yeats had fled, she could see no sign of the girl. When she emerged into open space, an expanse of grassland with a couple of football pitches and a kids' playground lay ahead, the next block of houses on the far side. Yeats was halfway across, glancing over her shoulder as she ran. Tara wondered if she were worth chasing. They could pick her up later; she would have to return home at some point. But why had she scarpered in the first place? Why was she avoiding the police? That was worth finding out. She carried on across the playing fields. When Tara reached the playground, her feet beginning to throb from continually snagging her heels on clumps of grass, she saw Yeats making for a gap between two blocks of flats.

The gap between the flats was more of a laneway with lock-up garages at the far end. Tara continued to run, but she had lost sight of the girl. The lane opened into an area of rough ground that had suffered from fly-tipping of building waste and a couple of burnt-out cars. As she emerged in the open space, she felt a heavy thud across her back. The blow sent her sprawling hands-first into a puddle of water. Winded, she struggled on to her knees. Yeats stood over her, wielding a heavy baton of wood in both hands like a mighty sword.

Tara tried to get up. Her head buzzing, she gasped for breath. She saw two Lynseys towering over her. As she attempted to get to her feet, the girl struck again. Searing pain on the back of her neck, she slumped to the ground. This time her hands failed to save her face from hitting the wet gravel. She had no strength left to rise. Lynsey stood over her, her weapon raised above her head. Tara slowly turned and, looking up, she saw fiery hatred in the eyes of the young girl who was about to end her life. She could do nothing but wait for more pain. She closed her eyes.

Suddenly, Yeats cried out. Eyes opening, Tara saw her hit the ground beside her, the baton of wood falling out of reach.

'Leave her alone.' A man's voice. Tara heard it. It wasn't Murray.

Yeats screamed angrily and struggled to her feet. She attempted to retrieve her weapon, but the man beat her to it.

'Mind your own fucking business,' Lynsey yelled.

'You better leave now, while you can still walk.'

Yeats grunted at her attacker. She seemed to consider taking him on, but when he wielded the baton of wood, she thought better of it.

'Stay away from me, bitch,' she spat at Tara, who was only vaguely aware of what had taken place. Yeats fired a threatening look at the man. 'I'll get you done over for this, dickhead.'

The man feigned a swipe at her head, and she backed off then gathered her two plastic bags and took to running once more, soon disappearing beyond the lock-ups.

Tara felt strong hands gripping her arms, raising her, firstly to her knees then all the way to her feet. Sharp pains surged around her neck and shoulders. She couldn't stand unaided, but he took a firm hold of her waist. He peered into her scratched and muddied face. She tried hard to focus.

'You?' she said.

CHAPTER 48

Guy

That bastard Cranley, my supervisor, gave me a verbal warning. He said he didn't think for a minute that I was sick. I was a slacker.

'And there's only one thing worse than a slacker,' he said, quietly, so no one else could hear him. 'That's an Irish slacker. A lying Irish slacker.'

He turned his nose up at me, like I was shit on his shoe. I wanted to down the bastard. Down him so he would never get up. Back in Belfast they have a good way to deal with assholes like him. Take out his knees. Soon cleans the cheek out of the bastards. But I didn't. I held my nerve. Couldn't afford to lose the job. Not yet anyway. Someday I would sort him.

Instead, I apologised, I grovelled.

'I'm really sorry, Mr Cranley,' I said. Didn't even use his first name. Very respectful. 'I was genuinely sick; I have a bad stomach, like. Think it's an ulcer. Have to go to the hospital for tests.'

'You're in a bloody hospital, sunshine. And it pays your wages. So, this is the last time you mess me about. Once more and you're down the road. Clear?'

'Won't happen again, Mr Cranley.'

He pissed off down to A&E, leaving me to collect a stiff from Ward 12 and take it down to the mortuary. Nice job, eh?

So, it was nearly a week before I could get daytime off to keep tabs on Tara. I was struggling to get by with bloody porn DVDs. I needed the feel of a good woman. The harder it became to snatch her, the more I wanted her and the more I was determined to have her.

It was a pissing awful morning, when I tailed her and that big eejit she hangs around with. I followed them all the way from their station out to Netherton and on to one of those stinking housing estates. I hoped this was the type of place that Cranley lived. Would serve him right to get done over by a couple of crackheads or his wife to get raped by some sexual deviant.

I watched them park their car outside of a house. I didn't reckon it was the sort of place I was ever going to have the chance of snatching Tara, so I drove on, stopping for a drink and a bag of crisps at the mini-market beside the park. I'm not usually all nostalgic for Northern Ireland, couldn't care less about the place, but you do get better cheese and onion crisps there. Stuff you get in England is shite.

I was just getting back in my car when I spotted a figure trotting across the football pitches. A girl, dark hair, from a distance not that great-looking, wearing jeans and a black leather biker jacket. She was carrying a plastic bag in each hand. Didn't think much of it. Then I saw another girl further back. She was running too. I munched on me crisps and watched her approach. She wasn't exactly dressed for jogging: dark jacket and skirt, tights and shoes. Blonde hair tied back in a ponytail. Tara.

By now the first girl was out of view, but Tara was still running. She crossed the road right in front of me and ran down a lane between blocks of flats. Thought I should take a look. See how my girl earns her living.

That's when I found her. Sprawled in the muck, the other girl about to smash her head in. Looked like a wee slapper or one of those crackheads I was hoping would kill off Cranley. She soon pissed off, though. I stuck my boot in the small of her back. She went down like a sack of spuds. Full of cheek when she got back to her feet, but she didn't fancy taking me on.

I could hardly believe it. Tara in my arms once more.

'What was that all about?' I asked her.

She could barely speak. Amazed to see me. Her eyes weren't focussing properly. Looked like a girl after a hen night in Matthew Street. I tried to wipe some of the muck off her cheeks, but she winced at every touch, and her legs, in ripped tights, were giving way beneath her.

'You?' was all she said.

'Aye, it's me.'

'What are you doing here?'

'Stopped at the shop for a drink, and then I saw you charging across the playing fields. I wondered what was going on. Where's your big mate?'

She regained some strength, enough to sort of push me away. I didn't much like that. I'd just saved her life, and there she was pushing me off her. I was only trying to hold her steady. I wasn't going to do anything. I let her go. I walked with her as she limped to the road beside the park, and from there she spotted the big-lig cop wandering about on the football pitches. Two arms the one length. Big ganch.

'Thank you, James,' she said, emotion or nerves cracking her voice. 'I think she might have finished me if you hadn't come along.'

'You have a very dangerous job, Tara. Who was she?'

'No one important. At least I didn't think so until now.' She was trying to tidy herself as her mate approached, out of breath and carrying two plastic bags.

'Did you get him?' Tara asked.

'Na, disappeared, into a mate's house I imagine.'

The cop looked from me to Tara and back to me, except this time he was glaring.

'What happened, ma'am?'

'Yeats sprang a surprise for me.'

'You need to get to a hospital, Tara,' I said.

The cop continued to glare; he was definitely unsure about me.

'I'm fine, honestly, just winded. If it hadn't been for James here, she would have really hurt me,' she said to her mate.

'You two know each other?'

'We met recently,' I replied, knowing it would irk the big bastard. Thought he might have remembered me from that night in the pub. But maybe cops like him don't have much between the ears. I'm quite sure he'd been wanting to have a go at Tara himself and got nowhere. Then he held up the two carrier bags.

'The reason they scarpered when they saw us.'

'What is it?' Tara asked.

'Ecstasy, thousands of them. Enough to blow the minds of every kid in Liverpool.'

Tara looked at me and smiled. Probably forced, not genuine.

'Thanks again, James. We have to go now.'

'Don't you need a statement from me or something? I saw what happened.'

Wasn't I the upstanding citizen?

'I'll get to it soon enough. I've got your number.'

I nodded. The big shite smirked. I knew a fuck-off when I saw it.

'Right. Look after yourself, Tara.'

'I'll be in touch,' she said.

I watched them from my car, walking across the playing fields, Tara managing only a slow pace. I'd just saved her life. Boy, did that feel surreal. I was supposed to be the guy who ends it.

CHAPTER 49

Tara

She got home early to a hot bath and a long soak. Murray and Tweedy insisted that she got checked out at the hospital. All fine. She would have a couple of nice bruises on her neck and shoulders, her knees were skinned, and she had a few grazes on her right cheek when she'd hit the gravel face down. What was almost worse than her injuries, was to run into Kate as she was leaving the Royal, and Kate was going on duty. She had to cough up the whole story. Now Kate would tell Aisling. She was just going over this in her head when the doorbell rang. It had to be Aisling on a mission of mercy. Tara climbed out of the bath, wrapping her towel around her twice.

'Hi, Aisling,' she said deliberately cheerful, so her friend wouldn't come over all judgemental about policing and morbid about her chosen career.

'Don't "hi, Aisling" me,' she said, barging in. 'You promised to call me if you ever got into bother. Instead, I had to find out from Kate.'

She tossed her coat on the sofa and made for the kitchen. Then she noticed the black and purple bruises on Tara's shoulder.

'Oh my God, Tara. Look at those bruises. They're horrible.'

'I'm fine, Aisling. Don't fuss.'

'People don't go to A&E if they're fine. Tell me what happened, and I'll pour us a nice glass of chardy. If you have some?'

'Yes, it's in the fridge. Let me get dressed first, and then we can talk.'

Ten minutes later the pair sat at opposite ends of the sofa, glasses of wine in hand. Tara retold the events of her day, well diluted. No point in giving Aisling more cause to go on at her about packing it in. She did, however, confess to feeling strange about James turning up from nowhere.

'Just as well,' said Aisling. 'That bitch could've killed you.'

'I realise that, but don't you think it's odd, him showing up like that? What was he doing in the middle of Netherton, in the middle of the Treadwater Estate? He lives in Toxteth and works at the Royal. Do you think he was following me?'

'Maybe he's your guardian angel?'

'I just find it weird that he could be there. He's a bit weird.'

'What has he ever done to you that was weird? He's been a perfect gent, if you ask me.'

Tara wasn't prepared to get into an argument with Aisling over her feelings. She knew how she felt about this man, and she knew she had never felt this way about anyone before. James was not your usual bachelor; he was not your usual lad, cheeky, witty, brash and randy. Something deeper lay within this man. It gave her the shivers to think about it.

* * *

The pain ran across her shoulders and down her left arm. She'd managed little sleep. An intense ache gripped at her forearm and was accompanied by episodes of pins and needles as she turned from her back to her left side and then to her right. It was just gone six when she gave up, slipped from the bed and padded to her bathroom. A hot shower at first provided some relief, but with constant movement the discomfort in her forearm returned. For a while she sat on the sofa, wrapped in a towel and eating two mandarin oranges. Her throat ached too, and she'd noticed the bruising on her shoulder had spread around the base of her neck. No one in the office would be surprised if she didn't show this morning, but what was she to gain by staying at home? She wasn't sleeping; it was too painful to lounge on the sofa, and more than that it was too frustrating to be sat still while a posse of theories rampaged through her head.

Rising from the sofa, she moved to the window and opened the curtains to reveal a grey sky leaning heavily upon the river and the dull buildings of Birkenhead. Didn't add much inspiration to her day. Staring blankly upon the river scene, she thought about Lynsey Yeats, a girl who might well have killed her. Was she capable of murder? Did she have a strong motive for killing Terry Lawler? They'd had a relationship together. But had there been real love? She doubted it. Perhaps it had been one-sided. Maybe Lynsey had seen Lawler as her meal ticket, her way out of Treadwater to a better lifestyle. From what she'd learned so far, it appeared that Lawler was not averse to using people if it helped him get his story. Would her anger at being used in this way have been enough for Lynsey to murder her ex-boyfriend? Perhaps Danny Ross helped, or he'd carried out the killing on Lynsey's behalf. Suddenly, she wondered if yesterday's events had brought her closer to solving the case.

Driving was more awkward than she'd expected. She'd hardly managed to change gear and at times remained in third, her car whining on the longer stretches of road from Wapping Dock. Her whole body sighed in relief when she drew into a parking space at St Anne Street. Her early rising meant that she entered the operations room to see only DC Wilson seated at his desk poring over a stack of files.

'Morning, ma'am,' he called across the office as she made her way to the whiteboard she'd adorned with theories the day before.

'Any news?'

'All quiet.' She studied the arrangement of names on the board. This morning, those of Yeats and Ross seemed to stand out in 3D.

'No arrests overnight?'

'Nothing relevant. If you're wondering about the Yeats girl, uniform didn't find her at home.'

'Surprise, surprise. I'm quite sure that young lady has plenty of places to hide. Anything on Ross?'

Wilson shook his head and returned to his study of a bunch of files.

She lowered her handbag to the floor and stood transfixed by the names in front her. Such a cosy alibi for the Blackleys, Sullivan and Doreen Leitch. Were they really such good friends? The deaths of Terry Lawler and Paul Macklin would most likely make business easier for Evan Blackley and his involvement with Matt Sullivan. But what about Doreen Leitch? Her affair with Sullivan may remain a secret for the time being, but did she have more to hide, or more to lose? Tara had been a little surprised to learn that Doreen's name hadn't featured in the Sullivan-Lawler libel case. Then again, her stance on planning laws appeared to be diametrically opposed to that of her lover's. So, what exactly was going on between Leitch, Sullivan and Evan Blackley? When Murray joined Tara at the board, she was lost in thoughts of Gwen Blackley.

'Morning, ma'am, how's your back feeling?' Murray was not his usual dapper self. He stood in blue jeans, a brown cord sports jacket and a wrinkled blue shirt beneath.

'Hi, Alan,' she said, vacantly. 'Very painful. Yesterday is not a day I would like to repeat.'

'Me neither. That was my best suit ruined, traipsing through the muck. I don't suppose uniform have managed to grab either of those reprobates?'

'Not yet. Tell me what you make of Gwen Blackley?'

The question caught him on the hop.

'Well.' He paused. 'Nice-looking woman…'

'Yes, Alan, let's skip the obvious attractions for you. How does she fit in here?' Tara placed her forefinger on the board below Gwen Blackley's name. 'Bearing in mind that she has lied to us at least once, does she have a motive besides that of being in league with her husband?'

'She was married to Lawler; they had a daughter together. She, Lawler and Macklin were long-time friends. They were on speaking terms right up to Lawler's death.'

'Do you think it's just a matter of her protecting Evan Blackley? Was she well used to battling her ex-hubby and his mate?'

'Or maybe she's become well used to fighting some of her present husband's battles?'

'What if the husband is protecting the wife?'

'Why think that?'

'Just a thought,' said Tara.

Seated at her desk, she continued to ponder the women connected to her case. Murray had slipped off to chat with Wilson, and from the sounds of their exchange, not so much was said on the murders and more on Everton's chances against Arsenal for the coming Saturday. Her left arm throbbed, launching spikes of pain through her neck into her head. It was going to be a hard day.

Gwen was a long-suffering wife, firstly to Terry Lawler and then to Evan Blackley. Both men had a blight upon their character. Lawler, according to Aisling, had a roving eye, but he'd also possessed a single-minded streak when it came to gathering a story. Little else mattered, including his wife and daughter. His career, combined with a predilection to be unfaithful, had destroyed his marriage. Perhaps it was that stubbornness that got him killed.

Gwen had moved on to Evan Blackley, a once famous footballer with a tarnished record, or at least a hefty element of doubt hanging over his sporting career. How had the pair got together? Through Terry Lawler's investigation of the ex-footballer. She'd done well to start over. She was now comfortably off, nice big house and spare time on her hands. She was no longer struggling to maintain a home and raise a daughter. She would have had a lot to lose if her ex-husband had continued to make things difficult for her new man. If she had killed Terry Lawler, then an interfering Macklin would have been easy meat.

Tara rose from her desk; she couldn't get comfortable and wandered across the office to Murray and Wilson. It was well after nine, and the room was filling with staff and the noise level was steadily rising. She had an idea to run by her colleagues. Football stories would have to wait.

'Tell me what you think of this,' she said to them both, resting her body gingerly at the edge of Wilson's desk. 'The night before Lawler was killed, he called in at the Blackleys', and he also spoke to Gwen. On the day we questioned her about Lawler and her husband, Paul Macklin was in the house with her. Why?'

'Paying his respects,' said Murray, getting into a Mars bar. 'They used to be mates.'

'What if the lovely Gwen is at the centre of all this? Rather than she being the wife trying to protect her husband's business interests, what if she passed information, firstly to Lawler and, after he'd been killed, to Macklin?'

'Why would she do that? She would be risking her new lifestyle to pass on titbits to a reporter.'

'It can't be a good marriage, though. Blackley's too much of a showman, and he never seems to be home.'

Wilson, with nothing to add to the discussion, had continued his examination of the contents of a large brown envelope. The folders and papers strewn across his desk had all been removed from Paul Macklin's flat. Simultaneously, Tara and Murray noticed that Wilson was staring intently at two press cuttings, his eyes jumping from the one in his left hand to the one in his right.

'What have you got, John?' Tara asked.

Murray snatched the cutting from Wilson's left hand and glanced at the story. Wilson offered the other to his DI. All three officers looked at each other.

'Wow,' said Murray.

CHAPTER 50

Tara

She'd telephoned prior to her arrival at the house in Lymm. A one-to-one chat was needed, not a confrontation. Tara had convinced herself that Gwen Blackley was at the centre of all that had transpired between her ex-husband, her present husband, a pair of city councillors and Paul Macklin. It wasn't so much that Gwen Blackley was holding back potentially useful information, it was more a case that so far, Tara had not been asking the right questions.

'I want you to stay in the car,' she told Murray.

'Why's that, ma'am?' he replied with a tone of complaint.

'It's best that I speak to her alone. She might be more forthcoming on a woman-to-woman basis.'

Murray couldn't stifle his scoff.

'You can make yourself useful by checking on the progress of the search for Ross and Yeats.'

She slammed the car door to let him know he had been irritating and approached the front of the house. Gwen Blackley answered without her having to ring the bell.

'Hello, Inspector Grogan,' she said, stepping back to allow Tara to enter.

'Thank you for agreeing to see me again, Mrs Blackley.'

The woman didn't reply, but merely led the way through to the bright kitchen at the rear of the house. A large window afforded views across the fields in the direction of the M6. A hefty woman with long mousey hair was seated at the kitchen table, her head down studying a collection of photographs. When she glanced at Tara, there was no greeting or acknowledgement. The woman's face was quite plain, ruddy cheeks devoid of make-up; she seemed indifferent to Tara's presence.

'Inspector, this is Beth, Terry's sister. Beth, say hello to Inspector Grogan.'

The reply was barely audible, and the woman dropped her head and continued to fidget with the pictures scattered over the table. A glass of strawberry milkshake and a plate of Jaffa Cakes sat close by.

'Hi, Beth,' said Tara. 'It's very nice to meet you.'

There was no further response, and Gwen Blackley rolled her eyes.

'Can I get you tea or coffee?'

'Coffee would be great, thank you.'

Tara was invited to sit at the island bench closer to the centre of the kitchen, putting a few feet between them and Beth. Gwen poured two mugs of coffee from a percolator, filled a small jug with milk and placed it all on the counter between herself and Tara.

'I'm assuming you don't take sugar.'

'No, I don't, thank you.'

'Evan is in London. Beth is staying with me for a few days; she has no one else now.'

'Company for you.'

'Mm, difficult at times. Moody. She hasn't taken the news about Terry well, and I'm not quite sure how to help her understand. Hasn't made it any easier that Terry never told her the truth about her sister. As far as she's concerned Ruth is backpacking in Australia.'

'Do you think she is still alive?'

Gwen shook her head then drank some of her coffee.

'I doubt it. I'm guessing that you see a link between Terry's death and Ruth's disappearance?'

'I have been considering that possibility.'

'Why are you here, Inspector? What is it you want from me?'

Tara sipped at her coffee, hot and a little strong for her taste.

'I was thinking over the case and realised that you lie somewhat in the centre of all that has happened.'

Gwen's face reddened; she looked alarmed.

'Are you suggesting that I'm your prime suspect?'

'Not at all.'

'You think I killed my ex-husband? He is the father of my daughter, for goodness' sake.'

'Please, Gwen, let me explain.'

'You believe that I could kill someone in the way that Paul was murdered?'

'Please, let me finish.'

Gwen at last halted her rant.

'What I am trying to say is that you connect all the strands of the story we have so far gathered.' Tara could see that the woman was still a long way from accepting what she was trying to say. 'As you have said, you were once married to Terry, and Paul was an old friend to both of you. Also, your present husband was receiving threats from Terry and Paul. But yet they came to you each time they wanted to get at Evan. I suppose what I am asking of you, Gwen, is for you to think hard about what both men said to you. Did they mention anyone else who had a reason to harm them? Did Terry mention any details about his sister's disappearance that gave you cause to wonder or to be concerned?'

'I still loved Terry after all this time, after all he'd done to Maisie and me. But I hated him with equal measure. He destroyed our marriage, and it didn't do Maisie a lot of good. I left him when Evan started paying me attention. Ruth never forgave me for that. But Evan is a good man, Inspector. He has a temper, he has a poor reputation with the press, and he despised Terry.'

'Enough to kill him?'

'No way. And believe me, a lesser man would have throttled Terry a lot sooner for the things he tried to do. But do you think a man who took Maisie and me on, treating her like his own daughter, would stoop so low as to murder?'

Before Tara could respond, a telephone rang.

'Excuse me, Inspector. That'll be Evan.'

Gwen lifted a handset from its cradle on the worktop and stepped quickly into the hall. Tara could hear only a muffled voice of the wife speaking to her husband. She gazed across the kitchen to where Beth continued to sort through photographs and news cuttings. Tara approached and watched as Beth lifted a black and white photo from a cardboard box, placed it on the table then swiped her palm heavily over the print in order to smooth out wrinkles on the paper despite there being none. It was a picture of Terry wearing motorcycle leathers, holding a crash helmet and standing next to a Suzuki motorbike. The wind had blown his hair across his face, but he'd managed a wide smile for the camera. Beth then placed the picture in a small pile with other black and white photos. She repeated the exercise with a couple more pictures before moving on to a colour shot of herself with a girl, Tara assumed, was her sister Ruth. If it were indeed the missing Ruth, she had been a beautiful girl, short dark hair, chirpy smile, confident and happy with eyes filled with fun or mischief. Hard to say which.

Beth continued her activity while ignoring Tara looking on. At one point Tara thought she'd managed to provoke a smile, but in an instant it became more a sneer, a derisive scowl of a child trying her best to tell you to go away and leave them alone. Tara was about to do just that when she glanced at a news cutting sitting off to the side from the piles of photographs that Beth had arranged. She reached out to lift it, but Beth slammed her hand down hard upon the paper.

'Mine!'

'I just want to have a look at this one, Beth.'

'No, mine.' An angry face glared up from the table.

'Please, Beth.'

'Beth, don't be rude,' said Gwen Blackley returning.

'Mine.'

'You know fine well they're not yours. They belong to Terry. Don't they?'

'No. Terry's dead.'

'Yes, they do. Now let Inspector Grogan have a look at whatever she wants. Go and put your empty glass in the dishwasher.'

Reluctantly, and with little grace, Beth stamped across the kitchen and opened the dishwasher. Tara seized her moment to study the article that had caught her eye. It was a photo cut from *The Echo*, no date but at least the legend beneath was intact. "Councillor Doreen Leitch," the caption read, "pictured with staff, volunteers and users of the new drop-in centre." Tara studied the faces in the grainy shot. In addition to Leitch, she recognised only two others, but it was enough. At last, she had her first real lead.

CHAPTER 51

Tara

'Have they picked up Ross yet?'

'Not yet,' Murray replied, startled by Tara hastily jumping into the car.

'Back to the station, quick as you can. At last, I think we might be getting somewhere.'

Tara filled Murray in on what she had discovered among Beth's photographs.

'Put that together with what Wilson had, and I think we have our killer.'

She could hardly contain her thoughts as Murray rushed them back to the city. On the way, she phoned Wilson and urged him to speed up the search and arrest of Danny Ross. Gradually, however, the implications of what she had uncovered began to conflict with her first thought, that Ross was the killer. Suddenly, it wasn't so clear-cut. Yes, he was pictured with Doreen Leitch at a drug rehab centre; the picture had been part of a story reported by Terry Lawler. But Wilson had found a couple of others in among Paul Macklin's belongings, pictures taken by Lawler during his investigation of the drug activities on the Treadwater Estate. Ross, in these shots, had not been identified by name, but it was the same youth each time. Had Ross been trying to suppress the stories of his drug dealing? The obvious answer was yes, and he'd killed Lawler and Macklin to prevent further publicity. But the longer she held that view the more Tara wondered about a third party.

When they got back to St Anne Street, she allowed Murray to go for some food, while she formulated a list of questions to put to Ross when eventually he was brought in.

The afternoon dragged on. She updated Tweedy on her recent findings. He, cautious as ever, did seem convinced that it was progress. A sickening feeling took over in her stomach. She was hungry but couldn't face food even when Murray returned with sandwiches, enough for two. He had no trouble in scoffing the lot. Her head throbbed. Her neck still ached from the attack by Lynsey Yeats. She'd noticed the spreading bruise across her left shoulder, and by this stage in the day regretted not heeding the advice from Tweedy to take some time off. And still she had the nagging unease about the motives of her rescuer, James. The coincidence of his just being there was simply too much for her to swallow. There was something about the murder of Terry Lawler and all the connections to it that continued to make her feel uneasy. She couldn't help wondering if somehow, bizarrely, James was involved. The curious yet foolish thought quickly dissipated.

It was close to midnight, when Murray phoned her at home to say that Danny Ross had been arrested in Treadwater. Members of a Matrix team had cause to interrupt a house party on the estate following complaints by other residents of noise and brawls in the street. Tara hoped the youth, when he arrived at St Anne Street, would be in a fit state to face questions, but somehow that seemed unlikely given the circumstances of his arrest. Danny Ross, most likely, would be stoned out of his head. And later, as she suspected, she received word that Ross was hardly able to state his own name. Her questions would have to wait until morning.

She didn't sleep. A shower, a bowl of muesli, a cup of weak peppermint tea and then she tried to look presentable for the day ahead. Not that she had to impress a drugged youth who most probably had slept it off in a holding cell, but she had to feel professional in herself, and she had to look in control to those around her.

Gathering the scraps of paper on which she'd scribbled further questions and sketched out more scenarios on this case, she pulled on a black leather zip-jacket and hurried from the flat. She reversed her car from its space in the square and over-revved as she sped to the barrier. As she swept around the curve of the drive leading to Wapping, she noticed a black car, a small Peugeot hatchback, sitting half on the pavement half on the road, its driver crouched low down in his seat. For a fleeting moment she thought it was James, but by the time she'd reached the junction she had heavy traffic to negotiate and her planned questioning of a murder suspect, and so the notion left her.

Murray was ready and waiting in the operations room when she arrived. He looked fresher than she felt, but she could never allow him to sense it. He drew too much satisfaction from seeing her struggle at times. At least that's how she felt about her subordinate. A friend on occasions, hopefully when it mattered most, but also a man resentful at seeing a woman, a younger woman, fast-tracked into a job she'd never had the experience for.

'Morning, ma'am. I've put Ross in room two. He's all yours.'

'Right then, let's get on with it.'

She dumped her bag by her desk, retrieved the files she would need from the cabinet and allowed Murray to lead the way downstairs.

Biting his nails, Danny Ross didn't seem concerned when first Murray then Tara entered the interview room. Ross's blue checked shirt was ripped at the seam on the left shoulder, he needed a shave and there was congealed blood gathered around the gold stud in his right ear. There wasn't much of him, Tara thought, although he'd given the arresting officers a rough time the night before. Presumably that was how he'd ripped his shirt and had dried blood on his ear. Murray dealt with the preliminaries, reading Ross his rights and explaining about the interview being recorded. Ross was unmoved, didn't seem to care, didn't set his gaze upon Murray or Tara.

'Well, Danny, let's begin with Terry Lawler, shall we? How well did you know him?'

'What you talkin' about?'

'How well did you know Terry Lawler?'

'What's this got to do with last night?'

'Last night?'

'That's why I'm here, innit. I was at the party when the Matrix shut us down.'

Tara grinned at Murray, who took it as his signal to continue.

'Don't worry about that for now, Danny. I'm sure the drugs boys will catch up with you soon enough. We want to ask you about the murders of Terry Lawler and Paul Macklin.'

The thin face of Danny Ross turned white; his mouth dropped open after spitting a fingernail across the table.

'Don't know nothin' about no killings.'

'OK, Danny, let's get back to the first question,' said Tara. 'On our visit to Lynsey's house, when we first met you, it was clear that you knew Terry Lawler. How well did you know him?'

'Saw him about the estate and that.'

'Did you have conversations?'

'No.'

'You never spoke with him?'

'No.'

'Did you visit Lynsey's house while Mr Lawler was living there?'

'Might have done. Don't remember.'

Tara could sense Murray's impatience kicking in: first a sigh, then him sitting way back in his chair. Ross was going to be hard work, but she was hopeful of getting what she wanted from the youth. Drug dealer he may be, but he was still only a teenager. She was certain that he wouldn't want a murder charge pinned on him. For now, Murray would have to bide his time.

'You left something behind when you ran off the other day,' Tara continued.

Ross shrugged.

'Bit of a haul, wasn't it, Danny? Ecstasy. Must have been worth a lot to you, and yet you left it behind?'

'Thought you weren't bothered about the drugs,' said Ross.

'Depends on how you help us with other things. Terry Lawler worked on a story about drugs on Treadwater. Did he ask you any questions, Danny? About your supplying schoolkids?'

'I never told him I supplied kids.'

The face of Ross became flushed. He sat forward in his seat, squaring up to Tara. She was pleased to see him so animated. Now she was getting somewhere.

'Then what did you and Lawler talk about?'

'Asshole followed me all over the place. Wanted to see how I struck deals. He asked me to show him some of the dens on Treadwater.'

'Did he take photographs? Like these?' Tara set two enlarged prints on the table. Ross examined them for a few seconds showing little emotion. 'This one,' said Tara, lifting the one to her right, 'is a picture of you making a sale with an eleven-year-old girl.'

'That's not me.'

Tara set the picture back on the table and pointed firmly with her finger to the youth pictured in the second photo.

'But that is definitely you, isn't it, Danny?' It would be difficult to deny, given that it was a clear frontal shot of a youth wearing a grey hoodie while staring directly at the camera.

Ross didn't respond.

'Terry Lawler took that picture of you, Danny. On the same day he also took this one. Your back may be turned slightly, but that is you selling drugs to a child.'

'Didn't sell her drugs, just gave her some sweets.' He sat back looking pleased with himself.

'Is that why you killed Mr Lawler, because you thought he would use those pictures in his newspaper story?'

'What you talking about? I didn't kill him.'

Tara paused for a few moments, allowing Ross to settle, and hopefully giving time for the seriousness of what he was facing to sink in.

'Do you take drugs, Danny?'

'Sometimes,' he replied in a croaky voice.

'What do you take?'

'Whatever. Tabs, speed, blow when I can get some. Nothing much else to do round our way.'

'How do you feel when you get high? Are you happy? Sad, depressed? Do you ever get angry? Want to do someone harm? You'd have to be off your head to do this to someone, wouldn't you, Danny?'

Tara revealed a photo of Terry Lawler after he'd been removed from the hole in the sand at Crosby Beach.

'To bury a person head-first so that they suffocate, then to cut off their privates and let them bleed to death. Have to be someone on drugs, wouldn't you think?'

'Wasn't me. Didn't kill him.'

'How about this one?'

She set down a picture of Macklin tied to a wire fence and slashed to death. Ross shook his head, no.

'One final picture for you, Danny.' Tara left the other photos on the table and produced a copy of the picture she'd discovered in Beth's collection. 'Apart from yourself, do you recognise anyone?'

Ross did little more than glance at the picture, but he didn't seem inclined to answer the question. Tara pointed to one of the people in the print.

'Councillor Leitch, you know her, surely?'

Ross feigned another look and wiped his hand across his mouth.

'She helped to set up the day centre on the estate.'

'You ever meet with her?'

'Nope.'

'Despite standing three feet away from her in this picture, you never spoke to her?'

'No. Not my type.'

Tara smiled at his quip.

'What about Lynsey? She's right there beside you. Did she ever speak to the councillor?'

'Don't know. Might have done.'

Tara searched the face of Danny Ross. She needed only one slip, but the scrawny teenager had sufficient confidence to stare back at his interrogator. She was already convinced of his guilt, but she had to unearth the proof.

'One last question before I turn you over to my colleagues interested in your drugs activities; how many times did you meet Paul Macklin?'

'Never met him,' said Ross swiftly.

Tara wasn't prepared to go through a list of questions regarding Macklin only for Ross to scoff with his denials. Instead, she pointed to the photo of the lacerated body of Macklin on the table.

'Did you do this, Danny?'

CHAPTER 52

Guy

'Hi, is that James?'

'Aye, it is.'

'It's Tara. I'm sorry I haven't called sooner, but things have been hectic round here. I just wanted to thank you for coming to my rescue the other day.'

'No problem. How's your back?'

'I have an enormous bruise across my shoulders, and I'm a bit stiff. Apart from that I'm fine.'

'Maybe when you're fit, we can repeat our night out?'

She hesitated, but I thought it was worth asking. I'm not a complete animal, you know. I'm just a bloke looking for real love.

'Maybe,' she said at last.

'Did I do something wrong last time?'

'No, no. It's just me.'

'I understand; you don't want to get into anything heavy?'

'That's part of it. My job doesn't do much for personal relationships.'

'How about no strings, just dinner and a couple of drinks. You talk, I'll listen. See where it takes us.'

Another silence at her end.

'How about tonight?' I asked.

'Can't this evening.'

'Tomorrow then?'

'Next week would be better.'

'Monday or Tuesday?'

'Tuesday at the same place as last time, seven o'clock?'

'All right, see you then.'

She hung up, and I danced around the corridor. Didn't give a shit if Cranley saw me; I was dead chuffed. This copper was doing something to my head. I was coming over all tingly and romantic like. Couldn't wait to see her again. Couldn't believe she'd agreed to go out with me for a second time. Maybe my life was turning round, and I wouldn't have to take a girl ever again. Then, as I pushed an oul doll in her wheelchair back to the ward, I began to worry. What if I couldn't stop? What if I ended up in a proper relationship with Tara and I still had to go out and snatch girls? I'd be rightly screwed up. And just as I was thinking these things my head was filling up with visions of the wee blonde I'd spotted near the police station. Funny how the mind works.

To stay focused on Tara, I decided that after work I should pay another visit to her apartment block at Wapping Dock. Maybe I could spot her driving home.

CHAPTER 53

Tara

Murray, cheese roll in hand, caught up with her on the stairs as she was leaving.

'What did you make of Ross? Didn't give much away.'

'Didn't really expect him to, not yet anyway,' Tara replied.

'I don't get it. You still think he's the killer, don't you?'

Tara stopped before the bottom step, looking up at Murray who'd paused several steps higher.

'Who do you reckon has the strongest motive?' She continued on her way, assuming that Murray would follow.

'Could be any of them,' he said, following her.

'Yes, all of them had a reason for wanting Lawler silenced.'

'But yesterday morning you were suggesting Gwen Blackley was at the centre of things.' Murray held the door allowing Tara to pass through.

'I know, but then I saw the photo that Beth had.'

'So, now you're convinced it was Ross?'

'Not exactly. I'm thinking more of Lynsey Yeats.'

Murray took a bite of his roll as he and Tara wandered across the station yard.

'What evidence do we have that Yeats is the killer?' he said at last.

'No more than we have for any of the suspects. Tell me, we agree that whoever killed Lawler and Macklin either had to be off their heads or they actually enjoy the killing process?'

'True. And you think Yeats fits the bill?'

Tara nodded.

'Based on her attack on you?'

'Her attack on me certainly supports the argument.'

'But you don't think she acted alone?'

'She had help, and my guess is that Danny Ross was the source of it. And then comes the question of motive. Lynsey kills Lawler because he pissed her off in some way; used her to get a story on drugs, treated her badly or whatever.'

'Why kill Macklin?'

'Exactly. Yeats and Ross, as far as we know, had no reason to butcher Macklin. It is likely that they didn't even know him.'

'But you still think they killed him?'

'Yes, if they were acting on someone else's behalf. Which brings me back to the picture I found belonging to Beth. Doreen Leitch in the same shot as Yeats and Ross. A woman with good reason to see Lawler *and* Macklin dead.'

Tara beeped her car open, climbed inside and with a wry smile drove off, leaving Murray to cogitate on her theory and to finish the remainder of his cheese roll.

As soon as she reached home, she immediately checked with St Anne Street for news on Lynsey Yeats. The girl who had seemed intent on killing her was proving difficult to find. She realised her theory was entirely founded on the picture she had taken from Beth. She couldn't prove anything until Lynsey was in custody.

Lingering in the shower for much longer than usual, her mind rolled from one thing to another, from Yeats to Murray, to Aisling, to a vision of Paul Macklin's body ripped to shreds and hanging from a wire fence. Wrapped in a towel, she dropped into her sofa and stared vacantly at the folders she'd left on the coffee table for the past three days. Something about their contents haunted her. It felt like disappointment. If the conclusion of the Lawler case now lay with Lynsey Yeats, then where could she go with the files on all of those young women? Terry Lawler had been onto something. Every girl within those folders had disappeared without trace, and as far as she was aware not one police officer was searching for any of them. Surely the families of every girl deserved the truth, deserved closure. As sleep began to take hold, she was telling herself that when Lawler's case was complete, she would look into this story, even if she had to do it in her own time.

A brief glimpse of the car parked on the pavement outside her apartment building flashed through her mind. She blinked it away only to see those girls posted on the bedroom wall of Lawler's flat. Recently, it seemed that all her nights were filled with the horrors of her days. In the bedroom, she dropped her towel to the floor and climbed into her bed, wrapping the duvet closely around her.

CHAPTER 54

Tara

Doreen Leitch stared at the two pictures lying on the table. Eventually, in answer to Tara's question she said, 'No comment.'

Her solicitor, a confident-looking woman in her mid-thirties with ash-blonde hair and blue-grey eyes, smiled at her and her client's intention not to co-operate with Tara's investigation.

'Councillor Leitch, you are in the same photograph as Lynsey Yeats, do you know this girl?'

'No comment.'

'Can you please confirm that you are acquainted with Danny Ross and Lynsey Yeats?'

'No comment.'

'How many times are you going to rephrase the same question, Inspector?' said the solicitor. 'My client can be of no further help in this matter. If you have nothing else to ask, I suggest we bring this to a close.'

Leitch sat impassively, while Tara considered one final question.

'I find it more than coincidence that a person with a strong motive for killing Terry Lawler and Paul Macklin has had a recent association with another person who also had reason perhaps for wanting Mr Lawler dead.'

'That's all you have, Inspector? No evidence? This meeting is over.'

Tara let the pair leave. She sat for a while at the table, gazing at the blank wall. Until they found Lynsey Yeats, they had no case, except for what they might squeeze out of Danny Ross.

Before lunch, she and Murray drove out to Treadwater and parked outside the house that until recently was home to Lynsey Yeats. They'd gone prepared, a search warrant and a jemmy to force the door if necessary. It didn't take much for Murray to slip the bar between the door and its lock. One sturdy thrust, the wood splintered, and the lock eased from its catch. Murray took the upstairs, while Tara inspected the living room and kitchen. She had no real objective for things to find. Just a look for something that might hint at where Lynsey was hiding, a clue to suggest that she was capable of two murders or that she did have an association with Doreen Leitch.

The living room had a dank closed-up smell of cigarettes and cooked food, and was cluttered with odd pieces of furniture, a worn multi-coloured carpet and a gas burner at the fireplace. A coffee table was littered with sweet wrappers, two empty cigarette packets, half of a chocolate biscuit and several letters, some of which remained unopened. Tara lifted the papers and leafed through them. Mostly junk mail, a charity circular, a credit card application and a bank statement. Surprisingly, the envelope was addressed to Lynsey Yeats. She wouldn't have thought Yeats would be in a position to have a bank account. A cursory glance down the list of transactions didn't arouse any suspicions. No major lodgements or withdrawals to suggest that someone had paid her a hefty fee to commit a murder. A tidy account, really, in balance at two hundred and fifty-three pounds and twenty-six pence. She would not have thought Lynsey capable of managing her finances well; she apparently made such a poor effort of looking after herself.

There was little else of interest in the room, a bottle of gin, one third full, and a stack of DVDs on the same shelf to the right of the television. Maybe her suspicions of Lynsey were unfounded. An ordinary girl, maladjusted certainly, and having problems dealing with a drug habit.

'Find anything?' she called up to Murray on her way to the kitchen.

'Not a lot.'

The kitchen was tidy and clean, again not what she would have expected to see. Her first impression of Yeats was that she cared about little except her next fix. She didn't think that keeping a clean house was a priority for the girl barely out of her teens.

Everything was in its place. The cooker, slightly battered, was clean; the fridge wasn't full but held the essentials, milk, butter, some cheese, a pack of sausages and three eggs. No dishwasher but the washing machine was full of clothes. Cupboards were quite sparse, a variety of plates and dishes, not a single set, a few mugs and some glasses that looked as though they'd been nicked from the local pub.

'Ma'am.'

'Coming,' she replied, and as she turned to leave the kitchen, she glanced at a wooden knife block holding only two of its four knives.

When she reached the bedroom, Murray was standing over a chest of drawers gazing into one that was empty.

'Very few clothes about,' he said.

'Do you think maybe she's been home and gathered some things to take with her?'

'Have a look for yourself. Very little in the drawers or the wardrobe.'

Tara again wouldn't have imagined that Lynsey possessed a vast array of fashionable clothes. Each time they'd met she'd been wearing only black jeans, a T-shirt and a biker jacket. A few pairs of trousers were hanging in the wardrobe, two pairs of trainers lay at the bottom. She found some underwear in a drawer, a few shirts and sweatshirts, but the room gave little impression that a young woman lived there. Lying at the bottom of a drawer was the driving licence belonging to Terry Lawler. Tara reckoned that either he had left it here by accident or it had been hidden after Lawler was killed.

'Seems like she's scarpered,' said Murray.

'What are we going to do, Alan? Until we find her, we've got nothing on this case.'

'What if someone doesn't want her found?'

'Like Doreen Leitch?'

'If you believe she's behind the killings then maybe she's had to silence young Lynsey.'

Tara shivered. Didn't think she could bear another murder in this case. If Leitch was incapable of killing Lawler and Macklin, having got Danny Ross and Lynsey to do it, then surely, she wouldn't be up to dispensing with Lynsey? Best for now if she could hang onto that thought. Soon, though, it was clouded by the notion that Lynsey had joined the list of missing women.

She immediately ordered the re-arrest of Danny Ross. He had been granted bail in relation to the drug charges. They stopped on the way back from Treadwater for a quick bite of lunch at a KFC. Ross was already waiting in an interview room when they arrived at St Anne Street. She told herself that this would not be a repeat of the first interview. She glared at the youth who sat with arms folded looking set once more not to co-operate.

'Do you know where she is, Danny?'

He grinned, smug and evidently enjoying pissing this copper off.

'It would be better if you told us, you know. She could be in danger. Do you realise that?'

Ross glanced from Tara to Murray. He looked confused. Tara spoke quietly and earnestly.

'Danny, whatever she might have done, I believe that someone else is behind all this. If I'm right, then Lynsey could be next to die. Do you understand? If you know where she is hiding and you're happy that she's safe, fair enough. But if you aren't sure that she's completely safe then you must tell me.'

'Did you kill her, Danny?' Murray asked.

'No, I didn't bloody kill her. Don't know where she is.'

'Do you care for her, Danny?' said Tara. The youth dropped his head and pinched his nose between his eyes. 'Tell us what happened, Danny. You don't want Lynsey to get hurt. Is there anywhere she could have gone? A friend's house? Has she left Liverpool?'

Ross slammed his hands down hard on the table.

'Don't know nothin',' he shouted. 'Leave me alone, will ya?'

Tara felt her own anger rise. She wanted to slap this kid. To him life was cheap. She yelled back in his face.

'You didn't care when you killed Lawler and Macklin, but if you don't help us the girl you love is going to die, you little shit.'

Murray stood with Tara in the corridor outside the interview room. Tara looked close to tears.

'He doesn't know, Tara. He looks every bit as confused as we do.'

'He may not know where Lynsey is, but he is aware that something is going on. I intend to drag it out of him.'

'Then why don't we charge him? Maybe he'll crack after that.'

'We can't, Alan. What do we really have on him besides a possible connection from a photograph to Doreen Leitch? We have no hard evidence. No prints, no DNA, weapons, nothing. It's all my supposition. Tweedy will not be impressed if we try to charge Ross.'

'Then let him go for now. He might lead us to Yeats.'

Tara was already strolling away from the interview room, her mind on other things.

'Ma'am?'

'Yes, let him go. When you've finished with him, we're going after that Leitch woman.'

CHAPTER 55

Tara

She told herself that if this didn't work not only would she have failed in tracking down a killer, but Councillor Leitch would probably go straight to the Chief Constable to complain about one of his DIs. Murray drove the car. She was glad of his help, for his company even. They'd never been close, both harbouring a slight resentment towards the other, but she felt that he was loyal to her. He'd try his best to help her.

They pulled up outside the electric gates of the Leitch house in Birkdale. A man answered the intercom and told them that Doreen, his wife, was not at home. She had council business in the city. Tara decided not to bother the husband any further, thanked him and told Murray to drive back.

'I suppose that means she could be anywhere,' said Tara.

'Maybe we should have forced the issue, demanded to check around the house, see if Doreen had suddenly come over all shy.'

'I'm thinking that she's off seeing her lover Councillor Sullivan.'

'You want to drive to Sullivan's house, catch them *in flagrante delicto*?'

She couldn't help smiling at his rather formal turn of phrase.

'A nice thought, Alan, but no, we should check out the town hall first. She could be anywhere for all that her husband knows.'

'Which is why I'm suggesting she's enjoying a little afternoon delight with Sullivan.'

'OK, we'll try Sullivan's house after the town hall and council offices.'

On the drive back to the city, Tara phoned Wilson and asked him to check with the town hall to see if anyone there knew of the whereabouts of Doreen Leitch and Matt Sullivan. Wilson drew a blank and reported back to Tara.

'You win,' she said to Murray. 'Let's call at Sullivan's house.'

Sullivan's home was a modern double-fronted red-brick with bay windows, close to the racecourse at Aintree. There were two cars in the drive when Murray pulled in.

'Looks like he has company,' said Murray with a smirk.

Tara sighed at the quip but felt a strange relief in hoping that they had tracked down Doreen Leitch.

Immediately she opened the car door, the screams of a terrified female filled the air.

Murray bolted to the front door of the house, Tara close behind. The wooden door was locked. He raised his foot aiming it at the lock. Three kicks and eventually the door flew back against the inside wall. Upstairs, a female voice battled against the rampant screams from another.

'You said you'd help me.'

Murray and Tara charged up the staircase. Reaching the open door of the master bedroom, they halted at the sight of a naked Doreen Leitch, drenched in blood. Her screams were uncontrollable, fuelled by fear and panic, driving her into a fit. She cowered against the wall in the far corner of the room. There was blood on her hands, her face and smeared across her bare flesh. Tara couldn't process the vision. Lynsey Yeats stood over Leitch, brandishing two knives. One dripped with blood.

'Shut up, you fucking bitch,' she cried. 'I didn't want to do this.'

For a second, Yeats was oblivious to the presence of two police officers. Her business, her attention, was sharply focussed upon the hysterical Leitch. Tara and Murray were separated from Yeats by the width of a king-size bed, the bloodied and unconscious body of Matt Sullivan sprawled across it.

'Lynsey!' Tara called out above the screaming. 'Put the knives down. There's no need for this. We can talk quietly. Just drop the knives.'

Yeats rotated her stance to cover both Leitch and now the two police officers. Tear-streaked mascara down her face, her bare arms splashed in blood. She pointed the knives, one in each hand, towards Murray.

'Stay back or I'll fucking cut you up. Bizzies don't scare me.'

Doreen Leitch slid down the wall to the floor. Tara could tell advanced shock was taking hold of the councillor. No time for coaxing Yeats. She couldn't see how badly wounded Leitch was, but she realised the woman would die if they didn't get her out soon. Sullivan may already be dead. Tara stepped toward the bed, intending to check him for a pulse. It panicked Yeats who lunged with the knife in her right hand. Tara drew back; the knife skimmed her shoulder, ripping through her jacket. Murray seized his chance, rounding the bed and moving behind Yeats as she attempted to lunge again. He clasped both his arms around her and pulled tight in a bear hug. She was trapped.

'Get off me. I'll fucking kill you. All of you.'

She could do nothing. Her hands were now useless with the weapons. Tara, stepping towards her from the side, gripped Lynsey's right wrist and twisted hard. The knife dropped to the floor. She did the same with the left hand and the second knife fell on the carpet. Murray bundled Lynsey to the floor, face down and, with Tara's help, they soon had the girl secured with handcuffs. She resorted to angry screams and foul threats against Tara, then Murray.

Doreen Leitch, bleeding profusely from a slash wound that ran from her left shoulder to her right breast, was delirious, her lips trembled, and rapid sobs expelled bubbles of saliva from her mouth. Tara placed her hand at Sullivan's neck and found a pulse. He was bleeding heavily from a stab wound just below his right shoulder. His eyes opened when Tara removed her hand.

'It hurts like hell,' he said in a laboured whisper.

Murray pulled a pillowcase free from a pillow and pressed it against the wound. Tara made the call for help.

'You're going to be fine, ambulance is on its way,' she said.

She pulled a sheet from the bed and wrapped it around Doreen Leitch. The woman's skin was cool to the touch as she continued to shake. She stared aimlessly at the floor, showing no signs of being aware of Tara and Murray's intervention. Lynsey, the side of her face pressed to the floor, had ceased her rant and spoke quietly.

'I was only trying to help you, Doreen. Why wouldn't you listen to me?'

Doreen seemed incapable of listening now; she'd withdrawn to a place within herself.

Thirty minutes later, Doreen Leitch and Matt Sullivan were on their way to hospital, and Lynsey Yeats was seated in the back of a patrol car. Tara and Murray waited for back-up to arrive in the form of scene-of-crime officers to gather evidence on what had taken place. Fresh questions were running through her mind, like the reason why Yeats had been attacking Leitch and Sullivan. Did that mean they had their killer?

It would be a while, she imagined, before Leitch would be available to interview; Sullivan would be much sooner, she hoped. Once forensics turned up, she could be on her way back to the station.

They called a doctor to St Anne Street to examine Lynsey before any interviewing could take place. The girl's agitation had waned, replaced by tears. She'd asked to speak with Danny Ross but was refused. When the doctor had finished, he declared that Yeats was fit enough to be questioned.

Tara and Murray sat opposite Lynsey and a duty solicitor named Michelle Roberts, a forty-year-old woman with shoulder-length dark brown hair and deep-set brown eyes. She sat impassively, pen and paper at the ready. Yeats sat with her head bowed, rubbing her feet together, caressing her hands between her knees. The preliminaries to the interview had been explained by Murray, who started the recording and then waited for Tara to ask her first question. It was going to be a long night.

'Tell me why you were at the home of Matt Sullivan.'

Without lifting her head, Lynsey shrugged a don't-know.

'Did you go there to see Doreen Leitch?'

Another shrug.

'It would be better if you tried to answer the question, Lynsey. We just want to get the truth. Two people have been injured; it would help your situation if you told us what happened.'

Tara glanced at the solicitor, but she didn't seem inclined to intervene. She decided then on a different approach.

'Tell me about you and Danny.'

Another shrug, but at least she did look up for the first time.

'Are you close?'

'Not like we used to be.'

'What happened?'

'We were living together for a bit before…'

'Go on.'

'Before Terry came to Treadwater. They didn't like each other much.'

'And you liked Terry? You lived together for a while?'

'Terry wanted to get a story about drugs and crackheads on the estate. I thought he was dead cute. He bought me stuff, he took me out and gave me money.'

'What did Danny think about that?'

'He took off. Said he didn't want no part in stories about drugs.'

'Was that because he was involved in supplying?'

'Yeah, said he'd come back when Terry had gone.'

'And he did, isn't that right? He was with you when we came to speak to you about Terry's death.'

Lynsey didn't reply and once again took to contemplating her shoes.

'Was Danny jealous? Was he responsible for killing Terry?'

Lynsey shook her head and began to cry. She wiped her eye with the back of her hand. Murray passed her a tissue.

'Did you kill Terry, Lynsey?'

The girl placed the heel of each hand on her temples and squeezed, raising her eyes to the ceiling. Beyond her dramatic pose there was no response. Tara paused for a moment until Lynsey dropped her arms.

'Did you get Danny to help you?'

Her eyes widened suddenly. A switch flicked, a light coming on. She glanced from Tara to Murray.

'Was Doreen Leitch involved? Did she ask you to kill Terry?'

Neither officer could have predicted what happened next. Both hands gripped the edge of the table. Lynsey thrust upwards as she jumped to her feet. Her scream bounced around the bare walls. The table landed on Tara and Murray. Plastic cups of water and Tara's files dropped to the floor. Michelle Roberts attempted to push herself backwards on her chair, but Lynsey, flailing her arms, caught the solicitor across the face with the back of her hand. Blood spurted from the woman's nose, and her scream joined with Lynsey's. Strong hands suddenly gripped Tara's throat. Lynsey's momentum sent the pair of them tumbling backwards to the floor. But Murray, having righted the table, hurled himself at Yeats. He grabbed her by the waist and tried to pull her off Tara. Eventually, her hands slipped from Tara's neck but caught hold of her blouse. It ripped open in her hands. The screams brought two uniformed officers to the door. They and Murray wrestled Yeats to the floor and held her down until another uniform appeared with cuffs. Tara felt powerless. She looked on with her blouse ripped open, her throat burning as Lynsey writhed and moaned on the floor.

'Leave her alone. Do you hear me?' Yeats shouted. 'Leave her. She didn't do anything. She helped me.'

One of the uniforms had Lynsey's face pressed to the floor.

'Get that doctor back in here,' Murray called.

Tara looked despairingly at her sergeant.

'What do we do now?' he said.

'Get her back to a cell.'

It was well after ten by the time Tara felt sufficiently calm to make the journey home. Too much excitement, too much heartache for one day. The doctor had attended to Michelle Roberts' bloodied nose, and Yeats was under observation in a cell. Tara and Murray had tried to talk through the day's events over strong coffee from the vending machine in the corridor, but they were too shaken by the latest incident, called it a day and made for home. In the back of her mind, though, she had the feeling that she'd forgotten something.

She clicked the key to lock her car as she strolled to the lift to her apartment. Exhaustion and hunger were uppermost in her mind until she glimpsed a car driving off. It hadn't been in the car park for she would have passed it on her way in. It had been on the pavement to the side of the building. Not the first time she'd been aware of someone waiting there. Once inside her flat she dumped her bag and jacket on the sofa and made straight for the fridge. The notion of scrambled egg on toast occurred to her at the same time she realised what she had forgotten. This was the evening she was supposed to meet up with James. She'd stood him up.

CHAPTER 56

Guy

Bitch. Stood me up. Can you believe it? But I'm the stupid bastard, allowing myself to think that she would show. That she wanted to see me. That we would become a couple, a proper couple, Sunday walks in the park, coffee shops and reading the papers, cuddling by a warm fire and watching an Arnie DVD. What a dipstick.

I got to the bar nice and early, found a seat facing the door. I'd even bought a new shirt, pale blue with a thin purple stripe. The whole evening panned out before me: a couple of drinks then round to that Italian in Castle Street. A nice meal there and back to her place. I tried my best not to think of us laying together. Didn't want a lovely picture of her spoiled by visions of needles, holdalls and her body sinking beneath the waves. I was going to make gentle love to her, and she was going to love me back.

After half an hour of waiting, I told myself not to worry, it was only just past our arranged meeting time; she wasn't yet late. Fifteen minutes later I was wringing my hands, praying that she was going to show, that she was just delayed getting away from work. I ordered a second pint and waited. The bar was filling up. By half past eight I was fuming. No call from her to say she was running late. I tried calling her, but I only had a number for St Anne Street station, and some asshole answered so I hung up.

I left the bar at nine and drove to her apartment block, parking up on the pavement opposite the electric barrier. I walked into the parking area, looking around for a blue Focus. No sign. I considered waiting for her. But what the hell for?

I knew what would happen next. If I didn't get my way with Tara, then some other wee skirt was going to pay for it. But I realised that nothing else was going to satisfy me. I'd got myself in a state over this sexy cop, and I was scared of what I might do next. I sat and fumed in the car, well down in the seat. It was nearly eleven when the blue Focus drove through the barrier. Obviously, I was not of sufficient importance for her to have even called to tell me the date was off. The thought of me probably hadn't entered her head. Soon, very soon, she would be thinking of nothing else but me.

CHAPTER 57

Tara

They sat in a corridor waiting for the doctor and nursing sister to finish their morning round in a general ward at the Royal. Tara looked on as her colleague played a fantasy war game on his mobile. She couldn't even settle to read *The Express* that Murray had offered her and now was tucked inside his jacket pocket.

'I wonder how much Sullivan knows about the whole thing,' she said, her eyes now fixed upon a wall poster spelling out the list of ailments one can acquire from an idle lifestyle. 'Would he have even known Lynsey Yeats when she turned up on his doorstep wielding a couple of knives from her kitchen?' Murray remained entranced by his game. 'My preferred conversation this morning would have been with Doreen Leitch.'

'That's not going to happen for a while,' he said at last, his eyes still fixed on his mobile. 'Be surprised if she can remember her name after yesterday.'

'Doctor said her wound wasn't too serious. Not deep anyway, although she'll have one hell of a scar.'

'Her husband's been on the phone to Tweedy this morning, demanding to know the exact circumstances of the attack on his wife.'

'He's going to regret asking that question when he finds out that she's been unfaithful.'

The ward sister, a slight woman in her forties with brown hair in a ponytail, emerged from a private room and told them they could now see the patient. She pushed open the door to reveal Councillor Matt Sullivan sitting propped up on the bed, a padded dressing covering the area below his right shoulder where he'd suffered two stab wounds from the attack by Lynsey Yeats. Tara had some sympathy for the young, attractive man who'd just had a narrow escape, but she was in no mood for skirting around the reason why she was there to speak with him. She and Murray stood on opposite sides of the bed.

'Can you tell us what happened?'

'I got stabbed by a nutter, that's what happened, Inspector.'

'From the beginning, mate,' said Murray, he too in no mood for messing around.

Despite his injury and discomfort, Sullivan, true to form, had his eyes lingering on Tara's chest. His trauma hadn't affected his eyesight. Tara was now pleased to have worn a plain black jumper this morning. It didn't exactly advertise what lay beneath.

'She broke in. Doreen and I were, you know, in bed. I heard a window smash downstairs at the back of the house. She was in my bedroom in a flash. I'd hardly made it out of bed, and she comes in waving those bloody knives.'

'Did she say anything?'

'Told me to get out. She'd come to speak with Doreen. I told her to give us a minute, but she wasn't for waiting. I was naked, for God's sake, and so was Doreen. Then she just lost it. She went for me with both knives and got me in the shoulder. Would have been a lot worse if I hadn't swung around.' He paused, looking up at Tara. 'That's about all I can remember. I must have passed out.'

'So, you don't know why Doreen was attacked?' Tara asked.

He shook his head. 'She was already screaming the place down when Yeats burst in.'

'Were you acquainted with Lynsey Yeats before this attack?'

'Met her for the first time a few days ago. She'd been staying with Doreen at her house. Doreen said she needed a place to lie low for a while. Then Doreen's husband came home from Dubai, and she asked me to look after the girl for a few days until she could sort something out.'

'And did you agree to this?'

'I did, but I wanted to know why she was helping her. She told me the girl had a drug problem, and some guys on her estate were after her.'

'That was all?'

'I didn't push it, so yes, that was all.'

'So, Lynsey was staying at your house when she burst in on you and Doreen?' Murray asked.

'Not exactly. I have a cottage in the Lake District, Ambleside. I thought it was a good idea to put her there for a while, until whatever trouble she was in had blown over.'

'Did she go?'

'Oh yes. Doreen and I drove her up on Friday morning. Got her settled in with groceries and things. She seemed happy enough, and we left her on Friday afternoon. Next time I saw her was in my bedroom yesterday.'

'Did Councillor Leitch tell you anything more about Lynsey? Did she mention what sort of relationship they shared?'

'Relationship?'

'Are they friends, for instance?'

'Inspector, you don't go around slashing your friends with a knife after they've done you a favour. As far as I know, Lynsey was simply a girl with a drug habit who sought help at one of Doreen's rehab centres.'

'No connection then between Doreen, Lynsey and the murders of Terry Lawler and Paul Macklin?'

Sullivan suddenly winced, and instinctively his hand located his wound.

'My God, is that what you think? That Doreen had something to do with killing people? You lot really are a piece of work. First you chase after Blackley, then me, and now you're out to get my... closest friend. Who's next, eh? Me nan's eighty-two with Parkinson's; want to have a go at her, do ya?'

'We're trying to get to the truth, Mr Sullivan. Two people are dead, and I think someone is protecting the killer. But thanks for your help. Get well soon.'

Tara marched out of the room and into the corridor. She had her killer, she was sure of that, but still she was searching for the reasons. Murray, who'd stopped to speak with the ward sister, caught up with her near the hospital exit.

'Doreen Leitch is still under sedation,' he said. 'Do you want to have another crack at Yeats?'

'Not right now. I reckon Danny Ross will have more to say when he hears that Lynsey is in custody.'

They found him easily enough this time, walking a small dog across some open ground close to Treadwater Primary School. Thankfully, Tara thought, he didn't make a run for it when he saw Murray and her coming towards him. The youth called his dog then turned to face them as if prepared for the inevitable.

'Hiya, Danny,' said Murray. 'We need another word, mate.'

The three of them walked to a bench at the edge of the green, Danny finding himself bracketed by the two detectives.

'We found Lynsey,' Tara began. 'She's in a bit of a state, Danny, but we know she killed Lawler and Macklin.'

'Shanks, come on, boy.'

Ross dropped his head as his dog came to his call. He stroked the dog's back as the mongrel tried to lick his hand.

'We need the truth, Danny. From your side. Lynsey might not be capable of straight talking for a while.'

'What do you mean?'

'She's had a breakdown. We're taking good care of her.'

It was clear to Tara that Ross, from his silence, was running through his options.

'My brief says I don't have to tell you nothin'.'

'Might be better for you in the long run if you did.'

'You've got nothin' on me, cop, so just fuck off and leave me alone. Come on, Shanks.' He ran off, his dog racing ahead across the green.

'Will I go after him?' Murray asked her.

'Leave him. Unless we charge him, he's not going to talk. Surprising loyalty towards his girlfriend. True love and all that.'

Late in the afternoon, around four, Superintendent Tweedy called Tara and Murray into his office. Time for an update, Tara was thinking as she took her seat beside Murray. Tweedy looked rather serious, his hands clasped as if in prayer.

'Chief Constable has been on the phone. He's just had to deal with the irate husband of Councillor Leitch. Seems he can't get straight answers as to what happened to his wife yesterday.'

Tara accepted her cue to explain the events of the previous day.

'So, her husband is in for another shock when he learns that his wife has been having an affair?' said Tweedy.

Tara noticed her boss's gaze land for a second on the Bible at the corner of his desk.

'We believe she is also implicated in the murders of Lawler and Macklin,' said Tara.

'But you don't have proof?'

'We're not able to interview either suspect. Yeats has been placed in a secure ward undergoing psychiatric evaluation; Leitch is under sedation. Sullivan denies any knowledge of his lover's involvement in the killings. Danny Ross won't help; his brief got to him. Obviously, he doesn't want to implicate himself by telling us the truth about Yeats.'

'Bit of a stalemate,' said Tweedy. 'Have you reviewed any of the forensics in light of what's happened?'

'Not lately, sir, but we believe we now have the murder weapons. We took two knives from Yeats when we arrested her. I think she'd brought them from her kitchen; there were two missing from a set of four when I was last there.'

'Can't prove anything with forensics when it comes to Doreen Leitch,' said Murray. 'Or Matt Sullivan for that matter.'

'You're going to have to hope you can interview Leitch and Yeats again soon,' said Tweedy.

Tara agreed with her boss, but at the same time she worried that they may never be able to get to the truth if neither woman was prepared to confess.

CHAPTER 58

Tara

Tara sat with both elbows perched on her desk, her fingers intertwined and supporting her chin. Lost in thought. Well after nine and she should really be home in front of the telly. Instead, she sat alone in the office, lights out but for her desk lamp shining down on a file much too thin on evidence. Hard evidence is what she really needed in this case, not all this scuttling around listening to stories which amounted to little more than malicious gossip.

Who had the greatest reason to see Lawler dead? Had a drug-crazed young lady acted on her own? Or did Ross give her a hand and had Doreen Leitch put her up to it?

Tara knew the version of the story that she preferred. Murray agreed. Could they sit back and hope for Leitch to eventually tell the truth? Tara wondered if she would even recognise the truth when she heard it. There had to be something she'd missed. Something said by one of the suspects, a piece of forensic evidence as Tweedy had suggested, or a vital clue lurking in the home of one of the victims or suspects.

Her thinking was interrupted by a text from Aisling.

'Can we go out this week?' it read. She replied immediately with a yes, but she added nothing to suggest a time or a venue. She really couldn't see beyond her sitting at this desk until a solution to this case landed in front of her.

'Thurs 8 at Malmaison then on to Club 66. Don't drive, taxi,' was Aisling's reply.

Setting down her phone, she opened another file on this troublesome case and began reading through, first her notes and then Murray's. After a while she got up from her desk and went to the whiteboard. In the semi-darkness, she peered at the connections drawn between each suspect and the victims. She had a line running from Yeats to Lawler and from Leitch to Yeats and to Sullivan. Ross was also connected to Yeats and Leitch. Nothing new occurred to her. Both deaths, Lawler and Macklin, involved knife wounds. Yet another link to Lynsey Yeats. There was nothing to suggest any connection between the Blackleys and Yeats, so she drew a line through the names of Gwen and Evan. In that vein there was no longer any reason to include the mystery man, if he existed at all, who may have abducted more than twenty women. She drew a line through that also.

Her brief text communication with Aisling sailed through her head. *Malmaison... Don't drive, taxi.*

She tried to list the similarities in both killings. Knife wounds, crazed attacks, lonely places, planned executions rather than spontaneous attacks. Why those places?

Macklin certainly was killed at the building site to draw attention to Blackley, although she had yet to figure out why. Lawler was killed on Crosby Beach. Why go there?

Suddenly, an exciting thought gripped her. Something they hadn't considered before and yet it was so simple. So damned obvious. Tara took a seat and continued to stare at her work on the board. If Yeats was the killer, how did she get the victims to the place where they died? Macklin's car was found close to the scene, so he had probably driven there himself to meet someone. Perhaps one of the people he was blackmailing? That brought in all of the suspects once again, including the Blackleys. But what of Lawler's murder? No car was ever recovered from Crosby Beach. They hadn't found a car belonging to the victim. How did Yeats get Lawler out of the city, in the dead of night, to a beach four miles away? Did she drive? And what about Ross? If he was her accomplice, did he drive and does he own a car? She raced to her desk, lifted the phone and called Murray.

'I need you in here; we have work to do.'

'What's up, ma'am?'

'The blooming obvious has just dawned on me, and I can't believe we didn't see it before. Now hurry up.'

She cut the call and sat down in front of her computer screen. By the time Murray arrived twenty minutes later she had discarded Yeats and Ross as car owners, certainly licensed owners anyway. She didn't allow Murray to remove his jacket or take a seat.

'Let's go.'

'Where are we off to?'

'You should enjoy it; we're going to look at some cars.'

CHAPTER 59

Tara

Rain was coming down hard upon the bonnet of her Focus as they drew up by the gates of the Leitch family home. There were lights visible at two of the upstairs windows. Someone at home and still awake, she hoped. Thankfully, she reached the intercom without having to get out of the car. It took nearly a minute before a male voice answered.

'Yes, who is it?'

'Inspector Grogan and DS Murray. May we speak with you, Mr Leitch?'

'It's eleven o'clock, don't you people stop working for the night?'

'It's very important, sir, otherwise we would be home at this time.'

The intercom switched off, and the gates began to swing open. When Tara drew up close to the front door, she noticed just one car, a dark-coloured BMW, parked in front of the house. Off to the right, the doors of the double garage were closed.

A tall man, close to seventy with silver hair, a square jawline and tanned face, stood at the open door of the house. He wore a striped dressing gown and brown leather moccasins.

'What's this about? Is Doreen all right?' His voice was assertive, with no local accent apparent.

'As far we know, sir,' Tara replied. 'May we have a look at the car your wife usually drives?'

'What for?'

Already Tara had felt some similarity in the attitudes of man and wife. Not entirely obstructive but needed some pressure to gain co-operation.

'If we could take a look, sir, it will help with our case.'

'Do you have a warrant?'

'No, but if you would prefer that I got one, I should be back here about two o'clock.'

Without further comeback, Leitch disappeared inside the house, returning a few moments later with a set of keys which he handed to Tara.

'There's one car in the garage. The BMW is mine. Her usual car is parked at the home of Councillor Sullivan. I'm sure you're aware of that, Inspector. If you don't mind, I'll wait here. Not getting soaked for the Merseyside Police. Side door of the garage should be open.'

Tara and Murray walked briskly through the rain to the garage. Once inside, Murray found a light switch, and before them sat a white Range Rover.

'Look for anything that might indicate the car was used to ferry a dead man or a man knocked unconscious.'

'Blood, you mean. I get it, ma'am.'

'Not just blood. Hairs, mud from shoes, sand if this thing has been to Crosby Beach. Anything, damn it.'

Tara was angry at herself for not having realised Doreen Leitch's car was parked at Sullivan's house. She could have saved them the trouble of driving out to Birkdale. Still, it was worth taking a look at the Range Rover. Murray removed a small torch from his jacket pocket and set about a thorough inspection of the boot. Tara began at the front. There were a few loose-leaf papers lying on the passenger seat. Council memos, nothing she found of any interest. A green waterproof anorak lay on the back seat. Apart from that the car interior was pristine, hardly a speck of dust.

'Find anything?'

'All clean here,' Murray called out.

'Right then, let's get over to Sullivan's place.'

They returned the keys to a disgruntled Mr Leitch and headed to the Sullivan house at Aintree.

The house was in darkness and hidden from the street by a neat row of leylandii. There was little natural light at all on such a damp night, so Murray used his torch from the moment he stepped from the car. A silver Mercedes belonging to Sullivan was parked to the left side of the house. This time they had no keys, and so managed only a cursory look through the window. Nothing seemed out of place. Doreen Leitch's car was parked farther along the drive toward the back of the house, an attempt perhaps to hide it from prying eyes, Tara thought. Murray tried the door handle at the driver's side and found it locked. Neither of them lingered on the fact and set about an inspection of the interior of the Audi by shining the torch through the window.

'Never seen cars so bloody clean, except in a showroom. She must have them valeted regularly,' said Murray.

Tara sighed in frustration and disappointment. She hadn't thought of the vehicle perhaps having been valeted since the murders.

'I'll get forensics to check over both cars just in case. Sorry to waste your evening, Alan. I was sure I had it sussed.'

'No problem, ma'am. Wasn't doing much.'

'How the hell did Yeats get Lawler out to Crosby Beach?'

'Let's ask Ross. This time we'll bring him in.'

'First thing in the morning,' said Tara. 'Time we were home in our beds.'

* * *

A beleaguered-looking youth sat before them in the interview room. His shirt was blood-stained and a cut one inch long sat above his left eye. He was a very reluctant witness at nine-thirty in the morning. Tara allowed Murray to handle the questions. Ross's solicitor, a young man, fresh-faced and recently qualified in legal aid by the name of Josh Hegarty, grey suit, white shirt and blue and white striped tie, sat in silence. His blue eyes were fixed on Tara, not in the blatant manner of Matt Sullivan, more in admiration of her stature. He'd been appointed to the case when Ross had been interviewed in relation to his drugs activities.

'Okay, Danny,' Murray began. 'We know you helped Lynsey Yeats to kill Terry Lawler and Paul Macklin. We know she probably did the cutting, but we want you to tell us why and how you took Lawler all the way out to Crosby Beach.'

Ross looked at Hegarty for a lead, but the solicitor signalled for him to respond. It seemed that Ross had now resigned himself to being implicated in the murders. Little did he know, however, that Tara was still without hard evidence to prove it.

'Lynsey wanted to do him there. That's where they used to go when they were together, for walks and stuff.'

'Do you have a car, Danny?'

'No.'

'Does Lynsey have a car?'

'No.'

'How did you get Lawler out there?'

'Drove him in the boot of a car.'

'Whose car, Danny?'

'I don't know. Lynsey borrowed it.'

'Where did she get it? Was it stolen?'

Ross seemed reluctant to answer. He glanced again at the solicitor who remained impassive, continuing to have eyes only for Tara. She smiled thinly as if to acknowledge his interest in her.

'All I did was drive the car, right. I didn't do nothin' to the bloke. Lynsey did the killin'.'

'I'm quite sure you did a lot more than that, Danny, but for now just tell us about the car,' said Tara.

'Who owned it, Danny?' Murray repeated.

'It was Doreen's,' he said with a sigh. 'She let Lynsey use it.'

Murray shook his head.

'I don't think so. We've checked her cars, or did you get it cleaned out afterwards?'

'What are you on about, cop? I told you we used Doreen's car.'

'What make of car, Danny?' Tara asked.

'BMW, a big black one. Dead expensive and that.'

Tara looked at Murray. Again, they had slipped up. They'd walked past the BMW, ignoring it because it belonged to the husband.

Tara left the interview and went straight to the operations room, where she ordered a uniformed patrol car and a forensic team out to the home of Doreen Leitch. Now, hopefully, she had all the parties involved in the murders of Lawler and Macklin, and she might have some forensic evidence too.

CHAPTER 60

Tara

'Danny, you don't have to protect Lynsey any longer.'

Ross sniffed back his tears and rubbed a shirt sleeve across his mouth and nose.

'We know she killed Terry Lawler and Paul Macklin, but we need you to tell us why, Danny. We can't help you if you won't explain what happened.'

The youth rested his head on folded arms upon the table, trying to shut out the voices circling in the room. His once tough exterior, his foul tongue, full of threats and bravado, had deserted him. Murray's impatience was mounting as Ross remained silent, but Tara knew that soon she would squeeze the truth from the young monster. She had already assembled the truth for herself; she just needed his confirmation. For the moment she allowed Murray to continue with his questions.

'We know the car you used, Danny. We know who drove it. We know who owns it.'

'So what?' he said, lifting his head from the table.

'Like I said, Danny, you're not protecting Lynsey any longer. We know you care about her, mate, but why should she go down for murder and you as an accessory when someone else is behind it all? You aren't gaining a thing by trying to protect them.'

'It don't help Lynsey by telling you lot anything.'

'Lynsey is ill, Danny,' said Tara. 'She might never be well enough to stand trial. Any information you give us will help your case. Could be the court will look kindly on someone who was only trying to protect the girl he loves.'

'What do you mean ill? Sick in the head, like?'

'She's suffered a breakdown. It'll be a while before we know how well she might recover.'

'But she will get better, won't she?'

'I can't say for sure. But I think you owe it to her to speak the truth, Danny. Do you think it's right that the person behind these killings stays free, while you're in prison and Lynsey is kept in a hospital?'

'She was only trying to help Doreen, to pay her back. She was good to Lynsey, getting her off the shit, lending her money, trying to get her a job, a new start, like. And Lynsey said she could help me get out of the racket, stop selling an' that.'

'How did Lynsey first meet her?'

'Lawler brought her to one of the drop-in centres to try and get her clean. He wrote all about it in the papers. Took pictures of us. Lynsey thought it was a laugh. That's what she told me. She only went to please Lawler. Turned out, all he cared about was getting a story on us crackheads. Then the cold bastard broke up with her, and she went straight back on the stuff, but she kept going to the centre. And that's when she met Councillor Leitch. She helped her big time. Got her off heroin and on to some medicine that was really helping her. She gave her money, let her stay over at her house. Lynsey was really happy, and she came looking for me and we got back together, we used to be close an' that, since school, like. She told me if I really wanted to have her for good then I had to give up the dealing and Doreen would help me get a proper job.'

* * *

They entered the private room on a ward at the Royal, where Doreen Leitch lay awake staring into space. She had a dressing over her chest wound and a couple of stitches on her forehead. She did not acknowledge her visitors.

'Councillor Leitch, I'm told you should be well enough to speak with us this morning?'

'Go away.'

Tara pulled a chair close to the bed and sat down, cutting off the woman's view out of the window.

'I'm afraid that's not going to happen, Councillor. We already have sufficient evidence to charge you with the murder of Terry Lawler and Paul Macklin, but we would like to hear your version of events.'

'And neither is that going to happen, Inspector.'

Tara examined the woman's face. She didn't look quite so attractive without make-up and hairdo, but it seemed like Doreen Leitch had lost so much more than mere looks. She was a woman stripped of all dignity, vacant of any warmth, compassion or pride. She didn't have much farther to fall. Tara decided to test her, to see if any grains of humanity were left within.

'Danny Ross told us about Lynsey and how you had been helping her.'

Leitch didn't even blink.

'But you used the young girl to get rid of a troublemaker, didn't you, Councillor?'

'You may as well stop calling me councillor. Very unlikely that I will attend any council meetings in the future.'

'I suppose the same can be said for Councillor Sullivan?'

'What do you mean?'

'Surely his reputation has also been shattered by recent events, not to mention his future once he is convicted.'

'Convicted of what, Inspector? Matt had nothing to do with any of this.'

'But Lawler was blackmailing him, threatening to discredit him in the press. He had just as much motive for murder as you had, Doreen.'

Leitch suddenly managed a smile which quickly became a grimace as she attempted to rise.

'You don't know much about what happened, do you? You have no evidence to prove anything.'

'We have your husband's car. Looks as though it's teeming with evidence, things that can be traced to Lawler. Won't be long before we have some results from the lab.'

'My husband's car was stolen a couple of weeks ago.'

'Did you report it stolen?'

'That Danny Ross took it. He brought it back a few days later.'

'After it had been used to carry the body of Terry Lawler?'

'I wouldn't know, Inspector.'

'Mr Sullivan told us that you had Lynsey staying with you?'

'On occasions, yes. She needed help. She wanted to get off drugs. I thought it best to get her away from that awful estate.'

'Why, then, did she attack you and Mr Sullivan?'

'She was upset, because she wanted to continue living at my home. I told her that was impossible. Obviously, she didn't like being told no.'

'Ross told us that Lynsey would have done anything for you.'

'Including murder? Is that what you think, that I asked her to kill Lawler?'

'You both had strong reason to want to harm Terry Lawler.'

'So did half of Liverpool. The other half, sadly, regarded him as a bloody hero. If you have nothing else, Inspector, please get out, I want to rest.'

Murray treated Tara to a coffee from a vending machine in the hospital foyer. She didn't really want it but appreciated his gesture. She sipped from her cup as Murray began to express his latest doubts over the case.

'Could we be wrong about Leitch?'

'It may come down to what evidence we get from the car.'

'It might prove that Lawler was in the motor, but we'll have a hard job proving that Leitch sanctioned his murder. What if Yeats acted on her own? What if she thought she was doing Leitch a good turn?'

Tara shook her head.

'No, she had to have someone help her.'

'OK, she had Ross, he drove the car and helped to bury Lawler in the sand, but what I mean is she acted alone. Leitch wasn't yanking her chain.'

Again, Tara shook her head. She tipped the remainder of her coffee into a bin.

'We need to lean hard on the others, Lynsey, Ross and Sullivan. Leitch is as guilty as sin, and I'm damned if she is getting away with it.'

Back at St Anne Street, she read the lab report confirming that Terry Lawler had been in the boot of the BMW. What's more, he was probably alive at the time because his prints were all over the interior, along with traces of his blood. Seemed likely that Lawler had been abducted and beaten before being placed in the boot of the car and driven to Crosby Beach, where he was rendered unconscious, buried and castrated.

Other prints taken from the car were a match for Danny Ross, Lynsey Yeats and Mr and Mrs Leitch. Tara realised that prints of the owners proved nothing. She sat forlornly at her desk, having finished the report, staring at the Merseyside Police screensaver and wondering what else she'd missed that could bring about the arrest of Councillor Leitch.

As far as Lynsey Yeats was concerned, her wheels had come off big time. She had inflicted terrible carnage on both of her victims. She killed Lawler, her ex-boyfriend, at a place they used to visit together. She chose his place of execution; she performed the killing and she castrated him. But what of Paul Macklin? Her only motive for killing him surely was to oblige her friend Doreen Leitch. Lynsey and Ross wouldn't have been aware of the significance of where they killed him. They didn't know anything about Evan Blackley and his building sites, nor would they have known of his association with Matt Sullivan. It had to be Leitch or Sullivan who decided that Macklin should be found at one of Blackley's building developments. Were Sullivan and Blackley not cohorts in the property business? Why, then, would Leitch or Sullivan wish to implicate Blackley in the murder of Paul Macklin?

'Murray!'

'Yes, ma'am,' he said, while trying to stuff the remainder of his Subway roll into his mouth.

'We're off to see Evan Blackley, and you're driving.'

They managed to track down the property developer to his golf club in Lymm, where he was to be found in the members' bar, having just finished his round of nine holes. On the way to the golf club, Tara explained her thinking to Murray. He didn't appear enthusiastic.

'Bit of a long shot, don't you think?'

'You're the football fan, have you never seen a goal scored from a long shot?'

They'd been told by his secretary that Blackley was off playing golf. Tara didn't doubt that the secretary would have alerted her boss to the impending visit by Merseyside Police. He was alone by a table at the window overlooking the eighteenth green when Tara and Murray barged in.

'Here we go again. What have I done now?'

'Nothing to excite yourself about, Mr Blackley. Just a few questions, that's all.'

His bloated face seemed to relax slightly in reaction to Tara's remarks. His apparent bemusement at the young girl before him playing detective hadn't waned since they'd first met. She and Murray sat on a sofa directly opposite the former footballer.

'So, ask away, Inspector,' he said, taking a healthy gulp of his vodka and tonic.

'Your association with Matt Sullivan. I want the truth, Mr Blackley. I'm not here to deal with a matter of corruption. I'm trying to catch a murderer.'

'What do you want to know?' He finished his drink and signalled to the bar for another.

'Was Matt Sullivan in your pocket?'

'Is that what he told you?'

'Just answer the question. Were you paying Councillor Sullivan for favours in relation to your planning applications?'

'Do you mean was Lawler right in what he printed? No, he was off his friggin' trolley.'

'Was Councillor Leitch also in receipt of payments from you?'

'What? Are you mad? She's dead straight, building her political career, she can't be seen to be mixed up in that sort of business.'

'Was she aware that Sullivan was taking bungs?'

'I have no idea. I know he was giving her the sausage, but I wasn't privy to their pillow talk.'

'Thanks, Mr Blackley, you've been very helpful.'

They left him to enjoy his next drink. Tara would make sure he got a call from her colleagues in Fraud when she'd finished with this murder case.

'Right,' she said with a buzz. 'Another word with Matt Sullivan and my longshot may just score me a cracking goal.'

Murray laughed as he swung the car out of the golf club and headed back to Liverpool.

They didn't spend long with Sullivan. One question from Tara and his reply was sufficient to send her scuttling down the hallway, across the hospital to the private room of Doreen Leitch.

Her bed was empty.

CHAPTER 61

Tara

Tara was drained. Another long day. Even Murray seemed to wilt as they sat in Tweedy's office reporting the latest developments and how their suspected murderer had given them the slip. Tweedy's understanding tone merged with deep concern over the disappearance of Doreen Leitch. It seemed that she had simply walked, un-noticed, out of the hospital wearing what little clothes she'd had in her locker.

'Neither Ross nor Yeats have implicated the councillor?' said Tweedy.

'No, sir,' Tara replied. 'We know that a car belonging to Mr Leitch was used to transport Terry Lawler to Crosby Beach, and he was probably still alive at that point.'

'And who drove this car?'

'Danny Ross,' said Murray.

'The point is, sir, Doreen Leitch and Lynsey Yeats had strong reason to kill Lawler, but if Yeats murdered Paul Macklin, it had to be at the behest of Leitch. Yeats had no other motive to kill the solicitor.'

'I agree, Tara, but I take it you have no proof that Leitch ordered Yeats to kill either man?'

'No, sir, but Macklin's body was found tied to a fence on a building site owned by Evan Blackley. Why would that be? Coincidence? Or was someone trying to implicate Blackley in the murders? Again, no reason for Yeats to do that. I believe she had no knowledge of Blackley's activities. But Macklin had taken over where his mate Lawler had left off in trying to blackmail Sullivan and exposing his affair with Doreen Leitch. It's clear now that Sullivan received bribes from Blackley. I think that Doreen Leitch, in having Macklin killed, was attempting to rid herself and her lover of a blackmailer and at the same time trying to blame the killing on the man who was controlling Sullivan by his bribery.'

Tweedy eased his glasses back up his nose. Although she hoped for his approval, Tara often thought that her boss looked to be carrying a burden much too great for a man of his years. He looked weary. She waited for his response.

'I don't disagree with your reasoning, Tara, but we need evidence, or at least we need the Yeats girl to confirm that she acted under instruction from Doreen Leitch. Without it, I'm afraid we can proceed only with the case against Yeats and Ross. Any news on the whereabouts of the councillor?'

'No, sir,' Murray replied. 'We're never going to get Yeats to shop Leitch.'

'I know,' Tara replied with a deep sigh as she settled back at her desk. 'The girl's practically gaga and dangerous with it.'

'Go home, ma'am. You can't do much more tonight.'

Her headed pounded, her shoulders felt locked tight around her neck.

She sat at her desk after Murray left her. She wondered where Doreen Leitch had taken herself.

* * *

An injured woman who flees her hospital bed with what little clothes she had is never likely to get far. By midnight, the call came into St Anne Street that Doreen Leitch was trying to gain access to her home. Her husband, however, had no intention of letting her inside. He'd made the call to the police, demanding that his estranged wife be removed from his property. A car with three officers was despatched to the house at Birkdale, and the distraught woman was brought to St Anne Street station. Tara, by this time, was sound asleep in bed. When she arrived for work at nine o'clock next morning, Murray was waiting for her in the foyer.

'We have Doreen Leitch in custody, ma'am.'

'Has she been charged with anything?'

'Not yet. I thought you might like a word. Duty sergeant has had her checked by the doctor. She's a bit fragile but should be up to answering some questions.'

'Good. Although why do I get the feeling we'll be wasting our time?'

While Tara went to collect some files from her desk, Murray prepared an interview room and requested that Leitch be brought up from her cell. Tara was taken aback by the woman's appearance, when she joined Murray and Leitch in the room. The once glamorous councillor's hair was dirty, unbrushed, her face was smattered with red blotches and she had a bruise forming below her left eye.

'How did you get the injury to your eye, Doreen?'

'Guess?' She sat partially slumped over the table scarcely able to hold herself upright, wincing from the pain of her knife wound.

Tara glanced at Murray for the answer. He merely shrugged.

'Were you in a struggle with police officers?'

'Yes, I was. They were trying to take me away from my home, Inspector. But I got this from my darling husband.' She touched her left cheek with her forefinger. 'Thirty-four years married. Nice memento, don't you think?'

She looked at Tara with despairing eyes.

'I know you think I deserve it, Inspector. Me having an affair with a younger man, not much more than a boy is Matt. But my husband, in going about his business, has screwed his way around the world several times.'

Tara wasn't particularly interested in the marital infidelities of the Leitch family. She was there to get answers to why two men had been murdered. Strangely, though, Tara got the impression that Doreen Leitch was now up for some serious talking. She would indulge her, now that she was at least prepared to co-operate.

'Tell me about your relationship with Matt Sullivan.'

The woman smiled.

'A real sweetie is Matt. You know, Inspector, you could do a lot worse than finding a man like my Matt.'

Tara cringed at the thought. The creep could hardly look her in the face.

'What did he think about his lover arranging the murders of Terry Lawler and Paul Macklin?'

The question was a deliberate side swipe at Doreen Leitch, and for a moment the woman did seem shocked by Tara's callousness. She fiddled with the sleeves of her sweatshirt, pulling them down over her hands. Then she sat back in her chair, raised her arms and drew her hands back through her hair. She groaned, however, from the pain of the knife wound across her chest.

'I realise I have nothing left now, Inspector. I've lost my home, my family, my lover and my career. Did you know that I was set to be the next MP for Sefton Central?

I could have done great things at Westminster. Perhaps even made a cabinet minister. And now look at me.'

She grimaced in pain, and her hands settled gently on her chest.

'Can I get you anything, Doreen? Do you need a doctor?'

She laughed.

'Doctors can't cure what I've got.'

'I think it's time to explain your part in the killing of Terry Lawler, Doreen. We know he was threatening to expose your affair with Matt Sullivan…'

'I went into politics to help people; did you know that? I just wanted to make a difference.'

'So, what happened?' Murray asked.

Doreen smiled at him, her eyes beginning to sparkle in the presence of the hefty yet attractive detective sergeant.

'You know, Sergeant, if you're a free agent, I could teach you a thing or two.'

'I'll keep it in mind, Doreen. Now tell us what happened.'

'What happened? Evan bloody Blackley, that's what happened.'

CHAPTER 62

Tara

Their arrival at the house in Lymm was timed perfectly with a torrential downpour. Murray didn't slow the car, and it splashed through the open gates, coming to a halt as close to the front door of the house as he could get it. Gwen Blackley stood at the open door, her daughter, Maisie, and her ex-husband's sister, Beth, were beside her. It seemed to Tara like they were expected. She dashed from the car to the welcoming party.

'We'd like to speak with your husband, Mrs Blackley.'

'As would I, Inspector.'

'Do you know where he is?'

'Not exactly, but my guess is he's out of the country. Would you like to come inside?'

She and Murray went indoors, both Maisie and Beth stayed close to Gwen Blackley as she led the way into the sitting room. Her face was pale, eyes red, she clutched her arms as if freezing cold. Dressed in black jeans and ruffled T-shirt, not the appearance of the woman that Tara had come to expect. Beth switched on the TV and flopped down between Tara and Gwen on the sofa.

'Not now, Beth, please,' said Gwen. 'Go and watch it in the kitchen.'

The heavy woman stamped out of the room, grunting under her breath as she went. Tara noted that Maisie had no intention of following suit.

'I take it that you have no idea if or when your husband intends to return home?'

Gwen held both hands to her face, stretching her skin backwards.

'He told me nothing. All he said was that he had to get away.'

'How long has he been gone? Can we stop him at the airport?'

The woman shook her head and sighed.

'Yesterday afternoon.'

'Just after we spoke to him at the golf club?' said Murray.

'How much trouble is he in?' asked Gwen.

'Soliciting to murder,' Tara replied. 'We believe he ordered the deaths of your ex-husband and of Paul Macklin.'

It was clear from Gwen Blackley's reaction that she had no prior knowledge of her husband's activities. She cried sorely, burying her head in her lap. Young Maisie fell to her knees beside her mother and cried also.

'Do you know which airport, Gwen?'

The woman shook her head. Murray stepped into the hall and called the station. They might well be too late, but still they had to confirm with airports and ports if Evan Blackley had skipped the country.

By late afternoon, Tara and Murray had presented Superintendent Tweedy with a statement given by Doreen Leitch in the presence of her solicitor. Tara summarised the facts of the case, filling in those details they previously had not deduced but now were confirmed by the disgraced councillor.

'Blackley had been paying Sullivan for favours for a number of years, but Sullivan was desperate to end the arrangement, especially after being hauled through the courts when he'd been forced to challenge Terry Lawler's accusations.'

'What about Doreen Leitch, was she accepting bribes also?'

'No, sir. Her only involvement was her affair with Matt Sullivan. When Sullivan tried to end his dealings with Blackley, Blackley told him that he knew all about his affair with Leitch. He threatened to expose them both if Sullivan didn't continue to do his bidding.'

'How did the murder of Terry Lawler come about?'

'Lawler had threatened to publish fresh allegations against Blackley regarding his bribery of Sullivan, but he'd also uncovered new evidence about Blackley's activities while playing football in Italy. There had always been rumours of his involvement in the match-fixing scandal. It was all too much for Blackley, and he ordered Sullivan to get rid of Terry Lawler.'

'Lawler had also threatened to expose the affair between Sullivan and Leitch?' said Tweedy.

'Exactly. But the plans to kill Lawler were already in place before Lawler turned up at Sullivan's house and saw him with Doreen Leitch. Sullivan had told Leitch about Blackley's instructions and, fortuitously, Doreen knew just the person to carry out the killing. Lynsey Yeats, a drug addict who had become very much dependent upon the friendship and care of Doreen Leitch, also had strong motive for killing Lawler. He was her ex-boyfriend, and she wanted retribution for him dropping her as soon as he'd got his story on the crackheads in Treadwater Estate.'

Tweedy, as always, seemed to take revelations such as these at a deeply personal level. He sat in his chair, his brow furrowed, hands clenched together on the desk. Tara believed she knew what he was thinking at that moment. That nothing so trivial could ever justify the taking of human life. No matter how bizarre or frantic the circumstances, no one in that circle of friends and associates deserved to have their lives ruined.

She realised that Tweedy had his own way of dealing with these experiences. Otherwise he would not have survived in policing for all these years. She had learned also that she and Murray and the other guys in the squad all must develop their own mechanisms to deal with the stark realities of murder.

'I take it that Paul Macklin got himself involved in a situation where he put his own life at risk?'

Tara allowed Murray to continue the report.

'Macklin tried to take over where Lawler had left off. He threatened both Evan Blackley and Councillor Sullivan. Seems he was too stupid to realise he was dealing with the people who'd arranged the murder of his best friend. When Blackley instructed Sullivan to dispose of Macklin, it was Leitch's idea to have the body placed at one of Blackley's building sites. She hoped that it might help implicate Blackley in the murder. They all gave themselves an alibi by having dinner together on the night that Macklin was killed. Interestingly, according to Leitch, if Macklin had not surfaced after Lawler's murder, the intention was to have Yeats kill Evan Blackley.'

'A lucky break for Mr Blackley. And how does Councillor Sullivan fare in all of this?'

'Well, sir,' said Tara, 'he shared his worries with Doreen Leitch over his involvement with Blackley. She took charge of the whole affair. Despite his denials, and Doreen's insistence that he knew nothing of the murders, I'm certain he was well aware of every step Doreen was taking.'

'She'd have been much better off ending her love affair with Councillor Sullivan.'

'Seems it was quite a serious relationship; both have remained quite defensive of the other.'

'But why such brutal killings?'

'All down to Lynsey Yeats. Ross told us that she was hyper on drugs when she carried out the killings. She dug a hole in the sand with her bare hands just to bury Lawler. I don't think she even remembers exactly what she did to her victims.'

The bustle in the operations room had died to the hum of a laser printer and the odd tapping of keys at a computer. Murray was putting the finishing touches to the statements taken so far from Doreen Leitch and Danny Ross. Interviews were set for the following day with Matt Sullivan and Gwen Blackley. It was doubtful that in the near future they would get anything sensible from Lynsey Yeats, and the whereabouts of Evan Blackley remained unknown.

Tara, alone at her desk tried to come to terms with the outcome of the investigation. Seldom did they ever have a completely sharp end to a case. All the loose ends tied up. This one was far from satisfactory. The killer was no longer in her right mind, and the man who'd called the shots was, for now, scot-free.

Murray came over to leave the statements with her. He looked tired and, as she had come to notice recently, he tended to fall rather quiet and withdrawn upon the closure of a murder investigation. His way, she supposed, of dealing with the horrors of human behaviour.

'What are you doing, ma'am? Time to get off home. We've done enough for today.'

Spread across her desk were the twenty or so photographs of the missing women taken from the wall of Terry Lawler's flat.

'Can't help thinking there's a lot of unfinished business out there.' She lifted the picture of Ruth Lawler. 'Some families seem to corner the market on tragedy. First Ruth, then Terry and now poor Beth is left on her own.'

'I'm sure Gwen Blackley will take good care of her.'

'I suppose you're right. I just can't help wondering if Terry Lawler was really onto something when he went searching for his sister. Is there a serial killer out there? Someone who's murdered more than twenty young women?'

CHAPTER 63

Guy

Game on. Tonight's the night, baby. Tara is going to have one hell of an evening and so am I. Pity it has to be her last but that's life, isn't it?

I was dragging myself into work for another night shift, and I bumped into the wee redhead nurse, Kate, the one who's friendly with Tara. I'd kept watch on her house several times when I couldn't keep tabs on her friend. I don't know which of us was the more surprised. First time we'd met she'd seemed very friendly, very tasty.

'Hi there,' she said, a strange look of shock on her face. I wondered if Tara had filled her in about me. Maybe she was just distracted. Eventually, she smiled and asked how I was doing.

'Dead on,' I replied. 'Just starting a shift. How about you?'

'Finished for today, thank goodness.'

'Home to relax?'

'Not tonight. Out with the girls for dinner.'

'Very nice. How's Tara doing? We seem to have lost contact.'

'She's as busy as ever. It's hard getting her out for a night. Half the time she cancels.'

'I suppose it's the nature of her job. Tell her I was asking after her.'

'Will do. Have to fly. I don't want to be the one who's late.'

'Where are you going?'

'Malmaison first then on to Club 66.'

I watched her hurry on down the corridor, coat in one hand, handbag in the other. Suddenly, the notion of working scarpered. I waited for the girl to disappear then headed for the exit. When Tara arrived at the restaurant, I would be waiting for her.

My van was parked way out by Knowsley. I'd left her in a lay-by in the middle of an industrial estate. After running into Tara at Treadwater, I thought it best not to leave the van there any longer.

I had to speed through evening traffic, but at least I was already well-prepared for the night ahead. The van was kitted out with a new mattress, holdall, gaffer tape, a heady supply of China White and syringes. Mother Freedom also was well-prepared, fuelled up and ready to go.

All I needed for the party of a lifetime was for the cutest police inspector I've ever laid eyes on to come sallying down the street all alone with not a care in the world.

CHAPTER 64

Tara

'He looks promising,' said Tara as best as she could. If she were counting, she reckoned they were into double figures of various cocktails: Mojitos, Tequila Sunrise, Sex on the Beach, Manhattans and the latest concoction, A Slow Comfortable Screw Against the Wall. Aisling beamed, while Kate hurled another drink down her throat.

'I'm going to give him the time of his life,' said Aisling as the six-and-a-half-foot, broad-framed Australian returned from the bar carrying another tray of drinks.

He set each glass on the table and handed the tray to a passing waitress.

'Here we go, ladies,' he said. 'Get those down you, put hairs on your chest.'

All three giggled like teenagers at a school disco. Chris, bleached hair, sturdy jaw and slightly cauliflower ears sat next to Aisling, immediately slipping his muscular hand onto her bare thigh. She didn't seem to mind.

'Chris has invited us to watch his match on Saturday,' said Aisling.

'Whish mash?' Kate just managed to ask.

'I play a bit of footie,' Chris replied with a broad smile. 'Some of my teammates will be along later.'

'Are you playing at home?' Tara asked.

'No, he's playing away,' said Kate, bursting into laughter.

Suddenly, Tara and Kate were bystanders as Chris and Aisling began kissing, the rugby player's big hands getting to grips with Aisling's shapely figure.

'Time we weren't here,' said Kate. 'Let's go find some talent of our own.'

Both girls could do little more than hobble towards the bar. Kate wore five-inch heels, a short maroon leather skirt and a pink camisole vest, her current hair colour wasn't far from a match to her skirt. Tara also wore very high platform heels in patent black and a body contour mini dress with black lace which sat off her shoulders. By the time they struggled to the bar, nudging through the crowd, they were ready for another drink.

'Better make this one the last,' said Tara. 'It's time I was home in bed.'

'My point exactly,' said Kate, swaying. 'Just pick your fella and then you can go home.'

'Very funny.'

'Go on, there's plenty here to choose from. Or maybe you want to wait for one of Chris's friends to show up.' Kate patted Tara on the shoulder. 'What about him?' She blatantly pointed toward a man of at least fifty, bald, overweight and red-faced as a young girl danced around him, rubbing her bottom against his groin. Twerking. Others in their company were in kinks of laughter. Clearly, it was a crowd out on a works do.

'Yeah sure,' said Tara. 'I'm not proud. I'll open my legs for any poor sod who'll have me.'

'OK, I'll go and ask him. See if he's willing to show my friend a good time.'

Both girls laughed as the actions of the man became more lurid. He now stood behind the girl, both his hands weighing her breasts. Another girl, taller than the man, stepped behind him and fondled his bum.

'I think he has his hands full already,' said Tara.

Barely able to finish whatever cocktail they had last ordered, she finally admitted defeat.

'Time to go, I think.'

'You're right, love, I don't feel so good.'

When they had paid a final visit to the toilets and signalled to Aisling that they were leaving, they battled their way outside in the hope of hailing a taxi. Rain was hurtling down, filling the gutters and bouncing on the pavement. Tara donned a white leather jacket over her dress, but Kate had nothing more than a scarf. There was a mix of people huddled under an awning by the doorway of Club 66 nightclub, some waiting for taxis, others having a smoke.

'Get me out of here. I'm finished with men.'

It was Aisling, shivering beside them in a pair of black shorts and sequined black vest.

'What's the matter, Aisling? Chris dumped you already?' said Tara.

'Bloody pervert. Wasn't content having me to himself. He had three teammates lined up for a gangbang. I might look easy, but I'm not that sort of girl.' She exploded into floods of tears.

'Come on, love,' said Kate. 'Of course, you're not.' She gave her friend a hug, allowing her to sob into her shoulder.

There were plenty of cabs coming and going, all pre-booked it seemed, as groups of three and four hurried inside the vehicles to escape the downpour. Tara then noticed a van a few yards away along the narrow street, parked up on the pavement. She could see a figure inside. As she was about to turn away to comfort Aisling, the headlights flashed several times. She looked around her in case someone had been waiting for their lift. The lights flashed again, and the driver climbed out. He waved, and suddenly Tara recognised her most recent date. It was James beckoning her to the van.

'Back in a sec, girls.'

Carefully, on her high heels, she stepped towards him. A crowd of girls on a hen night meandered past her, seemingly oblivious to the rain, the bride-to-be encouraged to offer herself to the man standing in the road. James was smiling wistfully as Tara approached.

'Hi, Tara. Can I give you girls a lift home?'

Tara stumbled on the cobbles, her head already spinning in the night air. James reached out to catch her. She smiled gormlessly at him.

'Hellooo,' she said. 'I know you, I think.'

She peered into his eyes, her hair dripping wet. Despite her drunken state, she felt a strange sensation from his hands holding her by the arms. He made no reply to her slurred phrases but continued to smile. She noticed the side panel of the van was open, and suddenly she felt a tightness at her neck. His hand gripped her under the chin, squeezing hard. She staggered backwards, but he had a firm hold. She tried to call out, but the sound died in her throat. He swung his left arm around her waist and hauled her to the open door of the van. Tara had still to realise exactly what was happening. She had pain in her throat, but somehow it felt they were playing a game. He was messing with her. She glanced down the street to the club. Kate was comforting Aisling, stroking her hair.

Now she was hardly aware of being out of the rain. She was in the van, and the door was closing. James wiped a cloth across her face. She had no fear. Only confusion. What were they doing? She heard something rip. There was a dim light above her. She was lying on something soft. She couldn't see James properly, silhouetted against the yellow light. Her head began to spin. Then hands were on her face and pressed on her mouth. At first, she tried to giggle, but now she couldn't speak, she couldn't open her mouth. She wrestled but lost as he pulled at her jacket until her arms slipped out of it. He took her hands and in seconds she could no longer pull them apart.

Fear replaced her drunken confusion. She tried to wriggle away from this man towering over her, but now he had her by the legs, and she could no longer move one foot without the other. She screamed, but only a dull whine was audible. She thrashed her body, trying to get away. And for a moment she was free as he fumbled in a bag. In a second he held something aloft then he turned and grabbed her once more by the throat, pinning her to the mattress. A sharp pain as the needle pierced her arm and then a burning sensation as the fluid entered her body. The van door opened then closed, and he was gone. She rolled towards the door and banged the side of the van with both feet. The engine started up. They were moving, and she was growing weak and drowsy.

'Where's Tara?' said Kate.

Aisling, having regained some composure, looked puzzled.

'What do you mean?'

The white van drove by.

'She went to speak to that bloke with the van, and now it's gone and so is she.'

'Woohoo, at least one of us has got a fella tonight.'

'Something's wrong, Aisling. Our Tara wouldn't do that. She wouldn't rush off without saying anything. I think it was that fella we set her up with, the one who works at the Royal.'

A black cab pulled up and two girls were about to climb inside. Kate barged past them, pulling Aisling with her.

'Sorry, girls. Emergency,' Kate said as they clambered in. 'Can you follow that white van, love? Please don't lose it.'

The cab roared away, the white van only forty yards ahead having stopped to give way at the junction.

Kate was suddenly remarkably sober, in touch at least with her rational thinking. Aisling remained in a daze.

'Where are we going? Is Tara going to be all right?'

Kate clasped her mobile in both hands.

'Quiet, Aisling. I'm calling the bizzies. That bloke's taken off with our Tara.'

'Oh my God. What are we going to do?'

'Shut up, Aisling.'

As the cab joined the late-night traffic, Kate managed to get through to St Anne Street station in the hope that somebody there who knew Tara would be able to help.

'What's going on, girls?' the taxi driver called out. 'This van seems to be heading for the tunnel.'

Kate mentioned Tara's name to the officer who answered the call, she asked to speak with DS Murray and was put through to his mobile phone.

'Just keep following,' she said to the driver. 'Our friend is in that van, and the fella driving is a friggin' weirdo.'

CHAPTER 65

Guy

It wasn't perfect, but I got her. I had Tara in my van. One of her mates spotted me, I think, but what was she going to do about it? They were so pissed I bet they didn't even realise their mate had gone. Tara was so wasted I hardly needed to give her any China White to knock her out. I hoped she didn't get a bad trip mixing the drugs with the drink. I wanted her mostly conscious when I did the business. I wanted her to know that the man she had dumped was still entitled to have her. I'd chosen her. I wanted her to recognise me and to be aware of what I was doing to her without having the strength to put up a fight.

I headed for Kingsway; traffic wasn't so bad, and my wee passenger had gone quiet. With all the weeks of waiting I had at least spent time planning for this night. I drove out to Wallasey, taking my time, couldn't afford any accidents or getting clocked for speeding. Remember, leave no trace, and you don't get caught. Soon I was in open country, with the Irish Sea on my right as I drove. I pulled off a lane into a car park at the Leasowe Lighthouse. A nice wee romantic spot. I parked in the section furthest from the entrance, behind the cover of the concrete bollards that divided the car park into sections. There were a couple of cars parked nearby, windows steamed up. Young lovers enjoying themselves. The rain was bouncing on the roof, not exactly the romantic clear sky and bright moon I had envisaged, but I wasn't about to let the British weather spoil my evening.

I jumped out of the driver's seat, slid open the side door and switched on the bulkhead light. Tara lay perfectly still. I climbed in and sat on the mattress beside her, watching for a while as she slept. Good enough to eat. Despite her hair being soaked, I ran my fingers through it, easing out the tangles. I rubbed the back of my hand softly on her cheek, and she moved her head slightly. Then both hands slipped over her dress, down her legs all the way to her trim ankles. I felt the stirring inside me. I was hard, too. But I knew I must wait. I wanted her to enjoy this as much as me. In the meantime, I got everything ready.

Cutting the cable ties on her hands and feet, I slipped off her shoes. Reaching behind her, I slid the zip of her dress downwards. Then, raising her arms over her head, I slowly peeled her dress upwards, tugging it until it came free. I sat back, admiring my handiwork. She lay motionless in a black lace bra and panties. I couldn't resist touching them, feeling the delicate lace between my fingers, exploring the line of her pants as it disappeared between her legs. It took all of my willpower not to slip my hand inside her.

I placed her dress and her jacket in the holdall that eventually would contain her lifeless body, ready for burial at sea. Next, I removed all my clothes and added them to the bag. Slowly then, savouring every moment, I undid the clasp of her bra and pulled it from her body. Unable to resist any longer, I ran my hand gently across her breasts taking a nipple lightly between thumb and forefinger. I touched myself with my free hand, and my heart began to pound. I felt a pulse in the side of my head as finally I took hold of her delicate panties and slid them down her legs. Both items, I placed in the holdall. Although I was now over-excited gazing at the vision of beauty lying there, I felt a chill in the air. As usual, I had brought a couple of blankets and, spreading them over Tara, I crawled beneath them and drew her close to me. Kissing her shoulder, I lay back to wait for some life to return to her wee body.

CHAPTER 66

Murray rushed from his flat and called for back-up on his mobile. Barely in control of his car, he weaved through traffic and jumped the lights a couple of times until he had a clear route to the tunnel. He called Kate to get an update.

'We can still see them,' she said through her tears. 'This is all my fault. I'll never forgive myself if anything happens to our Tara.'

'Don't worry, we'll get them. Where are you now?'

Kate asked the driver.

'Leasowe Road, just passing the golf club.'

'OK, I know it.'

Murray topped eighty through the tunnel. It wouldn't take long to catch them up.

Aisling and Kate sat in the taxi gripping each other's hands, both shivering and crying.

'I've lost them, girls,' said the driver. 'I can't see their lights with the rain.'

'Oh my God,' Aisling cried, tugging at Kate.

'Where do you think they were headed?'

'I don't bloody know,' Kate shouted. 'He's going to kill her; I know he is.'

They'd driven all the way along Leasowe Road, bearing left onto the straight section of Pasture Road. When they reached Moreton Station, the taxi slowed to a halt and the driver did a U-turn.

'He couldn't have got this far ahead. He must have turned off somewhere,' he said.

Kate phoned Murray again.

'What are we going to do, we've lost them?'

'Let me speak to the driver, Kate.'

She passed the phone through to the bulky frame of the driver.

'This is DS Murray, where are you?'

The driver explained that they were headed back along Pasture Road towards the sea.

'He must have turned off somewhere,' he said.

'I'm on Leasowe Road now, I reckon he's ducked into one of the lay-bys round here.'

'The lighthouse, maybe?'

'Keep looking, I'll meet you along the way.'

Murray slowed his car at every lay-by, junction and laneway, peering through the dark in the hope of catching a glimpse of a white van. On Pasture Road a beleaguered taxi driver was doing exactly the same, except that he had to endure the frantic cries of two girls in his cab.

The vehicles met at the bend where Leasowe Road ends and Pasture Road begins. Kate and Aisling, along with the taxi driver, ran to greet Murray.

'Anything?' said Murray.

'Nothing,' the driver replied. He was a heavy man, crew-cut head, thick neck and wearing a dark anorak.

Murray pointed at the laneway to his right.

'The lighthouse car park must be the only place left to go. When we find them, let me handle it. You girls stay in the cab.'

'But Tara needs us,' said Aisling.

'Stay in the cab until I tell you to come out.'

'Come on, Aisling, let's do as he says,' said Kate.

They were walking back to the cab when a patrol car pulled over beside them. Murray quickly explained the situation, and the two officers inside roared off down Lingham Lane.

The land to the right of the lane was open links until it met the sea. The old lighthouse lay dead ahead, and a few yards beyond was a visitors car park. By the time Murray arrived, and the taxi a little way behind, the uniformed officers had found a white van sitting in the far corner of the car park. Murray's car skidded to a halt on the gravel, and he was out of the vehicle, reaching the van at the same time as the uniforms. He banged on the side with his fist, calling out for Tara. There was no reply. He tried the driver's door; it was open, but there was no one inside, and the cab was self-contained, partitioned from the rear of the van. One of the uniforms slid open the side panel, but Murray was first to look inside. In the gloom, the face of a man peered out from under some blankets.

'What the fuck?' he said.

Murray yanked the blankets towards him, and his eyes widened in shock yet tinged with some relief. Both naked, Tara lay close to the man, in the spoon position. She didn't react to being exposed.

'Are you all right, ma'am?'

'What the fuck is this?' the man shouted in reply. 'You some kind of pervert? I'm trying to sleep with my girlfriend.'

'Get him the hell out of there,' Murray said to the uniforms.

But the man refused to let go of Tara. One of the uniforms managed to grip his feet, the other one joined him, and they pulled hard until the man slid out of the van, landing with a thud on the gravel. The two officers hauled him to his feet and, with his arms jerked behind him, they marched him to their car. Murray climbed inside the van, shining a torch. He threw one of the blankets over Tara's naked body then placed his fingers at her neck to check for a pulse. She made a slight groaning sound, and her head rolled to the side.

'Call an ambulance,' he shouted after the uniforms.

Kate, in bare feet, tiptoed from the taxi.

'Tara? Is she all right?'

Murray grabbed her before she could get into the van.

'She'll be fine, let's wait for the ambulance.'

'I'm a nurse for God's sake, let me see her.'

She pushed past Murray and climbed inside. Then Aisling came hobbling across the gravel.

'Kate, is everything all right? Where's Tara?'

'Keep her out of the way,' Kate said to Murray.

CHAPTER 67

Tara

A gentle breeze from the river wafted the curtain on her window. Not enough to make her feel cold, but mildly refreshed. It helped her headache, a pain she seemed to have constantly since that night. And that was all she had. It felt like a scrape across a shiny car bonnet. As if someone had taken their key and scored over gleaming paintwork. A part of her was flawed. Something deliberately etched into her very soul. She had no memory of what it was, but in the weeks since then, her friends had gently explained the source of her trauma. The doctors said she might get it back one day. The trouble was she didn't know if she wanted it to come back.

The reality might be worse than what she now imagined; her vision pieced together only by the little carefully told her by Kate. She learned that she had not been raped. A man she'd known briefly had snatched her as she left a nightclub, and she'd been drunk. But she'd felt little relief when she saw this man put away in prison. How long would her sentence be? How long before she felt able to return to work? Would she cope with being a detective inspector again?

A glass of chardonnay sat on the coffee table. She'd taken a few sips, but it tasted vile. Used to be her favourite drink with the girls. It did nothing to ease the hangover she'd suffered for weeks. At this late hour of the night, it meant nothing. It gave no comfort. She'd thought it might help her sleep, but how would she know if she couldn't drink it? A book, a light read by Wendy Holden, lay discarded beside her on the sofa. The television, showing a documentary on Alaskan homesteaders, had failed to hold her interest, and she had long since muted the sound. The images on screen were at least company at three in the morning.

Her hands slid one photograph to the top corner of the table. Then she moved another to the bottom. She'd added dates as labels to every picture, the dates when each of the women had disappeared. Having placed them in a timeline, she studied the photo of each one in chronological order. She didn't know why she was doing this except that it had been connected to the murder of Terry Lawler. That case was closed, or at least on hold until they managed to bring Evan Blackley home to Liverpool. But she'd held onto the photographs. They'd done nothing in helping them solve the murder of Lawler, but it didn't mean that these women had not gone missing. It didn't mean that somehow, they were alive and back home with their families. It meant that one person, perhaps several, had taken these women, and no one was doing anything to find them.

CHAPTER 68

Guy

She was just warming up nicely, and then that slimy git pulled the van door open. Talk about spoiling the mood. But I held Tara close to me. As far as they knew I was on a date with the wee cop. Only thing was that big eejit wasn't taking fuck off for an answer. Next thing I know I'm lying bollock-naked on the freezing ground and two assholes are pulling and hauling at me to get up.

Could have been a lot worse. I mean, what did they really have me for? I didn't kill her; I hadn't even made love to her. And most importantly of all, they knew nothing of my previous activities. See what I mean? Destroy the evidence; don't give them a crime scene to gawp at and don't keep mementos of your exploits. I was damned pissed off at myself for getting caught, all for the sake of wanting to have a nice policewoman, but it wasn't the end of the world.

I was taken back to Liverpool, and that big glipe, Detective Sergeant Murray, questioned me. He's a miserable sod. Never smiled once, not once. Then some aged superintendent, a bloody coffin-dodger, asked me questions. He looked as though he was about to croak, but at least he let me speak without interrupting, not like Murray who kept trying to put words in my mouth.

Both peelers wanted to do me for aggravated rape, but my legal aid brief was a turn-up for the books. I thought these cheapos would side with the cops, but this young guy was sharp, and he stood up for me. He told them they didn't have any proof to charge me with rape.

In the end they charged me with aggravated sexual assault. Seemed that aggravated was the word of the day. Nothing said, though, about how the peelers aggravated me. They searched my flat in Toxteth but didn't find anything. Surprise, surprise. Like I said before, I don't keep mementos of any of my girls. No research information, nothing. They didn't even find anything that could lead them to Mother Freedom.

My trial was a hoot and a half. Not only had my brief been on the ball at the time I was charged, but he got me a brilliant barrister. At one point I thought he was going to get me off completely. His plea to the court was that Tara and I had been engaged in consensual lovemaking which got interrupted by Merseyside's finest. But the sucker punch was the drugs. Tara was barely conscious when the police got to her, and my brief couldn't argue against the fact that she was not in a position to give her consent to intercourse while she was under the influence of drugs.

I sat in court gazing at her. She seemed to look straight through me before I realised that she didn't even remember me. Hadn't a baldy notion who I was except that I was in the dock, on trial for sexually assaulting her. My barrister told me that Tara had no recollection of the event. Not a thing. I wondered if they'd all been like that, every one of my girls. Would've saved me the bother of disposing of them.

The peelers even had a hard job proving I had abducted her. The only witnesses had been pissed out of their heads. Yes, they saw me driving away with Tara in the van. But they couldn't prove that I'd forced her inside, although they tried hard by producing the piece of tape I'd stuck on her mouth and the cable ties I'd used on her hands and feet.

In the end they settled for the fact that I had administered an intramuscular dose of fentanyl, that at some point I'd applied pressure to her neck, I'd removed her clothes and my own, finally placing my body against hers. They'd found nothing to suggest that we had sex, after poor Tara had been subjected to a medical examination. Really, she would have had a much better time if they'd let us get on with things. But, at the heels of the hunt, I got done for aggravated sexual assault. I had no previous record, and so I got three years. I'll be out in less than two.

I've been a good boy here in Altcourse Prison. The psychology department of the place assigned some kind of social worker to me. Young lad, straight out of uni. He talks a lot, full of shite mostly, but he suggested as part of my rehabilitation that I should write down my feelings over what I've done. He said it should help me to deal with my life once I'm out of here. I don't think so. My granny used to say that when you fell off your bike you should get back on right away. At the time I didn't understand why, I was only six, but now I know what she meant. And I just can't wait till I get back to what I do best. Taking women. I've written everything down, more than the wee social worker could ever imagine, but I don't think I'll ever let anyone read it. Might be a tad incriminating.

I have a lovely calendar on the wall of my cell. Nice wee girls bearing all. Keeps me sane, if you know what I mean? Only a few months to go before I can party. When I get out, I will definitely have another crack at Inspector Tara Grogan. You see, once I choose a girl I don't ever give up until I have them. Might even try one of her mates. That wee redhead, the nurse, had a lovely arse. Who knows, if you're a bit of a looker, I might even come after you.

If you enjoyed this book, please let others know by leaving a quick review on Amazon. Also, if you spot anything untoward in the paperback, get in touch. We strive for the best quality and appreciate reader feedback.

editor@thebookfolks.com

ALSO IN THIS SERIES

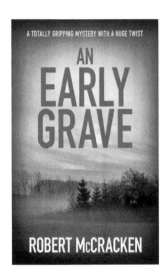

AN EARLY GRAVE (Book 1)

A tough young Detective Inspector encounters a reclusive man who claims he holds the secret to a murder case. But he also has a dangerous agenda. Will DI Tara Grogan take the bait?

Available on Kindle and in paperback!

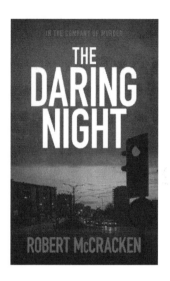

THE DARING NIGHT (Book 2)

Liverpool is on high alert after a spate of poisonings, but DI Tara Grogan is side-lined from the investigation. Yet when she probes into the suicide of a company executive, she becomes sure she has a vital lead in the case. Going it alone, however, has very real risks.

Available on Kindle and in paperback.

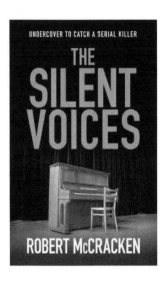

THE SILENT VOICES (Book 3)

When bodies turn up on a Liverpool council estate, DI Tara Grogan goes undercover to get inside information. But she risks everything when the cover story she adopts backfires. Can she work out the identity of the killer before she is exposed and becomes a target?

Available on Kindle and in paperback.

LETHAL JUSTICE (Book 5)

When a body is found, cruelly crucified on a makeshift wooden structure, DI Tara Grogan suspects it is the work of a secretive religious cult. Focusing on this case and with her guard down, she becomes once again the target of a man with murder on his mind, among other things. Will the wheels of justice turn quick enough to save her from an awful fate?

LETHAL MINDS (Book 6)

Following a murder, a drugs feud in a notorious Liverpool estate is kicking off when a missing woman's body is found in the Irish sea. DI Tara Grogan has her attention divided, and someone with a grudge to bear has her in his sights.

For more great titles, visit

www.thebookfolks.com

Printed in Great Britain
by Amazon

75543724R00163